Hot Mess

Also by Ed Decter

The One

VIP Lounge

Hot Mess

a Chloe Gamble novel

By Ed Decter
and Laura J. Burns

Simon Pulse
New York London Toronto Sydney

SIMON PULSE

An imprint of Simon & Schuster Children's Publishing Division

1230 Avenue of the Americas, New York, NY 10020

First Simon Pulse paperback edition August 2010

Copyright © 2010 by Frontier Pictures, Inc. and Ed Decter

For information about special discounts for bulk purchases, please contact Simon & Schuster

Special Sales at 1-866-506-1949 or business@simonandschuster.com.

The Simon & Schuster Speakers Bureau can bring authors to your live event.

For more information or to book an event contact the Simon & Schuster Speakers Bureau

at 1-866-248-3049 or visit our website at www.simonspeakers.com.

Designed by Mike Rosamilia

The text of this book was set in Adobe Caslon Pro.

Manufactured in the United States of America

2 4 6 8 10 9 7 5 3 1

Library of Congress Control Number 2010924617

ISBN 978-1-4169-5437-8

ISBN 978-1-4424-0661-2 (eBook)

For Cheryl Doherty, the best wife, mother, friend,
and writer I know; and Abigail Decter, the best daughter,
ballerina, violinist, and volleyball player I know
—E. D.

To Kathy Boutry, Drew Brody, Chris Pearson,
Matt Lopez, Brian Kiley, Rupa Magge,
and Joe Brouillette
—L. J. B.

Acknowledgments

I'd like to thank world-class editor Jennifer Klonsky for guiding me through two book series and making it fun the whole way, and also for introducing me to world-class coauthor Laura Burns who I am now honored to call friend.

—Ed Decter

Many thanks to Ed Decter for bringing me along on the fantastic roller coaster of Chloe Gamble's life.

—Laura J. Burns

chapter one

Police Report, July 5

Interview with Nika Mays of 8455 Fountain Ave., West
Hollywood. Employed by the Virtuoso Artists Agency.
Detective Matt Lopez interrogating.

Lopez: Can you describe your relationship with Chloe
    Gamble, please?

Mays: I'm her agent. I was, I mean.

Lopez: Were you familiar with her family . . . her mother,
    Earlene Gamble, and . . .

Mays: Travis, her twin brother. Yes, I knew Early and Travis.

Lopez: And the father, Lonnie Gamble?

Mays: I knew the rest of the family first. But I met Lonnie
    when he arrived in Los Angeles—

Lopez: From Texas?

Mays: I don't know. We weren't exactly making how-was-your-trip small talk. Chloe and Trav were not happy to see him. I assume he came from Texas. The Gambles were from a town called Spurlock, Texas.

Lopez: And you met Lonnie Gamble when?

Mays: I met him at Chloe and Travis's house, the same day everyone else met him.

Lopez: Who do you mean?

Mays: We were all there trying to talk sense into Chloe. It was me, Sean Piper—he was her lawyer. Um, Amanda Pierce and Jude Morgan—those were Chloe's friends who worked on her TV show . . .

Lopez: *Cover Band*?

Mays: Yes. Amanda did wardrobe and Jude was the set photographer. Then there was Max Tyrell, Chloe's boyfriend. Marc Duval, her publicist. And Travis and Chloe, of course. And Early was there, too. Oh! And Sasha Powell.

Lopez: The movie star?

Mays: Yeah. But she stormed out before Lonnie showed up. She and Trav had a fight about Chloe. They were dating, you know, and Sasha thought Chloe was a bad influence on Travis—

Lopez: Let's keep the focus on Lonnie, please. You say you were at Ms. Gamble's house?

Mays: Yes. Chloe and Travis had just moved into this great place in the Hollywood Hills and we were supposed to be having a housewarming party. But Chloe went and accepted a role in a movie—

Lopez: I'm sorry, keep to the facts about Lonnie.

Mays: I'm getting there. We were fighting, that's my point. Chloe was the star of the TV show Cover Band. She was under contract to the network. But Matthew Greengold offered her a role in his movie, and you know who Greengold is . . .

Lopez: Yes, Ms. Mays, even us cops go to the movies.

Mays: So you know he's the biggest director on the planet. Well, Chloe was ambitious. She wanted to be in his movie and she said she'd do it. But it meant she would have to break her TV contract and that would lead to lawsuits, so we all wanted her to change her mind. It was a tense situation. When Lonnie Gamble showed up, he walked into the middle of a . . . well, a kind of career intervention—

Lopez: I really have to ask you to focus. I don't want to hear about Chloe Gamble's career. I know you Hollywood people think the world revolves around the Business, but I'm investigating a murder.

Mays: Detective, I'm not trying to be difficult. I know that even the biggest movie is not as important as the fact that a human being is dead. But if you want

to understand what happened with the Gambles,
you have to understand Chloe's career. Everything—
everything—was about Chloe's career.

Nika Mays's Manuscript Notes: Prologue

The cops never did get it. They always wanted to put each part of Chloe Gamble's life into its own neat little box, as if that would help them solve the murder. Box one: her crappy family life. Box two: her too-mature-for-a-sixteen-year-old love life. Box three: her enemies. Box four: her fans. Box five: her bank account. Box six: Hollywood itself.

All of those things were the same to Chloe. All of them bled into one another until the only thing she knew was what she *wanted*. She wanted to be famous. She wanted her fans to love her. She wanted to destroy her enemies. She wanted men to desire her. She wanted to sing, to act, to earn, to conquer, to climb high above the nasty, dead-end life she had been raised to expect. Most of all, she wanted to escape from Spurlock, Texas. And from Lonnie and Earlene Gamble.

Chloe's career—Chloe's fame—was her *fuck you* to her parents, and it was also her entire reason for being. Chloe's *want* . . . that was her true self. Way down deep, that was her whole personality. It took over her career and her family, her friends and her lovers. It was everything to her.

Maybe the police could've solved the murder if they understood that the way I did. Maybe that's why I know who did it and they don't.

Looking back, it's clear that the day Lonnie Gamble arrived was the day it all began to go bad. At the time, he seemed like small potatoes to me, as my boss, Hal Turman, would've said. Chloe was being reckless—again—and she expected me to bail her out. I'd gotten the girl a starring role on a teen TV show, and it had made her famous. Then, when she broke her contract and recorded her own music instead of the show's, I'd renegotiated the contract. Every time Chloe went and did something stupid, I found a way to fix it. But this time I couldn't see a way out.

Maybe it wasn't the best idea to confront Chloe. She was never a girl who would cave in to pressure. But at the time, all I could think about was how she was going to ruin it all, everything that we had built together. It wasn't only her career at stake, it was everybody's—mine and Hal Turman's, because we had just sold our agency to Virtuoso, the biggest name in the Biz. If Chloe got herself sued by the Snap network for breaking her contract, then Virtuoso would be dragged into a huge lawsuit . . . and Hal and I would be out on our asses. It was Sean Piper's career, because he had scored a huge promotion at Webster and White, his entertainment law firm, based on our *last* renegotiation of Chloe's deal. And it was Marc the publicist's career, and Amanda the stylist's, and Jude the photographer's. And even Travis's career . . . would anyone really hire Chloe Gamble's twin brother if Chloe got blacklisted? Maybe some fourth-rate cable reality show, but otherwise it was the end of Trav's acting career too.

Chloe's stardom was the reason we were all so successful, and we didn't want anything to jeopardize our success. It's strange to see that in writing. It seems so selfish. But that day in the Hollywood Hills, I thought that Chloe was the selfish one.

She'd threatened to fire me and Sean: the two people most responsible for her current big-bucks contract with the Snap network. She said she'd dump us if we didn't find a way out of the contract. It still takes my breath away that she could be so awful, so ungrateful. So focused on getting what she wanted that she forgot everything I'd done for her. So focused on the next big thing that she was willing to sacrifice the big thing she already had.

But that was Chloe. What she had was never enough—she always, always wanted more. I'd been paying attention to myself in those days, concentrating on my relationship with Sean and on selling the Hal Turman Agency to Virtuoso. I was thinking of me, and so I forgot to think about Chloe and her need to keep climbing.

That all changed the second that Lonnie Gamble walked into the house. He had such a dark presence, such *gravity*. Just like Chloe did. I couldn't take my eyes off him, except it wasn't a good thing the way it was with Chloe. She practically glowed; all you wanted to do was stare at her. But Lonnie, he was fascinating because he just oozed . . . meanness. That's the only word I can think of. He was *mean*. But his face was perfect. He was a gorgeous man, there was no way around it. And yet all I had to do was look at him to know that it was a mask, that underneath that beautiful face was an ugly soul.

That's why the second I saw him, it all came back to me: Chloe wanted to get away from him. And from her mother, Early. And from her upbringing in Texas. She wanted to get so far away from her past that it could never touch her again.

She'd become so successful that I guess I figured she'd already escaped. But Chloe didn't think so.

Chloe was no idiot; she knew that her parents had both started out young and gorgeous and promising, and they'd ended up nowhere. Sometimes I think Chloe was terrified that she'd be just like them, that no matter how much money and fame she had, she would somehow fall into the same black hole that her folks had. That's why she wanted stardom as big as it could be, as fast as she could get it. Maybe she thought that once she had it all, she would be safe.

Poor Chloe. She got all the fame and money in the world, but it still didn't save her.

DADDY ISSUES

Once upon a time, there was a man named Lonnie Gamble, and he was the hottest damn thing ever to come out of Spurlock, Texas. That's what my mama had told me back in the day, before she hated him so much that she couldn't even say his name without swearing. Lonnie was tall and blond and gorgeous, and, more important, Lonnie was going places. He wasn't just some regular Spurlock nobody, he was a bona fide regional rodeo champion.

But by the time he showed up in my living room in Los

Angeles, he was nothing but a bona fide loser, and the hottest thing ever to come out of Spurlock, Texas, was *me*.

The day my twin brother, Travis, and me turned sixteen, we took our mama and left with only the clothes on our backs, and that's because there was nothing left in Texas that was worth a damn. And that included my daddy.

"Just what in the hell do you think you're doing in my house?" I demanded, soon as I got over the shock of seeing him again.

My daddy smiled his crocodile smile. "*Your* house? Well, ain't you fancy?" His face might have been grinning, but there was a sneer in his voice. "Y'all buy this place with some of that TV money?"

It was a rental, but I wasn't about to tell him that. "Nice, ain't it?"

"It sure is, Chloe-girl," Daddy said. He took a step toward me, like maybe he'd give me a hug. Like maybe we were a regular family having a reunion. For one second, I considered doing it. My daddy had never hugged me that I could remember. He always ignored me, except when he wanted something.

He wanted something now.

"Thanks," I told him. "You're not welcome in it."

"That's right, you get your ass outta here, Lonnie Gamble!" my mama shrieked. "You got a hell of a nerve showing up here after what you pulled!"

My daddy's eyes never left mine, even when he was talking

to Mama. "Nice to see you, too, Early. You want to show me to our bedroom now, or later?"

My mama opened and closed her mouth like a fish, but no actual words came out. "Mama don't live here, Daddy," Travis said. "Just me and Clo."

"And I wouldn't be sharing no room with you anyway!" Mama sputtered.

"Well, that don't make no sense," Daddy said with a chuckle. "Seeing as we're man and wife."

You could've heard a pin drop, at least in the two seconds before my mama hurled herself at him. That seemed to be some kind of signal for the men in the room, because all of a sudden my brother, my dreadlocked boyfriend, my sexy lawyer, and even my gay publicist were on their feet and moving to get between my mama and my daddy.

I didn't get involved. I was busy thinking about what Daddy had just said. No way was he really here to get back with my mama. They couldn't stand each other, and she hadn't heard a word from him since the day we hauled ass out of Texas nine months ago. Far as I could tell, the only reason they weren't divorced was 'cause neither one of them gave a crap about their marriage vows anyway.

But my daddy never said anything he didn't mean, in one way or another. He talked sideways, that's what Mama always said. I used to be pretty good at figuring out his doubletalk, but I hadn't seen the man in months. I was rusty.

Max and Sean managed to drag my mama away, practically throwing her at Travis, who held on tight. My daddy just laughed the whole time.

"Well, she is a hellcat, ain't she, boys?" he said. "Travis, how about you introduce me to your little posse here? I'd like to say thanks."

Travis turned away without a word, leading Mama out to the balcony for some air.

"Guess I'll have to do it myself." My daddy held out his hand to Sean. "Lonnie Gamble."

Sean ignored the outstretched hand. "My name is Sean Piper, and I'm with the law firm of Webster and White. We represent Chloe and Travis."

"Great! So you're our family lawyer?" Daddy said. "I'll have to get your business card."

"No, I'm Chloe's lawyer, and Trav's." Sean's voice was cold. "I am categorically *not* your lawyer, Mr. Gamble."

Daddy pulled his hand back, studying Sean's face. My whole body tensed up, and I wished Travis would get back in here to help me deal with this. My friends didn't know how to handle my daddy, they wouldn't understand that he was dangerous, that you had to move slowly around him, like you do around a rattlesnake. You never knew when he would strike. The sooner we got rid of him, the better.

"I told you to leave, Daddy," I said. "You're not wanted here."

"Hush up, Chloe, the grown-ups are talking," my daddy said. "I'm afraid I don't quite see how you can represent my little girl but not me, Mr. Piper. Chloe ain't got no legal rights on her own."

"I have the right to throw you out of my house," I snapped. My heart was pounding hard, but I kept calm on the outside. Me and Travis were emancipated minors, which meant Daddy had no power over us, though he didn't know it. I was hoping if I reminded myself of that often enough, it would start to feel true.

"Sweetpea, I don't even see how it's legal for you to live in this house without your mama or me," my daddy said. "That's why the lawyer and me need to talk things over."

"The only thing I need to explain to you, Mr. Gamble, is that from now on you'll have to go through me if you want to contact Chloe or Travis," Sean said. "My client has asked you to leave." He took a step closer to my daddy. "*Leave.*"

A couple weeks ago, that kind of speech to my good-for-nothing daddy might've made me want to jump Sean right there in front of our whole crowd of friends. But now, I couldn't help sneaking a glance at my agent. Sean's girlfriend. Or were they just fuck buddies? I didn't know, and I didn't care.

Nika wasn't looking at Sean, though. She was looking at me. "Clo, call the cops," she said.

I just stared at her. I'd called the cops a couple times back in Spurlock when my mama and daddy would get into one of their brawls. The cops never even bothered to come to the house 'cause they knew my parents would put on their every-thing-is-fine act as soon as they had an audience. Well, an audience besides me and Trav.

"You told him to leave and he won't," Nika said. "Call the police."

"I'll do it." My friend Jude—my first and best friend in Los Angeles—grabbed her cell and started dialing. I felt a little burst of warmth go through me. We'd all been in the middle of a fight when Daddy walked in here, and it had been all of them against me. But now they were on my side, and that's where I needed them. Too bad my daddy had to show up to get them there, but I'd take it.

Daddy was still in his pissing match with Sean. "I tell you what, I heard California was a strange place," he said, "but I didn't know I needed a lawyer to talk to my own family."

Before Sean could reply, my daddy did a quick change and turned to Max. It was a trick of his—leave people hanging, always get the last word.

"What about you?" Daddy asked Max. "You're no lawyer. What're you, Clo's hairdresser?"

I'd forgotten how my daddy could manage to make every single word out of his mouth sound disdainful, as if he was the hottest, smartest, most kick-ass guy in the world and you were nothing. Max wasn't me—he didn't have my steel, and he didn't know that it was all just an act Daddy put on to cover what a mess he really was. Max hadn't even opened his mouth to answer when I stepped up beside him.

"Max is my boyfriend," I said, taking his hand. Max glanced at me in surprise, and I knew I'd scored a point or two. When we'd first arrived at the house today, he'd been mad at me along with all the others. He'd been thinking I only wanted him to piss off his ex, Kimber Reeve. Truth was, I liked Max for himself. He calmed me down. But I don't think he'd ever heard me call him my boyfriend before.

Daddy gazed at Max's long hair. "If you say so."

"He's more of a man than you'll ever be," I muttered.

"Let's get this all out of the way," Marc piped up. He swished toward my daddy, looking way more gay than he usually did. "I'm Marc, I'm the publicist, and I'm a raging homo. I'm going straight to hell, I'm an embarrassment to real men like you, and I ought to have the crap beat out of me. You got anything else to add, Mr. Gamble?"

My daddy just stared at him, slack jawed.

"I didn't think so." Marc turned his back and headed for the kitchen, while Amanda just yelled from her seat on the couch. "Yeah, and I'm Mandy and I'm fat!"

I had to laugh. Marc had never struck me as a fighter before, but he'd nailed my daddy right away. And Amanda didn't ever seem to care what people thought of her, least not until she was alone. I'd interrupted her downing an entire pizza by herself once after a bad day at work on our

TV show, *Cover Band*, even though she'd been as brash as ever on the set.

"Well, you got yourself a nice collection of Hollywood freaks, Clo," Daddy said, turning back to me. "Who's the black girl?"

"I'm Nika Mays, Chloe's agent," Nika said. "And I'll be the one talking to the police when they arrive to throw your sorry butt out of here."

Daddy's eyebrows shot up. "No need to get angry, Nika. We're all on the same side." He gave her his good-ol'-boy wink, as if that would work on a classy girl like my agent.

"Everyone should stop trying to talk sense to him," Travis called from the balcony. "He don't care if the cops are coming."

"But these cops don't know you won that one tiny-ass rodeo back in the nineties, Daddy," I said. "They just might treat you like a regular deadbeat dad."

"Not when I've got a famous daughter," Daddy said.

"*Especially* when you've got a famous daughter," Nika replied. "That's what I'll be talking to them about, how Chloe doesn't want you here. And how their kids all have Chloe Gamble posters on their walls. Believe me, they'll take your daughter's side. Welcome to Hollywood, *Lonnie*."

"I see a black and white down the hill," my mama sang out.

"Guess I'll be going, then." My daddy didn't even have the decency to look embarrassed, or ashamed, or like he'd just had his ass handed to him. He gave me that typical, cocky, rodeo-champion grin of his. "Just wanted to let you know I'm here for you, Chloe girl. It ain't right to have the family split up like this."

"Go back to your little piece of ass in Texas, Lonnie," my mama called. "You got no family to rule over no more. The kids are emancipated now!"

For one brief second, I saw a flash of doubt in my daddy's eyes, and then it was gone. "I still got you, Early. You and me are family till death do us part. What's yours is mine, what's mine is yours."

Mama rolled her eyes. "You ain't even got nothing."

"Well, it appears that *you* do," he said. "That's a damn nice bracelet you're wearing, by the way."

Jude had to hold my mama back this time, but Daddy didn't bother hurrying. He just sauntered out the door like he had all the time in the world.

As soon as he was gone, my friends all started talking at once, trying to figure out how to deal with the cops, who would be here any second. Amanda lit up a cigarette right there in my nonsmoking living room, Mama headed straight for the bar, and Max rubbed my shoulders. I didn't listen to what anyone was saying, and I didn't listen to the conversation at the door when the cops showed up. Nika got rid of them pretty quick, now that there was no Daddy to throw out.

The whole group was buzzing like a bothered beehive, but only me and Travis understood what had really just happened.

Everyone else thought they got it, but they didn't. We'd been free for the first time ever, free of that man and his constant manipulations and his nastiness and his selfish, horn-dog ways, and even free of the way he made Mama into a worse version of her usual awful self. For nine magical months, we'd been free.

And now we weren't.

Trav and me stared at each other while they all flitted around acting as if there was something we could do, anything we could do to get free of Lonnie Gamble again.

"Just how smart is your dad?" Sean's voice broke in. "We told him to get out of the house, but will he try to see you again in public, or at work?"

"Ooh, in public would be bad," Marc said. "We couldn't get rid of him without making a scene, and a scene isn't good for your image, Clo."

"He's smart enough to do that," my mama answered. "He's no genius, but he knows how to get what he wants. If he can find a way to get to Chloe, he will."

"Well, that's not enough to get a restraining order against him," Sean said. "But we can hire some security if we don't want him around."

"I'll call the studio and make sure they put him on the watch list," Nika added.

I grabbed her hand before she could pick up her cell. "You don't need to call the studio," I said. "I'm not going back to work on *Cover Band*, remember? My jackass of a daddy won't be able to get anywhere near me once I'm in England."

Everybody stopped and looked at me.

"What's in England?" my mama asked.

"That's where we're shooting *Frontier*," I told her. "For the first month, anyway."

The warm feeling in the room vanished, just like that. For a long, long moment there was silence—the kind of judgmental silence I'd faced in Hollywood ever since my first disastrous "audition" at NBC. The kind of silence that most people couldn't bear . . . and the kind of silence that I didn't care about at all anymore.

"What?" I said. "Did y'all think that I was gonna turn into some well-behaved little simp just because my daddy showed up? I'm still doing that movie."

Nika sank down onto the couch. "Honestly, Chloe, I don't even know what to say to you anymore. You signed a contract. If you break it, you're out of a job on *Cover Band*."

"And so am I, and so is Jude," Amanda put in. "And Jonas, and little Maddie, and all the other actors on the show."

"And the makeup people, and the production assistants, and the cameramen," Jude said. "Think about it, Chloe. There's probably fifty people who have jobs right now just because of you. If you skip out on the show, you take all those people down with you."

"Why can't I just take all those people *up* with me?" I said.

"If I'm a big movie star, won't the TV show get even better ratings? Won't everyone be even more in demand because they work on a huge show with a huge star?"

Nika frowned, chewing on her lip.

"Technically, yes," Marc answered for her. "But that's only if you still *have* a show. If you get fired, so does everyone else. We were very successful in making it a Chloe Gamble vehicle, and that means there's no show without you."

"Come on, they won't fire me," I said. "I'm the Snap network's biggest star."

"And you're trying to ditch them," Nika pointed out. "They're going to do everything they can to keep you."

"What happens if I don't go back to the show?" I asked Sean. "Legally, I mean. What can they do? It's not like they can throw me in jail for breaking my contract."

"They'll file suit against you. And they'll prevent you from doing the movie," he said. "Matthew Greengold's company won't legally be able to hire you when you're bound to the Snap network."

"Oh." I felt a rush of fear. I'd worked too hard to land this movie role; I was not about to give it up just because of some stupid contract. "Fine, then, Snap has to say it's okay," I said. "How do I make them do that?"

"You don't. You tell Matthew you want to be in his next movie and you trust that there's a part for you. And you keep making the show that turned you into a star," Max said gently.

"Chloe, there will be another big movie. The timing is all wrong for this."

"There won't be a movie this big," I said. "It's an epic. It's a Greengold movie. And I know I'm supposed to do it." I turned to my agent. "Nika, remember how I targeted that NBC show?"

"Yeah. You crashed the audition, got tossed out on your ass, and landed on the Hollywood blacklist," she said drily.

"But I was right. That audition I crashed, that's why I have this movie offer now. The director who saw me that day recommended me to Matthew Greengold. My instinct was right. And when I recorded that song with you, Max, it got me in trouble with Snap," I went on, grabbing his hand. "But it was a fantastic song and now it's a hit. It's going to be the first track on the *Cover Band* soundtrack. I wasn't supposed to even write it, but I did. Y'all are always mad at me when I misbehave, but it always works out in the end."

"Chloe, every time you 'misbehave,' as you call it, more and more people in the Industry think that you're difficult. It gets harder and harder to clean up after you," Nika said.

"You telling me that Angelina Jolie always followed rules? Or Anne Lynch?" I said. "They're so famous that nobody cares if they're difficult."

"Well, you're not," Marc said flatly.

"Not yet. But I will be after I walk off with an Oscar for *Frontier*," I said. "Come on! Y'all used to believe in me! What happened?"

"We still believe in you, Chloe," Jude said, but she sounded tired. "But you're asking us all to take a huge risk just because *you* want to take a huge risk. And all the people on *Cover Band*, you're not even asking them."

"It ain't easy having people who depend on you, is it, sugar?" my mama sang. "Maybe now you can appreciate how hard it was for me all those years, trying to provide for my children."

"Yeah, using Chloe's beauty pageant money," Travis muttered.

"Y'all are not my children," I said. "You're grown people who know how to take a chance. You took a chance on me before. Listen to yourselves! You sound like a bunch of corporate drones, all talking about rules and jobs and contracts. What happened to the people who came up with the single most creative career launch in history? Don't you remember how we made me a star just by sticking our homemade music video on the Web?"

I glanced around the room. They all looked tired, pinch faced, and annoyed at me. It was time to change tactics.

"Look, I know I've been acting like a bitch and I'm sorry," I said. "We're a team, we always have been. I know I couldn't have done it without you, Nika. Without any of you. You've always had my back."

"Then why won't you listen to our advice now?" Nika asked.

"Because I want this so much!" I said. "Matthew Greengold

wants me in a movie. He wants *me* to act with Anne Lynch and Harlan Reed. *Me.* Just think about that. He didn't even make me audition, he came looking for me, to put me in a movie with an entirely A-list cast. Nika, that is incredible! It's beyond belief. It's a dream come true—it's every dream I ever had come true, only about a million times better."

For a few seconds nobody spoke. Then, out of nowhere, my mama came tottering over and flung her arm around my shoulders. "That *is* incredible, darlin'," she said. "Nika, can't you find some way to work this out for my Clo? You're always wheelin' and dealin' with them big network honchos, you must be able to pull some strings."

I couldn't believe it. Mama was pouring on her Texas charm and flattery . . . for me.

"You just don't want your gravy train to stop, Mama," Travis said.

"Well, neither do I," I told him. "I want the gravy train to go on forever, for all of us. And I know this is the right thing to do. I'm sure of it."

"You being sure of it doesn't magically erase all the legal obstacles," Sean said. Still, he sounded less stubborn than before.

"I know. But I trust my gut. I've been right every time I took a chance in Hollywood. I might go about things in the wrong way, but I always know the right direction to go in." I looked them each in the eyes, the way my mama had taught me to do when facing the beauty pageant judges. "Please, be on my side. Stop telling me how I can't do this. Start telling me how I can."

IM

GAMBLEGOAL: Sasha, baby, I'm sorry.

GAMBLEGOAL: That scene with my sister was bad, but Chloe's my blood and we stick together. I didn't mean for you to leave. I would've gone after you but my father showed up.

GAMBLEGOAL: Sash? Can I see you?

SPOWELLASST: Ms. Powell is unavailable. Please leave word at her office if you require a response.

GAMBLEGOAL: Srsly? Your assistant is returning IMs? That's cold.

SPOWELLASST: Ms. Powell is unavailable. Please leave word at her office if you require a response.

E-MAIL TO COOP

Coop, what the hell? Did you know my asshole father was coming to California? Dude just walked in like he owns the place. Not that he even noticed me—he was all Chloe, all the time. I forgot how much I hate him.

Whatever. When are you getting your butt out here? I need backup, now! I'll send you the money if you need it. Hell, you can fly first class on me.

Sasha Powell totally dumped me. She won't even take my calls, just because I decided not to move to New York with her. I think she thinks I chose my sister over her. But what was I supposed to do? Chloe's having a career crisis and everyone's kinda pissed at her, so she needs me here. You know how it is—we've got each other's backs. Even a girlfriend should understand that, right? But Sasha's treating me like I'm some stalker who she can just blow off with auto-reply messages.

Chloe told me that hanging out with Sasha was ruining my career—these days I'm in all the gossip blogs as "Sasha's boy toy" and nobody even calls me for auditions anymore. So what am I now? "Sasha's ex–boy toy"? You know what, screw that. I'm getting on the phone right now and getting myself some work.

Why is my sister always right?

Anyway, I could really use some sanity, Coop. Where are you?

Chapter Two

H Meter Blog

BUZZING UP: Blast from the Past HAL TURMAN finalized the deal to sell his boutique kiddie talent agency to monster agency VIRTUOSO. NIKA MAYS joins Turman at the new digs, and many say is the architect of the deal.

BUZZING DOWN: The SNAP network, on top of the world just two weeks ago with its hit show COVER BAND starring teen phenom CHLOE GAMBLE. Because . . .

BUZZING UP: Matthew Greengold, two-time Oscar-winning director, announced this morning that CHLOE GAMBLE will take over the role of Anissa Freelander in his upcoming film *Frontier*, a multigenerational epic based on the bestselling novel. (The role had been rumored to be a vehicle for KIMBER REEVE. Sorry, Kimber!)

BUZZING UP? DOWN? It's too early to call this one: CHLOE GAMBLE has accepted a plum movie role (UP!), but in order to shoot the film, she'll have to jump ship from the TV show that made her a star—and risk legal action from the Snap network (DOWN!). Only time will tell whether this GAMBLE will pay off for the starlet.

Nika Mays's Manuscript Notes: Risk

My new office at Virtuoso was big compared to my old office at the Hal Turman Agency. But when Hal himself was sprawled out on the couch, he seemed to take up so much space that the room felt tiny. Sean sat perched on one of the visitors' chairs, and I suppose I should have felt important sitting behind my power desk with a couple of suits there just to assist me.

But I felt like a little girl in her daddy's office.

Hal was the old-timer. He'd been dealing with stubborn starlets since before I was born. And I knew—I *knew*—that my new bosses at Virtuoso were expecting Hal to fix the Chloe Gamble situation. They hadn't said so. They still treated me and Hal as a team, since after all we were the only two agents acquired when they bought out Hal's old shop. But you don't get to be in my shoes at my age without knowing a thing or two about how to read people's unspoken cues. And when the calls came in the day before from the outraged execs at the Snap Network, all the senior partners in the room had turned toward Hal. They yelled at me, but not at Hal. And when Hal told them to shut up, they did.

He would be calling the shots, and I was supposed to listen to him.

So even here, in my own office, Hal was the big fish. And it made me furious.

"Are you telling me you've had sixteen hours to get control of that girl and you've just pissed it away?" Hal boomed.

"No," I said. "I have not pissed anything away."

"We explained to Chloe the legal ramifications of breaking her contract with Snap—" Sean began.

"You *talked*?" Hal cut him off, his voice dripping with scorn. "What the hell good is talking going to do? You want me to call Leslie Scott over at Snap and tell her we're *talking* it out?"

"Our client is Chloe, not the Snap network," I said. "And our client wants us to solve this."

"There's no *solving* it," Hal said. "There's *making it go away*. A contract is a contract, and that little diva signed one. We've renegotiated it once already because of her bad behavior."

We? I thought furiously. *Me. Me and Sean.* Hal hadn't been involved at all when Sean and I got the network to rework Chloe's contract so she could control her own music. That deal had been huge. It was the entire reason I'd been able to convince Virtuoso to buy the Turman Agency. Hal always took credit for the things his workers did, that was just his way . . . but I'd finally had enough of it.

"We renegotiated it to our own advantage," I snapped. "We just have to figure out how to do it again. Chloe's entire career has been unconventional. This is no different."

"Her entire career?" Hal scoffed. "She's been in the Business for about ten seconds, and she'll be right back out of it unless we make her toe the line. Listen, I don't give a fuck about that girl. What I care about is the fact that she's ruining my reputation in the same week that Virtuoso forked over an outrageous sum of money to *buy* my reputation."

"Most of that money was to buy Chloe," I said.

It was an insult, and Hal knew it. "Nika, if this thing blows up in our faces, we're both fired. Do you understand that?"

"Of course I do!" I cried. "But yelling about what a brat Chloe is will not help us solve this. Do you have any actual advice? Because if you don't, you can just get out of here and let me think."

Hal stood up then, and his old eyes were hurt. I didn't care. He was lecturing me, not helping me, and I didn't have time for that. "You listen to me, young lady," he said. "If you don't get control of Chloe Gamble right now, you will never be able to control her again. She'll know she can push you around, and so will everyone else in town. Once you've established that, you can kiss your A-list dreams good-bye."

Hal shuffled out of my office, and I finally felt like I could breathe again.

"You realize you're defending Chloe even though she's a complete nightmare?" Sean said.

"Yeah." I gave him a rueful smile. "It's a habit."

"No. She got to you, I could see it." Sean shook his head. "You want to make it work for her."

"Maybe." I sighed and leaned back in my Aeron chair. "She's only sixteen years old, but she can stand there in a room full of adults with college degrees and years of experience and tell us all that we're cowards. She's playing with her own life here, and she's willing to do things that we're not. She's got balls of steel."

"Or else she's got no idea how bad the world can be," Sean countered. "She's sixteen—she's clueless."

"You saw her father. You know her mother's a neglectful drunk. I think Chloe knows how bad the world is," I said. "She wants to be a movie star. And you know what? I want her to be a movie star. So why am I telling her no?"

"Because you know how high the stakes are. It's not only the Snap network, it's EdisonCorp," Sean said. "We can't fight them and win."

I nodded. The network's parent corporation was a huge international conglomerate. Chloe might be a big deal to Snap, but she was nothing to EdisonCorp—just one more cog in their machine.

"But what if we can?" I said. "If we find a way to work this deal, Chloe will end up in a gigantic, Oscar-caliber film . . . but you and I will end up *legends*. Think about it! Even Hal is afraid to find a solution here. Even my bosses at Virtuoso think it's a disaster. If we make it happen, then we're smarter and more inventive than the biggest people in the Industry."

Sean cocked his head to the side and let his

eyes run over me the way he did whenever I was naked. "Okay," he said slowly. "If you want to take a risk . . ."

"With a huge payoff," I said, getting up and walking around the desk.

"Maybe we are smarter and more inventive than anyone else." Sean's hands made their way around my waist, and I sat in his lap.

"We're a good team," I said, brushing my lips against his.

"Definitely true." He kissed me, deeply—and then I pushed him away.

"Great! Let's plan." I headed back to my desk chair, and Sean groaned.

"You're a tease," he said.

"The clock's ticking. Snap gave me a day to get Chloe in hand, and that day is almost over," I said. "No fun until the work is done."

"Fine. What's the plan?" Sean asked.

"EdisonCorp," I said thoughtfully. "You're right, they're the real problem. But they're the problem for Snap, too. If Leslie Scott loses her network's biggest star, she can kiss her head-of-network job good-bye."

"Can we get Leslie on our side?" Sean sounded doubtful.

"Probably not," I admitted. "She's hated us ever since that last Chloe debacle."

All the music Chloe created was supposed to be the property of *Cover Band*, because it was a show about a rock band. But Chloe wasn't about to be owned by anyone, so she'd snuck off and recorded her own stuff anyway. And released it online. And then pretended that she'd recorded it years before, and that she had no idea how it got onto the Internet, and that she wasn't basically telling Snap to fuck off.

"Well, Leslie *should* hate us. We went over her head," Sean said.

"I didn't know that extorting a settlement from her boss counted as 'going over her head,'" I said wryly. The CEO of EdisonCorp had indulged in an affair with none other than Early Gamble, and, luckily for us, didn't want his wife to find out. I doubt I'll ever know what Quinn told Leslie Scott when he ordered her to renegotiate Chloe's contract.

"Somehow I don't think we can go back to that well a second time," I said. "Unless Dave Quinn has been sleeping with somebody even worse than Early."

"Okay, so Leslie Scott's job is on the line

here. If Chloe bails on the show, Leslie's out," Sean said. "That means Leslie will play hardball. She'll try to bully Chloe into honoring her contract."

"Remember what Chloe said yesterday? *Cover Band* would get even higher ratings if she was a huge star." I frowned, thinking it through. "She's right about that."

"But first they would have to wait for her to make the movie, and for the movie to come out," Sean said. "Snap isn't going to shut down production on the show for a season just on the promise that Chloe will come back even more famous."

"Snap won't, but maybe EdisonCorp will," I said. "Dave Quinn has always wanted to be in the movie biz. What if this is his way in?"

"By letting his star out of her contract?" Sean shook his head. "I think it would be easier to extort him again."

"No, we let him extort us," I said. "If he helps us out, he gets Chloe for even longer. We extend her *Cover Band* contract for another year to make up for all the time she'll miss when she's shooting the movie."

"Why would he do that?"

"Because then he'll have a movie star in his

TV show," I said. "It's better for him to own a supernova than a starlet."

The phone rang, and I jumped, wondering if it was Matthew Greengold. He'd called me the day before to make an official offer on *Frontier* and I hadn't called back. It made me a little nauseous to think I was blowing off the biggest director in the world, but the truth was that I didn't know what to say to him yet.

"Marc for you, Ms. Mays," my assistant announced.

"Thank God." I hit speaker. "We're making a plan," I told Marc.

"To hypnotize Chloe and make her forget about the Greengold movie?" he asked.

"No, to get EdisonCorp on board," Sean said.

Marc snorted. "It's your funeral. But I'm calling about Lonnie."

"He's not secretly sleeping with Leslie Scott, is he?" I joked.

"You'll find out," Marc said. "You're going to hear everything you never wanted to know about the fine Mr. Lonnie Gamble soon enough. *TMZ* found him."

"Are you kidding?" I cried. "How?"

"Who knows? Maybe the cops we called tipped them off," Marc said. "Anyway, my snitch over there just sent me a link to the piece they're going to air tonight. Wait'll you hear the quote: 'When my wife took off with the kids, I figured I better just stay away and respect their decision to abandon me. I know I'm not a saint. But lately I been reading too much worrisome stuff about my Chloe, and I figured it was time for me to make sure she's got at least one responsible adult looking out for her. So here I am, and I plan to stay until I know my girl's all right.'"

"Oh, for Godssake," I muttered. "He didn't give a crap about his girl until she was filthy rich."

"Just thought you should know," Marc said. "Should I even bother getting a quote from Clo on this?"

"No, she might say something honest," I told him.

"That Lonnie seemed like a nasty little hick, but maybe he's smarter than we thought," Sean said.

"Chloe has to get it from somewhere," Marc said. "And he's spinning it just the right way—the concerned father. Gets everyone's sympathy." He chuckled. "I guess *that* runs in the family, too."

"Let's figure out a Lonnie game plan later. I need to concentrate on Greengold," I said. "Lonnie Gamble is small fish."

"Okay, *Hal*," Marc teased. "Big fish" and "small fish" were an integral part of Hal's worldview, and I guess of mine.

"That's not funny," I muttered. I hung up without saying good-bye.

"I've got a meeting with a judge, I can't move it," Sean told me, glancing at his watch. "I can come back for lunch and we'll talk Chloe."

"Daniel Shapiro wants me and Hal in his office at nine sharp," I said. The head of Virtuoso would want answers, and I didn't have anything concrete yet.

"What are you going to tell him?" Sean asked.

"That we have a bold and foolproof plan," I said. "Chloe always says that the best way to lie is to lie big."

"You think Hal will play along?"

"He has to, he's got nothing better to offer," I said. "Just outdated advice."

"Good luck spinning it." Sean gave me a kiss. "You'll need it."

I felt a flutter of worry as the door closed behind him. Hal Turman had said not to spin the situation, just to control Chloe. And Hal was almost always right, at least when it came to the Hollywood game. I'd never really gone against his advice before. But here I was, about to do just that, and right in front of Hal.

I wanted to feel confident, but instead there was a giant black pit of fear growing inside of me. If Hal was right—if I was wrong—I would take Hal down with me. And I wasn't sure I could bear that. Maybe Chloe wasn't only one with daddy issues, after all.

"They're waiting for you in Shapiro's office," my assistant buzzed in to say. "Are you ready?"

"Yup," I lied, trying to channel Chloe Gamble. "Born ready."

BIG TIME

"I am so sorry I'm late, Ms. Lynch. I only just got a call half an hour ago about having lunch with you," I said the second my butt hit the chair at The Ivy. "I sure hope I didn't keep you waiting."

"Long enough to have a glass of wine," said the best actress in the world. "So thank you."

"Thank *you*. I can't even believe you wanted to see little ol' me! I have been in awe of you since the very first time I saw you, in *Desert Sun*. You are just my absolute hero!" I gave her a pageant smile—I called it the "aw, shucks," which was a little wider and a little dumber than the "girl next door."

Anne Lynch raised one eyebrow, and it was like a smack-down. Her gray eyes held mine, and all of a sudden I felt like an idiot. That was not a feeling I ever allowed to stay for long.

"I just can't wait to watch you work. I am sure that I'll learn so, so much from somebody who's been in the business as long as you." This time I gave her the "bitchy cheerleader" smile.

"Miss Gamble. If you're trying to say I'm old, by all means say I'm old," Anne Lynch said dryly. "But don't try your beauty-queen tricks on me. I would have eaten you for breakfast on the circuit."

I wanted to say that no one—*no one*—could ever have beaten me on the pageant circuit. But instead I just took a sip of water. Anne Lynch wasn't some regular person I could mouth off to. She was a legend. "You did beauty pageants?" I asked innocently.

She chuckled. "Do you honestly expect me to believe that you don't know that?"

Of course I knew it. I knew everything about her, and whatever I hadn't known, I'd stayed up all night learning on the Internet. But nothing I'd seen had told me that she could read my mind.

"No . . . I mean, I think I heard you were a beauty queen," I said, flustered. I wasn't used to being off balance with people, and I honestly had no idea how she'd managed to make me that way in less than a minute.

Anne Lynch leaned forward, the "bitchy cheerleader" smile on her own face. "Don't lie to me and we'll get along fine."

I searched my mind for something to say, anything to salvage this conversation. But nothing came to me. I'd tried sweet, and I'd tried passive-aggressive. I couldn't be bitchy. So what was I supposed to do now? Be honest?

"Okay," I said. "I won't lie. I know you topped out as Miss Teen Connecticut and then you stopped so you could go to Yale. I've seen all of your movies, even though I think a lot of them were boring. But I know you've won Oscars and I know everyone thinks you're the brilliant one. And I'm going to be the next you."

Again she raised her eyebrow. "A lot of girls have said that. There is no next me. There is only you."

"You sound like my acting coach," I said.

"Then you have a good coach." She glanced across the dining room and a waiter appeared at our table instantaneously. "You know what I want," she told him. "Miss Gamble will probably have a salad."

"Only if there's a steak attached to it," I said. "I'm from Texas."

"Shall I bring another glass for the wine?" the waiter asked.

"Absolutely not. The girl's a child," Anne Lynch scolded. The waiter scurried off in terror.

"I'm actually emancipated," I told her.

"That doesn't mean you're legal to drink," she replied.

I shrugged. "Alcohol ruins your skin anyway."

"Emancipated . . . Is that why you're making such a terrible career choice?" she asked. "Your parents wouldn't let you do it, I imagine. My daughter loves *Cover Band*. She's devastated that you're going to destroy it."

"My mama probably wouldn't have let me do it, but that's just 'cause she likes steady money," I said. "I've got bigger dreams."

"Do you have any idea what a risk you're taking?" Anne asked. "Frankly, I'm surprised Matthew is willing to hire you, given all the legalities."

"I've been lectured by every single person I know, but I don't care. Matthew said if I wanted to do it, it was my head-ache," I said. "I don't care about legalities. I care about fame. This movie is perfect for me, and I don't want to wait."

She narrowed her eyes and studied me. "You're like a hungry little stray cat," she said.

"Is that a compliment?" I asked.

"I'll let you know," she told me.

"Anne! I heard you were here," Matthew Greengold called, striding into the dressing room where Anne Lynch sat enthroned on the leather sofa, watching as I stood on a podium surrounded by mirrors. She didn't bother to get up as he came over to kiss her.

"Little Chloe and I had lunch, and I thought I'd come to her wardrobe fitting," Anne said. "She's playing my daughter. It seemed like the motherly thing to do."

Her voice was clipped, and it was impossible for me to tell if she was being serious or sarcastic. It had been that way ever since lunch, and it was driving me nuts—because I knew she was doing it on purpose. I might not have loved all of Anne Lynch's movies, but I'd studied them enough to know she could play anything, anyone, any role at all, and she could act the hell out of it. You never could tell if you were seeing Anne Lynch the person, or the character she was playing. So she might be acting now, for all I knew. Usually I could read people. It's the thing I did best. It was my secret weapon.

But I couldn't read Anne. She was blocking me out on purpose. She knew that if she let me get some kind of insight on her, I would use it, and she didn't want me to. I could tell, because it's just how I handle my own mama sometimes. But there was not a thing I could do about it.

Anne controlled the room, even when I was in it.

"Ouch!" I yelled, jerking away from the wardrobe chick when she stuck me with a pin.

"Sorry," she muttered, lying.

"I didn't know you girls were having lunch. I would've joined you," Matthew said.

"Please, darling, you don't need to kiss my ass," Anne said. "And you certainly don't need to kiss Chloe's."

I glared at her reflection in the mirror in front of me, and Anne laughed. "I don't think she likes my version of mothering," she remarked.

"You should let her do it, Chloe," Matthew told me. "Anne's kids are the most well-adjusted Hollywood brats I've ever met. And I'm including my own."

"That's because they live in New Jersey," Anne said. "Far from the madness."

"Well, I'm not looking for a mother," I said. "I only just got rid of mine."

"Mmm." Somehow, the woman could make a single syllable reek of disapproval. I was starting to hate her. But she was the queen of Hollywood, and I had to make her like me. I could never, never be outright rude to Anne Lynch.

"Think about your role," Matthew told me. "Anissa's very close to her mother. It's what drives the romantic plotline— revenge against the tribe that killed her mother."

I glanced at Anne, my character's mother—*my* mother— and she burst out laughing.

"Little Chloe would like nothing better than to see me killed in a Native American ambush!" she cried, as if it was the funniest thing in the world.

"Don't call me Little Chloe," I said before I could stop myself. "I am not little. Jesus."

Anne gasped in delight. "There! The real Chloe Gamble appears."

I rolled my eyes. She was playing me, and I'd fallen for it. Some mother she was. But then Anne got up and came gliding over to me. She pulled my long hair back from my face and twisted it up into a bun so quickly that I could tell she had years of experience at doing her own kids' hair. "Look now," she said, nudging me until I looked back in the mirrors. The wardrobe girl had me in an ugly brown pioneer dress, but she'd pinned it here and there, noting my measurements, and somehow when I wasn't paying attention, she'd turned it into a tighter, sexier dress. It still looked authentic, but . . . better. And with Anne holding my hair up that way, I suddenly saw Anissa in the mirror, not Chloe.

"There's my girl," Anne murmured, beaming at my reflection. "You said you wanted to learn from me—and I know you were only blowing smoke up my ass, by the way. But if you do want to learn, you have to be open. Stop scheming all the time, Chloe Gamble. You're betting it all on this movie. You have to be the best you'll ever be."

"I will," I said. I smiled at her, and she smiled back. For real.

"Sorry, am I early?" a deep voice interrupted.

I didn't turn around. I didn't have to. Harlan Reed was standing behind me, checking me out in the mirrors.

"We're running late," the wardrobe chick said, unfazed by the fact that last year's Sexiest Man Alive stood not ten feet away.

"That's my fault," I said. "My mama always says I was born four days late and I been late ever since!"

I saw Anne smirk—she could spot a lie a mile away. Me and Trav had been born two weeks early, but that don't make as good a "Texas girl quip." Anyway, Harlan Reed laughed, and that was all I wanted.

"Hi, I'm Chloe Gamble," I said, turning toward him.

"Harlan," he replied, shaking my hand.

I'd known I would meet him eventually. Before Matthew even offered me the role in *Frontier*, I'd memorized everyone on the cast. Harlan Reed had the role of John Parrish, a French-Canadian kid raised by a Native American tribe in the nineteenth century. It was a meaty role with lots of fighting and three different languages and almost no scenes where his shirt was on . . . and one really steamy sex scene. With me.

The truth was, it was Harlan's movie. There was a big cast, and some big name actors, but he was the main character. He got to age from twenty to sixty-five, while the rest of us came and went in his life. My part was just there for the sex, I figured, even though I had a few scenes with Anne, too. It had to be mostly about the sex. That's what gets people to cough up their money for a movie.

Harlan and Anne were kissing each other on both cheeks, and I noticed that both of them seemed to automatically know to do it that way. Was there a signal that you should kiss someone twice? Everyone in Hollywood kissed hello, but usually it was just on the one cheek. Next time I saw Harlan, I'd have to kiss him twice. Noted.

"We can finish with you tomorrow, Chloe," the wardrobe girl said, which was code for "get out of here, this guy is much more important than you."

"Sure thing." I pulled my long skirt up and moved to climb off the podium, but Harlan grabbed my elbow before I even took a step.

"Let me help you, love." He smiled down at me, his perfect face even better in person than in the magazines. "Don't want you to trip."

"I never lose my balance," I said. But I leaned on him a little anyway, because who wouldn't?

"You work with Alan Leiber, don't you?" Harlan didn't take his hand off my arm.

"Yes. He's the best coach in the whole world," I said. "I haven't seen him lately, but I want to schedule a marathon session to work on Anissa. I only just got the part, and we start so soon."

"Alan taught me everything I know. Tell me when you're seeing him and I'll come along."

"You'd do that for me?" I asked.

"I'd do it for both of us. We're a team from now on, Chloe. You and I have some . . . delicate scenes. We've got to trust each other. I want you to feel comfortable in my arms."

Harlan had a voice that had sold a million products all

over the world, and he had a movie-star presence that sucked all the air out of the room. The man was so famous that I almost felt dizzy standing here with him, and all his attention was focused on *me*.

This is a whole other level, I suddenly realized. These people—Anne and Matthew and Harlan—they operated on a completely different plane of reality than I did. They were so famous, so rich, that it almost seemed as if the regular rules didn't apply to them. As if they were superhuman. I couldn't manipulate them the way I was used to. I was going to have to learn their rules, and fast.

I'd never been starstruck before, but right then, I had a hard time even thinking about Alan, my acting coach. I couldn't think of a clever, sexy thing to say. All I could do was nod, stare into Harlan Reed's ice blue eyes, and hope I wasn't making a fool of myself.

"Well, well," Anne's dry voice broke the spell. "Doesn't that just make your heart beat faster?"

Harlan laughed and turned to her. "You think?"

"Absolutely," Matthew added. "You were worried about me hiring Chloe with no test, Harley, but you were wrong."

"Test?" I asked, still a little dazed. "For what?"

"Chemistry, love. You can be the best actor in the world or the worst, but the thing that really matters is chemistry." Harlan's hand had slipped from my arm to my waist, and he bent to murmur in my ear. "At least for a wild pair like us."

I pulled away from him then and frowned. "And you were worried?"

"I'm not anymore," he said.

"Nobody's worried anymore," Anne put in. "In fact, Matthew darling, I think your film could use a little more of that. Don't you?"

E-MAIL TO COOP

Coop, what up? Got your message, I'm sending a car service to meet you at LAX on Thursday. Don't know how you convinced your mom to let you come here instead of college, but tell her I'm eternally grateful. You'll be the only sane person in Los Angeles (don't tell her that).

Here's the update: my freakin' father went and told some bullshit sob story to the gossip blogs. Last time I checked, dude doesn't even know my middle name, but now he's acting all fatherly. Only about Chloe, BTW. He could give a crap about me. Anyway, I see on this blog that he says he's living in a "cheap Hollywood motel" because he's trying to make himself look all poor and sad. So I called all the motels in Hollywood until I found him—and it's a Best Western right on the strip, so he's a liar if he thinks that counts as a seedy motel. And I went over there and knocked on his door.

You should've seen his face, man! He thinks he's the only one who can show up with no warning? Wrong. He had some old chick with him, she didn't even have her shirt on when I go in there, but then he tells me she's his lawyer. Yeah, I'm sure she's got great credentials. So he's like, "what do you want?" and I say I want him to get the hell out of LA. He had his chance to be a father for sixteen years, and he blew it.

Know what he says? He says, "You think you're the only one who can ride Chloe's coattails, boy? I'm a rodeo champion, I know how to hang on."

Nice. I bet you wish your dad was that awesome, huh?

IM

COOPERMAN: Trav, just reading your e-mail. Sorry.

GAMBLEGOAL: No big.

COOPERMAN. Your dad's a tool, he always was.

COOPERMAN: You should just ignore him. Make him go thru
   your lawyer.

GAMBLEGOAL: I'd love to see Sean's face dealing with Daddy's ho. I
   mean, his lawyer.

GAMBLEGOAL: Jesus. Daddy with a trashy lawyer, Mama with a
   porn king.

COOPERMAN: Classy. The porn king's worse.

GAMBLEGOAL: Wait till you meet him.

COOPERMAN: Hope Chloe won't mind me crashing on your couch
   while I'm visiting.

GAMBLEGOAL: Dude, be real. We have a guest house.

COOPERMAN: WTF is a guest house?

GAMBLEGOAL: Behind the house, there's a whole little cottage with a bedroom & a john. The realtor chick said our mama could live there & Clo laughed her ass off.

COOPERMAN: Okay, you know that you guys have left the planet earth, right? Guest house.

GAMBLEGOAL: I guess. But I won't have to hear your snoring.

COOPERMAN: Or see how many more girls I bring home.

GAMBLEGOAL: That reminds me, when you get here Thursday, we go straight out.

COOPERMAN: Where?

GAMBLEGOAL: I just left a film shoot—the assistant director of my Chanel spot is directing this indie and he got me and some other actors to shoot a crazy-ass scene where we play Russian roulette. Twisted. Anyway, the other guys were cool and they want to hit this new club opening on Thursday. You'll come with. You'll get laid.

COOPERMAN: Guest house. Laid the first night. Hollywood, here I come!

HOME SWEET HOME

"Any news on your show?" Max said, while he drove up the winding streets toward my house in the Hollywood Hills.

"I wish people would stop asking me that," I complained. "Ask me about my day with all the most famous people in the world instead!"

"Chloe, you love that show," Max said, like I hadn't even answered him. "It's *yours*."

"And now *Frontier* is mine," I said.

"*Frontier* is never going to be yours. It's Greengold's, and Harlan Reed's, and Anne Lynch's. You're not the star," Max said.

"Well, I'm getting to be," I said. "Matthew is going to expand my part! He said me and Harlan Reed have chemistry off the charts and he wants to capitalize on it."

"Oh." Max frowned.

"Don't worry, it's not real, it's just how we look together," I told him, running my hand along his leg. "Anyway, Anne talked him into it—she thinks my story should be bigger in the movie, even though it's really more her story in the book. But she told Matthew she doesn't even need half the scenes in the script. She was all, 'Darling, I don't need to say anything on this entire page. I can do that whole thing just with my eyes.' Seriously, she's the most incredible thing I have ever seen! You know, I thought I was going to hate her at first, but then she up and convinced him to cut her own part for me!"

"Wow." Max's eyes shot over to me, and I could see he was truly impressed.

"I know," I said, bouncing a little in my seat. "Plus, she said I should expect a lot of tabloid stories about how she and I are huge rivals because I'm stealing her screen time."

"But I thought it was her idea."

"She doesn't care, she'll still make a billion dollars for it, and she figures she can win an Oscar even if she's only onscreen for ten minutes." I smiled. "She's a lot more devious than I expected. She's never in the gossips, but she obviously knows how to work them. She said the hot young actress pushing out the grande dame is a classic gossip column story, and it will generate buzz for the movie."

"The hot young actress sleeping with the huge movie-star leading man is a classic story, too," Max grumbled.

I laughed. "From what I hear, Harlan goes both ways. And he barely even noticed me."

"Then why did they all think you two were so amazing together?"

I shrugged. "Anne says it just happens with some people."

Max pulled into the driveway and stopped. "Whose car is that?"

It was an ugly Viper, and I had a bad feeling I knew who it belonged to. I jumped out of Max's SUV and stormed through the front door. Kanye blasted through the house. "Turn that crap down," I told Max over my shoulder, and I headed for the French doors out to the pool.

My mama was buck naked in the hot tub, and her cockroach of a porn-producing boyfriend was buck naked on the diving board.

"Get the hell outta my pool!" I yelled at him. "And get the hell outta my house!"

"Well, hey there, darlin'!" Mama called. She wiggled her fingers at Max. "And you, too, Clo." She laughed like she was making a hilarious joke, and that loser Alex dove into the pool as if I hadn't just kicked him out.

"Trav and me moved out of the Oakwood so we wouldn't have to deal with your lowlife behavior anymore, Mama," I snapped. "This is our place. Go home."

"Your mother wanted to pay a visit, be nice," Alex said, popping up at the edge two feet from me. If he'd been a few inches closer, I could've kicked him.

"Don't you have some big, porny mansion you bought with the money you make exploiting wannabe actresses?" I asked him. "Or are you not that good a producer?"

"Sure, I do. But your house has a better view," he said.

I just stared at him, but Max rolled his eyes. "Dude, get dressed," he said. "If you want to pay a visit, don't do it in the nude."

Alex shrugged and climbed out of the pool, letting it all swing right in front of me. "Mama, you are disgusting," I said, turning my back on him. "And your so-called boyfriend is disgusting."

"Don't be such a drama queen," my mama slurred, waving her wine glass—*my* wine glass—around.

"Don't you realize how pathetic you look?" I said. "Like you're only with him so he'll put you in a movie. Except you're too damn old to make a porno."

My mama narrowed her eyes. "Don't you take that tone with me, young lady. I am still your mama no matter what the lawyers say, and I deserve some respect."

"I don't date adult actresses," Alex commented, pulling on his jeans.

"No, you just sleep with them," Max said.

"Yeah, but I don't *date* them. I'm with Early because I love her."

"Oh my God! Get out of my house!" I practically screamed. "And Mama, get a hold of yourself. It was one thing when Daddy was MIA, but now that he's in town you look like a cheating whore for parading around with this loser. Everybody knows you're still married."

"What the hell?" My brother's voice broke in. I turned to see him frowning at Alex, with Nika in the doorway behind him. "Mama, I told you he wasn't welcome here."

"Sugar, I can't exactly come visit without my ride," Mama called back. "Y'all took the Escalade and left me with nothing."

"Hang on," I said. "How did she even get in here?"

Travis shrugged. "I gave her a key."

I glared at him. "Sorry?"

"What? She's our mother, Clo, she gets a key." Travis glanced at Mama, then looked away. "Jesus, Mama, put some clothes on!"

"You give Nika a key, too?" I asked, eyeing my agent.

"Nope, we just ran into each other in the driveway. I've got news." Nika looked vaguely disgusted by the scene at the pool. "You haven't answered your phone all day."

"I changed my number," I told her. "Between Hal harassing me and everyone from *Cover Band* calling every two seconds, it was just too annoying."

"Hal's been calling?" Nika sounded astonished.

"I know he's old, but I think he's familiar with how to use a phone," I told her. "Tell you what, though, I am done with his threats. If I hear the words 'get your ass in line' one more time, I'll start shopping for a new agency."

"Hal said that?" Nika asked.

"Yes, Nika, Hal said that. And you've pretty much been saying the same thing, so don't act so shocked." I folded my arms and stared her down. "Are you here to try to talk me into ditching the movie? Because I won't. I had the best day of my life today."

Nika smiled. "Matthew Greengold says you have great chemistry with Harlan Reed."

"I do," I said, smiling back. "You talked to Matthew?"

"Yup. He's hiring Debra Baker to do a rewrite, beefing up your role."

"Who's she?" I asked.

"She's a script doctor, the best in town at women's dialogue. Matthew and Debra are old friends. It's a huge sign of confidence in you." Nika sounded excited, just like she used to.

Maybe we would make it through this thing, after all. Maybe I didn't care about her hooking up with Sean as much as I thought I did. I had Max, and I had a huge movie.

"What about Snap?" I asked.

"Sean and I have a plan," she said, and I decided to ignore the pang of jealousy I still felt. "I set a meeting tomorrow with the network honchos. It's do or die—my new boss at Virtuoso will be there, Daniel Shapiro. And Dave Quinn from Edison-Corp." Nika shot a look at Mama, but Mama was pretending not to listen. "So I need your okay to go ahead with it."

"Okay," I said immediately. "It's okay."

"No, Clo, you need to listen. There's a tiny chance this will work—*tiny*. But if it does, it will mean you have to stick with *Cover Band* longer than you expected."

"How long?" I asked.

"Another year at least, maybe two," she said. "We're asking them for a huge favor, it's going to cost us. We'll have to offer a contract extension."

"Okay," I said. I'd never pictured myself doing the show for that long, but whatever it took to make *Frontier*, I would agree to it.

"And you'll still have to do promotion and musical appearances for the show, even when you're filming the movie," Nika said.

"Fine, that's fine." I was bouncing again. "Nika! Will it really work?"

"Honestly, I don't know," she said, her voice serious. "I'm going to do my best, Clo. But if it falls apart, it will be bad. Are you sure about all this?"

"Sure as I've ever been about anything," I said.

"Okay, then I need your help tomorrow," she told me.

"This is fascinating, but can we please get this scumbag out of our house before we finish the Hollywood scheming?" Travis interrupted us.

I glanced back at the pool. Alex had planted himself in one of the lounge chairs, and he didn't even make a move to get up.

"What're you complaining about? You're the one who let him in!" I said.

"I told Mama he was not welcome," Travis growled. "In fact, I told Mama to stop hanging out with him."

"You don't tell me what to do. I am a grown woman," Mama said.

"Mrs. Gamble, everyone knows what Alex does for a living. Doesn't that bother you?" Max asked. He had this way of making everything seem so calm and reasonable, but it didn't work on my mama.

"I do not care how a man makes his money, just like he don't care how I make mine," she said.

"You make yours by leeching off of me," I said. "And if you want the money to keep coming, you do what I say, which is to dump the sleazebag."

"Ain't gonna be any money if you don't get your butt back to that TV show," Mama said. "'Cause your agent's big plan is for shit."

"Watch your mouth, Mama!" I snapped.

"You're a fine one to talk!" she yelled, waving her wine glass at me. "You try and act all snotty and better'n me, but you're the same trash you ever were."

Max reached for my arm; I guess after the last family scene in our house, he thought she and I might attack each other or something. But I was too happy about the guy I'd just noticed standing in the French doors. Watching the whole scene and shaking his head.

"Coop!" I cried. Our old buddy from Texas was a year ahead of me and Trav in school, so he'd just graduated.

"Coop!" Travis ran over and flung his arms around his best friend in the world—well, except for me. "You made it!"

"Yeah." Coop laughed and pounded Trav on the back, then shot me a smile. "And I can already see that the Gamble family has not changed a bit."

chapter three

From Nika Mays's Manuscript Notes: Texas Hold 'Em

"You'd better be right about this, Nika," Daniel Shapiro said to me in the EdisonCorp elevator. "Because this merger is looking like the biggest mistake of my career."

Well, as long as there's no pressure, I thought. But I just gave him my most confident smile and ignored Hal's accusing stare. "Daniel, I promise you, it will work. Look on the bright side—we've got the most successful director in history calling us for hourly updates."

"That's true." Daniel sucked on his teeth for

a moment. "But it only matters if we can work it out with Dave Quinn."

"I'm on it," I said.

The elevator doors opened, depositing us on the top floor of EdisonCorp's building in downtown Los Angeles. It was a strange place to have a meeting, and that was no coincidence. Quinn wanted to intimidate us. He wouldn't meet at Virtuoso, because that was our turf. And he wouldn't meet at the Snap network offices, because those weren't big enough. Instead he was making us all trek to EdisonCorp's Los Angeles headquarters, to make sure that we understood our place in this game: We were nobodies. EdisonCorp was huge beyond imagination, with skyscrapers in every major city on earth. Trying to fight with them and all their money would be like trying to storm a castle armed only with water pistols.

I was going to need a secret weapon.

"Let them know we're all here now," Sean said to the receptionist, then he came over to shake hands with Daniel and Hal. He'd come separately, and he'd brought Andrea Liddy, one of the senior partners at his firm. I shot him a look, and he tried to smile confidently. But he was scared, I could tell.

We were all scared.

The receptionist showed us into the boardroom, and we all took seats at one end of the twenty-foot-long table. Dave Quinn kept us waiting for a few minutes, and then he appeared with two other EdisonCorp guys who probably made several million dollars a year, and Rich Rawson, their head counsel.

Leslie Scott from Snap was there, too, but nobody seemed to care about her. The message was clear: this was a fight between the giant conglomerate . . . and Chloe Gamble.

"Let's get started," Quinn said brusquely. "We've agreed to this meeting as a courtesy to you, Dan," he nodded at my new boss, "but to be honest, I don't see the point."

"Chloe Gamble has a contract with Snap, and she is currently in breach of it. She hasn't been to work in three days now. That's three days that we've had to suspend production," Leslie said. "We all know how much money it's costing us. Would you like me to do the math for you?"

"That won't be necessary," I replied. "Chloe is terribly sorry for the inconvenience."

"Inconvenience?" Leslie snorted.

"We're not here to bicker about the production schedule," Rich Rawson cut in. "We all know the situation with the Matthew Greengold film. We're prepared to begin legal action against Chloe Gamble immediately."

"I was under the impression that you had a proposal for us," Quinn said. "If not, this meeting is over."

Daniel Shapiro looked at me. Hal Turman looked at me. Everyone in the room—all of them older, wealthier, and much more experienced than me—looked at me. I had only one ally here, Sean.

He cleared his throat. "We do have a proposal. You say you know about Greengold's movie; well, then you know it's a surefire hit."

"What you might not know is that Greengold himself has concerns about the budget," I added. "His original budget was $105 million, but with the economy tanking, two of his investors pulled out. He's had to cut it to $80 million. Being Matthew Greengold, he thinks he can make it work at this price."

"But to make his original vision a reality, he needs $25 million dollars," Sean said.

"We propose that EdisonCorp put up that money," I finished, my voice shaking a tiny bit.

Silence. They all just stared at us like we'd lost our minds.

"I'm sorry, but you're asking us for money at this juncture?" Quinn's number two guy piped up, his voice dripping with scorn.

I ignored him. Chloe always said, talk to the most important person in the room. That was Dave Quinn. "You've been wanting to find a way in to the feature business," I told him. "EdisonCorp even considered buying a studio last year."

"That deal fell apart," he said dismissively.

"Because it was too much money in a down market," Sean replied. "This is nothing compared to that. But it's an investment in a movie that will be on everyone's radar in the next year. I've done a model of this." He pulled a stack of papers from his briefcase and began handing them around the table while I spoke.

"Matthew Greengold is the most successful producer-director in history, financially speaking," I said. "I can count on one hand the number of Greengold films that didn't break even. If there has ever been a sure thing in Hollywood, he's it. Add to that Harlan Reed, literally the only star in the world right now who can open a movie. And Anne Lynch, who has two Oscars, five Golden Globes, and a boatload of other awards."

"Your typical big-studio feature film has a

fifteen percent chance of breakeven," Sean said, gesturing to his fancy-looking charts. "Combine Greengold, the all-star cast, and the fact that the film is based on a Pulitzer-Prize–winning novel with an already huge fan base . . . and *Frontier* has a sixty-five percent chance of breakeven."

I was happy to see that they were studying the charts, all except Leslie and Dave Quinn. Quinn was staring right at me. "You know how it works," I pushed. "Last in, first out. If EdisonCorp is the final investor, then they're the first to be repaid once the movie breaks even."

"So you're saying it's a good bet," he said.

"You won't get odds like this anywhere," Sean told him.

"And think of what it will get you. Matthew Greengold will be in love with you for allowing him to do this film the way he really wants to. The final product will be even more fantastic than planned—you could easily have a Best Picture winner on your company's resume. If that's not a way into the film biz, I don't know what is," I said.

"Excuse me." Leslie Scott's voice was shrill. "I thought we were here to talk about *Cover Band.* Not *Frontier.*"

"Mmm," Quinn murmured, nodding. "This is an interesting idea, but you're using it as a smoke screen. I can invest in *Frontier* regardless of Chloe Gamble. In fact, if Greengold is pissed at us for taking her away, investing is a nice way to smooth his feathers."

My heart began to pound. Quinn had seen right through me. Sean and I had known that was a possibility, and we had a backup plan just in case. But it was a backup plan that could easily end our careers.

"There's no reason we should lose a hit TV show just to get into movies," Leslie said, triumphant. "So let's get back to the topic at hand. Chloe's in breach. What do you plan to do about it?"

No choice. It was time for Plan B.

"I'd like to let Chloe answer that question," I said, shooting a nervous glance at Sean. He got up and went over to open the boardroom door.

"Excuse me?" Quinn asked.

"What the hell is this?" Hal Turman burst out. "Nika—"

But he was too late; my secret weapon had already appeared in the doorway. Chloe looked fantastic. She walked in to the room like she was strutting out onto a beauty pageant stage, a big, bright smile on her face. Her dress was adorable—cute and flirty and fun, just like a teenager's dress should be. And if it showed some leg, well, I didn't think the horny old men in the room would mind.

"Thank y'all so much for letting me come," Chloe said in full-on Southern belle mode. "Nika didn't want me to, but I just begged. I'm sorry if it's the wrong thing to do . . ."

"This is highly unusual," Daniel Shapiro cut in, a little panicked. Highly unusual was putting it nicely. In fact, it was absolutely unheard of. Even the worst agent knows that you never let your client into the room during a negotiation. You protect your client from people like Dave Quinn.

"I know it is, Mr. Shapiro, but I just feel so terrible about this mess I've made," Chloe said. She turned to Quinn and looked him straight in the eye—which can't have been easy for her, knowing the guy had used and dumped her mother. "Mr. Quinn, my mama raised me to take responsibility for my actions, and that means I simply had to apologize to you face-to-face," Chloe went on.

Sean shot me a glance across the table, his brows raised. Chloe had balls.

"See, I'm new at this. I thought if somebody

offered me a big movie role, I could say yes," Chloe said, turning back to face the rest of the bigwigs. "I don't know anything about all the legal stuff. I mean, Matthew Greengold wants me in a movie! I just got so excited that I wasn't thinking straight. Who ever would've thought that a girl who was living in a double-wide this time last year could be in a film with Anne Lynch and Harlan Reed?"

"The issue is the show," Leslie said.

"Ms. Scott, you know how much I love *Cover Band*," Chloe replied, wide-eyed. "That show is my whole life! I never in a million years wanted to hurt the show, or my bandmates, or any of the other actors. And the crew has always been so sweet and helpful to me, teaching me the ropes . . . well, I just love them. You have to believe me, when I told Matthew I would take the role, it didn't even occur to me that it could hurt *Cover Band*."

"Chloe, the shooting schedule conflicts." Leslie sounded exasperated. But all the men in the room were listening with sympathetic expressions.

"I know it does, but I just figured we could put off shooting the show for a little while," Chloe said. "I guess that sounds naïve. I didn't know it was all so written in stone. I thought I was doing something y'all would be proud of. I thought if I did a big movie and got really famous, then it would be even better for *Cover Band*!"

"Sort of like having Reese Witherspoon in your teen show," I agreed, smiling at Leslie. She stared daggers back at me.

"*Cover Band* has put me on the map," Chloe said, her focus back on Quinn now. "I understand how much I owe you, and Snap, and every single person involved with the show. I don't want to let any of you down. But I have a chance to be in a movie with two of my all-time idols—and I'm only sixteen years old. This is a dream come true, just like the TV show is a dream come true. Can't I do them both, please?" She took a step closer to Quinn. "I'll do whatever it takes. I'll do musical performances, and webisodes, and I can do a blog while I'm gone—maybe even in character. Maybe we could even write it into the show! Like, my character is going undercover for a couple of months and then if you check in online you can get clues to where I am!"

Chloe was smart. For that last part, she turned to Leslie, because Leslie was in charge of *Cover Band*. Quinn was just in charge of the money.

"I'm sorry, I still just get so excited about

the show sometimes. I know that part's all up to you and the writers," she said with a little giggle. "But what I'm saying is, I took the movie role, but it don't mean I'm leaving my show."

"Chloe is willing to extend her contract with Snap for another year to make up for any lost time," I put in.

"Of course I am!" Chloe cried. "And I promise—I *guarantee*—that when I come back, you will have a passionate, totally committed star for your show." She looked Quinn and his cronies in the eye, one at a time, as she spoke.

There was a moment of silence, and I held my breath. Then Chloe smiled again, dazzling the entire room. "Anyway, I'll get out of your hair now, I know I'm not supposed to be here. I just wanted to tell you in person how truly sorry I am for my screw-up. I know y'all expect me to behave myself, and I didn't mean to get it all wrong." She headed for the door, then turned to give them all one last look. "Thanks for listening to me. Y'all have a great day!"

When she was gone, Leslie dropped her head into her hands.

"Jesus, she really is just a kid," one of the EdisonCorp guys said.

"She's mature beyond her years, but we can't expect her to grasp the ins and outs of the Business the way we do," Daniel Shapiro jumped in. "If someone offered me movie stardom when I was a teenager, I'd've probably said yes without thinking it through, too."

"None of this solves our problem," Leslie pointed out. But Dave Quinn wasn't listening to her anymore. He was considering it, I could tell. And then suddenly he laughed.

"Well, that was quite a risk, Ms. Mays," he said. "Bring in the client and make me look like the big, bad wolf attacking a sweet young thing, hmm?"

"I told Chloe not to come," I lied. "But I have to say, she's right about one thing—if she becomes a movie star, it will raise the profile of *Cover Band*."

"It's win-win. If she's a bigger star, you own her longer, *and* you've got a hit movie," Sean said. "You make money off both things; you can spin it to look like you put her in the movie. You'll be a starmaker, not the big, bad wolf."

"Just think of the rebranding with *Cover Band* when it starts up again. Think of the concert tour with a movie star headlining the band!" I said.

"I want two years," Quinn said. "This is a disaster for Snap in the short term. I want a two-year extension on her contract."

"Done," I said.

"And we still get a piece of her—if I invest in the movie, they'll have to accommodate the needs of the show. The things she said, webisodes and musical performances, she can fit those in around her shooting schedule." Quinn nodded, as if he were convincing himself this was a good idea.

"There's also a soundtrack coming out," I said. "If we market it right, that will help keep *Cover Band* in the public eye while the show's on hiatus."

"Good." Quinn stood up, and that meant the meeting was over. "Tell Chloe she owes me one now," he said as he shook my hand.

My entire body was buzzing with some strange mixture of excitement and relief, and I wondered if my knees would buckle. Sean was flat-out beaming like a ten-year-old, but I just felt numb.

It worked, some little voice in my head was screaming. *It worked! It worked! It worked!* I'd known that bringing Chloe to the meeting could kill my career—or make it. It was the biggest risk I'd ever taken, and it worked!

"What the hell was that stunt, having the

client show up?" Hal growled as we all headed back to the elevators. "Have you lost your mind?"

It felt like a punch to the gut. "But . . . it worked," I said.

"The client in the room with the money!" Hal went on, his bushy eyebrows going overtime. "That is the cardinal rule, the one you never break. What in the hell were you thinking? She could've blown it all!"

My mind was frozen. Hal was yelling at me, schooling me in front of Shapiro, and in front of Sean and his boss. I thought it had been a victory, but I was wrong. The way Hal was looking at me, as if he'd never even seen me before, made my heart sink. I was fired. I'd saved the deal, but they would fire me anyway for pulling that stunt.

"That was the most unprofessional thing I've seen in all my years," Hal said, his voice dripping with scorn.

"It was brilliant," Daniel Shapiro replied.

I whipped my head toward him, astonished. Shapiro was grinning like the Cheshire cat, as happy as Hal was angry.

"Even Quinn thought so," Sean's boss agreed. "Those EdisonCorp guys are in love with all things Chloe now. I guarantee, by the time we get back to our offices, they'll think it was their idea to put her in the movie!"

The elevator opened and we all got in.

"We'll be there to remind them that we came up with it," Shapiro said. "And we'll take the credit with Greengold, too."

"I'm sorry I didn't tell you she was coming," I said, my heart rate slowing a little. "I knew it could backfire, and I didn't want you to take the heat."

"We figured you could just blame us if it was too unprofessional," Sean said. I shot a glance at Hal, who was still fuming.

"Very Machiavellian," Shapiro chuckled. "You've got balls, both of you."

"That's twice they've taken on Snap and EdisonCorp," Sean's boss said. "Impressive."

When the elevator opened in the lobby, Hal Turman stomped right out. But Daniel Shapiro stopped to let me go first. "I take it back, Nika," he said. "I think this merger is going to work out well . . . for both of us."

GOOD-BYE TO ALL THAT

"Did she call yet?" I asked for the third time.

"Clo, you gave me your phone so that you wouldn't have

to be stressed," Jude said. "You might as well obsessively check it yourself."

"Sorry." I grabbed a chunky Fred Leighton bracelet and tossed it onto my king-size bed. "It's just . . . how'm I supposed to pack when I don't know for sure I'm going?"

"Can't you just buy all new stuff once you're in England?" Travis asked, tossing a football back and forth with Coop.

"I don't know that, either, not until Nika calls," I said. "Maybe I got no money at all now. Maybe I'm out of a TV show and out of a movie."

"Nobody's fault but your own," Jude muttered.

"Thanks, pal," I said sarcastically. "You sure you want to come with?"

"Yeah. If you go, I'll go," she said. "I've never been to Europe."

"It's incredible there," Trav put in. "Girls will just have sex with you for no reason at all."

"Dude!" Coop cried, eyes wide.

"It's okay. I'm hoping I have that experience, too." Jude laughed, and my brother's best friend turned beet red. He hadn't quite figured out how to talk to Jude yet—she might like the ladies, but she's not an actual guy. It blew Coop's mind the same way it used to blow Trav's.

"Why hasn't she called yet?" I complained. "Gimme the phone."

"No need, I see Nika's car," Trav said, peering off the balcony attached to my bedroom. "She'll be here in a minute."

"Is that good or bad?" I asked Jude. "Do agents give you bad news in person?"

"If the news is 'you're out of a job,' I think they try to stay as far away as possible," she said.

"I can't wait." I stalked out of my bedroom and headed for the front door. My entire future was riding on what Nika had to say, and it made me feel sick. I do not like uncertainty, and that's a fact.

"I've been waiting forever," I yelled as soon as she stepped out of her Mini. "Why haven't you called?"

"Girl's been busy taking over the world," Marc told me, climbing out the passenger side. He handed me a bottle of Cristal as he walked right by me into the house.

"What's this for?" I asked.

"It's a done deal!" Nika cried. I let out a scream, and flung my arms around her.

"I'm in the movie? I still got my show?" I yelled. "Nobody's suing me?"

"Not right this second. So let's get drunk!" Marc said. "Who's this little ranch hand?"

"I'm Coop," Coop said.

"Stay away from him," I told Marc. "You're not his type."

Marc just laughed, grabbing champagne flutes from a cabinet.

"Details before drinking," Nika said. "Your new Snap contract is for two more years—"

"I don't care." I cut her off. "I don't need to hear the boring stuff, that's why I have you. So I can do the movie, which means I'm going to England day after tomorrow, right?"

"Matthew Greengold wants you there for rehearsals, but they won't be shooting for two weeks," Nika said. "They're going to have a revised script for you to read on the plane."

"With my part bigger?" I grabbed a drink from Marc.

"Yup. And there's more." Nika turned to Travis. "Tell me I'm the best agent in the world."

"I'd like to, but I ain't exactly been working a lot," he said, shocking the shit out of me. My brother is not a whiner, and he's also not the kind of guy who rides his agent for work. That was me, not Trav. Maybe Hollywood had gotten to him more than I thought.

"That's going to change," Nika said. "When I spoke to Greengold today, he mentioned that one of Clo's new scenes introduces the character's brother."

"He dies before her family moves to the frontier," Coop put in. When we all stared at him, he shrugged. "I loved that book."

"I don't even remember that, and it's my own character," I said. "Maybe I ought to read it again."

Nika shook her head. "Just read the script. Anyway, it's a tiny role, but I thought who would be better to play your brother than your brother?"

"Hang on. You got me a part in *Frontier*?" Trav asked.

"Not yet, but I floated the idea with Greengold, and I reminded him that he now has $25 million more dollars to make his movie, thanks to Chloe Gamble," Nika said. "So he's looking at the dailies from that indie you did last week."

Trav frowned. "How did you get those?"

"Are you kidding? Call the director of a little indie film and ask if he'll send his stuff to Matthew Greengold . . ." Jude said. "Nobody's gonna say no to that."

"Exactly." Nika grinned.

"Didn't Travis get himself that part in the indie film?" Coop asked.

Everyone stared at him again. Marc gave a low whistle. "New boy learns fast," he said. "But don't forget, Travis is more interesting now that he's single again. I pushed that angle in the blogs. I want some credit for him getting any part at all."

"Dating Sasha was a lot more interesting for *me*," Travis muttered.

"But it made you lazy," Nika said. "And hard to sell."

"And boring," I added.

"So, yes, new boy, Trav got himself the indie part through connections he made on a job I got him," Nika explained. "And now I'm going to get him a more important part through connections I've made. Agents and actors work as a team." She looked at me, and I pretended not to understand what she was saying—that I should be a team player, too, with no more going off and making trouble for her. But far as I could see, I'd just made enough trouble to land myself a huge movie and keep my huge show.

I turned away and winked at Travis. "Let's just hope you did a convincing Russian roulette," I told my twin. "Did you look scared?"

"Who the hell knows?" Trav said. "I wasn't the one who ended up dead."

"Then we'll hope you looked really, really relieved," Nika joked. "Anyway, I think it's a good bet."

"What about me?" Jude asked.

"Set photographer," Nika confirmed. "Your agent has the details. It's not glam—you're shooting B-roll for the DVD extra on costuming. But it's the best I could do. Chloe's got some pull, but . . ."

"After this movie comes out, I'll get you a bigger job, promise," I told her.

Jude gave me a half-smile. "England will be fun."

"You know it." I downed the champagne in one gulp. "Now I can pack!"

"Actually, you can't. You need to get your butt over to the studio and start filming," Nika said. "Snap wants at least ten interstitials that they can air as teasers while the show is off."

"What's an interstitial?" Coop asked.

"Something between a commercial and a music video, I

think." Nika shrugged. "It's whatever they want it to be—the writers are banging out scripts even as we speak. Basically, anything that shows Chloe's face and can be edited into a fun little reminder of *Cover Band*."

"And I'm supposed to do that all today?" I asked.

"You're supposed to do it today, tonight, and tomorrow right up until you set foot on that plane. And you're supposed to do it with a smile and the attitude you wore to the meeting at EdisonCorp," Nika told me. "Quinn said to tell you . . . you owe him one."

I winced. That guy was a piece of slime no better than my daddy, he just had the money to pull it off. But if I wanted to have my movie, I had to play nice. At least for now.

"Hey, y'all think I can get Amanda to pack for me?" I asked. "She'll know what I need to wear in Europe."

"I wouldn't go there," Marc said, shuddering.

"No, you should steer clear of her," Jude agreed. "Chloe, she's out of a job now. Everyone is, with *Cover Band* on hiatus. It's not like they keep paying us when we're not in production."

"Oh." I bit my lip, thinking it over. "Do you think Amanda's mad at me?"

Nika and Marc exchanged a look. Jude just shrugged, and Trav stared at the floor. It was Coop who had the balls to answer me.

"Hell yeah," he said. "You got your friend let go from a

cushy gig? Then you suck, Clo. She's mad at you, and so are all the other people you got fired."

"Too tired to make love before you take off for a month." Max shook his head.

"I know. I'm a sorry excuse for a girlfriend." I yawned and leaned my forehead against the glass of the passenger side window. We were nearly at the bottom of the hill, with my house far up above us. It still didn't feel like home, though. I'd only been there a few weeks, and now I was headed for the airport to leave. "I've been channeling '*Cover Band*'s Lucie Blayne' nonstop for the last thirty hours. I am seriously going to sleep the whole way to London."

"The glamorous life of a movie star," he teased me.

Movie star! I thought, a little thrill running up my spine in spite of the exhaustion. "You could come," I said. "I promise I'll jump on you the second we get to my swank hotel."

Max turned onto Hollywood Boulevard, heading for the freeway entrance ramp. "What am I gonna do while you're shooting all day?" he said. "It's not like you're going on vacation. You'll be working all the time."

I shrugged. "You could write some music. Sleep in. Go sightseeing at all the places I'll be too busy to see."

"No thanks. I don't do the pampered, useless boyfriend thing," he said. "Besides, I've already been to London."

I was too wiped out to answer. Sometimes it seemed like

I hardly knew Max at all. He'd seen my family at its absolute worst now, but I'd never even met his. They lived in San Francisco, and from some things he said, they obviously had money. It was just plain weird to be with someone from such a different world, someone who had actually gone to Europe before, even though he was barely older than me.

He shot me a sideways glance. "Sorry, Clo, but I've got the band here. Just because you're a big shot, it doesn't mean I'm going to stop doing my own stuff."

"You could find a studio there and we could record a few more songs," I said.

He laughed. "The minute you get back, we'll go into the studio," he said. "I don't need to go to England to produce music."

I pouted. I couldn't help it. He was supposed to do whatever I wanted, wasn't he? Lord knows Sasha Powell had wheedled my brother into being a pampered boyfriend for her.

"You don't want that kind of guy," Max said, like he could tell what I was thinking.

"I just want a guy, period," I told him.

"You do not. You'll be so busy working you won't even miss me. If I was always hanging around in your hotel room, it would piss you off."

"Fine," I said. He was right, and I knew it. But it still annoyed me. I was three hours away from getting on a plane all by myself. I'd never done anything by myself before. There was always Trav and Mama. But now it was just me. Nobody else even to talk to. Truth was, it was just a little bit scary.

"Jude'll be there in a couple weeks," Max said. "And maybe even Travis, if he gets that role." He reached over and squeezed my thigh. "You'll be fine."

"Course I will. I'm always fine," I said, shaking off my bad mood. "I'm tired is all. Once I get there, I'll be ready for adventure."

"That's my girl." Max turned on to the freeway going north—away from the airport, and toward Burbank. "You sure you want to do this first?"

"She's a lush, but she's my mama," I said with a sigh. "If I don't say good-bye, she'll never let me forget it."

By the time we got to the Oakwood, I was just about ready to drift off. So pulling into the parking structure made me cranky, and climbing my tired butt out of Max's SUV made me even crankier.

"Will Alex be here?" Max asked.

"If he is, I just might have to do some violence," I muttered. The sound of my heels echoed off the concrete walls of the outdoor hallway as we headed for my mama's apartment. Strange to think that a month ago it had been my apartment, too, and Trav's. We'd lived at the Oakwood Apartments since the day we arrived in Los Angeles. It's where I'd met Max, and his ex, my biggest rival, Kimber Reeve. It's where Jude had taken my headshots, and where we'd all filmed my first

YouTube video, the one that made me an Internet star. It's where my whole career had happened.

Until now.

Now, I had the whole of Hollywood at my feet, at least when I was standing in the living room of our rental house. I had a dream job in a movie, and the Oakwood seemed like another lifetime.

"This place is a dump," I said.

"No, it's not. You're just getting spoiled." Max gave me a wink to show he was kidding. But he wasn't, not really.

"I hope I stay spoiled forever," I told him. I stopped at the door of my old apartment and rang the bell. "Mama! Wake up!"

"It's noon," Max said.

"That don't mean she's rolled out of bed yet," I muttered.

But Mama surprised me. She answered the door right away, all dressed in a silk floral blouse and skinny jeans. Her hair was combed, and she didn't smell even a little like a bottle of wine.

"Hey there, Clo!" She flung her arms around me. "I made you lunch. Don't want my girl gettin' on a plane all empty."

"I'm flying first class, Mama," I told her. "They'll feed me."

"It still ain't nothing like your mama's home cooking," she said, steering me over to the table. She had places set for me and Max, and she bustled around the kitchen like she was prepared to wait on us.

"Mama, you don't even know how to boil pasta," I told her. "Where'd you get all this?"

She glanced over the table, filled with fresh bread, and a huge bowl of chopped salad, and some kind of grilled fish all laid out on a platter with garnishes. Then she laughed. "You're right, I am not the domestic type." Mama sat her ass down at the table and pushed her long blond hair back over her shoulder, her signature seductive move. I couldn't tell if it was aimed at Max, or me.

"It's good, whoever made it." Max was already downing the salad.

"You won't believe it, but turns out Alex is quite the cook. He brought it over," my mama said. "I tell you what, he is a true catch. Money and talent."

"I think I've lost my appetite," I said.

"Darlin', you need to make an effort," Mama said. "He's the real thing. I just might move in with him."

"If you move into the porn mansion, I'm not paying you a percentage anymore," I told her. "I give you some of my earnings to keep you respectable. I can't have my mama living like a porn queen."

"Well, sugar, that's just what I wanted to talk to you about," Mama said, leaning toward me with wide eyes and a slight, tremulous smile. It was the "sweet young thing," one of the trademark beauty pageant smiles she had taught me back when I started on the pageant circuit. It's the look you used when you wanted the judges to think of you as pure and innocent. The Texas cow town judges liked their girls that way, though it didn't really fly in Dallas.

And it didn't fly with me.

"Mama, I can't stop you from hooking up with inappropriate men, but I will not allow you to drag my reputation down with you," I said. "You want the money, you steer clear of Alex."

"It ain't *my* money I'm worried about," she said. "Well, not how you think. It's your daddy."

That stopped me in my tracks. "What about him?"

"Sugar, you know that man. He ain't gonna turn tail and head back to Spurlock," Mama said. "He's here to stay."

"Did he call you or something?" I asked. Trav had gone to see Daddy, I knew, though it was a waste of time.

"He had some lawyer send me a letter," she said. "All about wanting access to my financials, seeing as he's my husband and our money is community property. Alex said that's a load of crap, so I tossed it."

"Okay, so what about it?" I asked.

"He wants a piece of the pie, Clo. He's your daddy, he figures he's entitled," my mama said. "Not that he ever did a damn thing to make you such a success."

"Like you did, you mean?" I rolled my eyes.

"That's right." Mama puffed herself up tall in her seat. "I taught you how to walk, and how to sew your evening dresses, and how to smile your way into all them pageant crowns. You wouldn't even be here if I hadn't put you onstage."

"I'm the one who wanted to compete," I said. "It was my only ticket out of Spurlock."

"And I helped you do it. I drove you all over creation. I showed you how to do your makeup," Mama said, sticking to her guns.

"Yeah, and you took all my pageant money," I said.

Max cleared his throat. "Chloe, if you want to get to the airport on time—"

"I used that money to support you children!" Mama cried, tears filling her eyes.

"Don't try that act on me, Mama, I seen it too many times," I snapped. "You pretend to be all motherly, getting sober and making me lunch, for what? What do you want?"

"I want you to cut your daddy in," she said, sticking her chin out like a stubborn toddler. "Give him a percentage just like you do with me."

"Not a chance in hell." I stood up, and so did Max.

"He's here to make trouble, Clo, and he's good at that," Mama said. "Don't think his lawyer's about to stop at me. You're the one with the movie-star salary. He's going to get himself a piece of it, even if he has to take us all down to do it."

"You're afraid of him," I said, disgusted. "But I left that man behind the day I left Texas. I'm an emancipated adult now, he ain't got no power over me. And it's pathetic, you letting him worm his way back in. You trying to get him what he wants."

"I don't want anything getting in the way of your success," Mama said.

"In the way of your money, you mean." I pulled open the apartment door. "So long, Mama. I don't know why I even bothered coming here."

Max didn't say a word until we were back on the freeway, heading down to LAX. Then he reached for my hand. "Try to understand her, Chloe. She really does seem scared of your dad."

"Then she's a loser, just like him," I said. "That man is a snake with only one tooth, and I am not about to pay him the attention he wants."

"Is she right? Is he just here for money?" Max's voice was quiet, and I could see that he felt sorry for me. Poor, white-trash Chloe with her nasty, white-trash family. I pulled my hand away. Sympathy was for girls with nothing, and I had everything.

"I don't care what he's here for, 'cause I'm leaving," I said. "And I am not gonna miss a single thing."

IM

GAMBLEGOAL: You on the plane?

CHLOE: This seat is like a sofa.

GAMBLEGOAL: I know, I flew business class when I did that shoot in Spain. First must be even better!

CHLOE: It's boring without you.

GAMBLEGOAL: You'll be asleep the whole time anyway.

CHLOE: Just called Matthew myself and asked about your role in FRONTIER. Say thank you.

GAMBLEGOAL: Why?

CHLOE: 'Cause I cried and said I was scared to be away from my family and that my brother and me were twins, so he can act as well as I can.

GAMBLEGOAL: So you lied.

CHLOE: And it got you the part. Say thank you.

GAMBLEGOAL: Are you shitting me?

CHLOE: Nope. He liked your dailies, and it's only one little scene. He probably figures he'll just cut it if you suck.

GAMBLEGOAL: Thank you.

GAMBLEGOAL: Holy crap. Thank you!

CHLOE: You and me against the world.

GAMBLEGOAL: Same as it's always been.

CHLOE: Don't tell Mama, and don't tell Daddy. They'll try and take your money.

GAMBLEGOAL: Don't worry about me.

CHLOE: You're soft on them. Don't let them talk you into paying. Tell Nika I said so.

GAMBLEGOAL: I ain't soft. Besides, Daddy can't touch us, we're emancipated.

CHLOE: I'm taking off now. Waking up in London with a whole new life!

"Chloe gone?" Coop asked from his spot on the couch. We'd been playing Halo nonstop ever since my sister left that morning.

"Yeah. She got me the part in her movie," I said.

Coop killed me, watching the explosion in silence.

"It's a big friggin' movie," I said, shell-shocked.

"You can do it," he told me. "And if not, you'll still get paid."

"Damn straight." I laughed, and he laughed with me. "This is an insane life, right?" I asked.

"Dude, I've been here for a week and I already had a threesome." Coop shook his head in wonder. "This is beyond insane. You and Chloe just think it's normal these days. But it is not normal. Y'all are different people now; you can't ever come back home to Texas."

"My parents are still the same," I said. "Chloe says not to tell them I got the part."

"You don't have to tell them anything. You're a free man." Coop held up his hand for a high five and I gave him one. But I didn't feel free. Mama and Daddy always found a way to fuck things up, and they would until the day I died.

The phone rang and I figured it was Nika calling about the part.

"Travis, I need you and Chloe both," Sean said when I answered.

"Well, you can't have us," I told him. "Clo's on a plane to England."

"Damn. I forgot." Sean was tweaking, I could hear it in his voice.

"Why? What's up?" I asked.

"It's your father," Sean said, like I knew he would. "Lonnie just filed a motion to have your emancipation reversed."

chapter four

THE NEXT LEVEL

"The bathtub in my hotel room is big enough for five people," I told Max. "We could have some real fun in there."

"Clo, I have a gig this week. I can't come to London," he said, laughing. "We'll just have to make do with sexting."

"No way. Number twenty-six on the list. No naked pictures," I said.

Max groaned, but I was distracted by the nearly naked thirty-five-year-old climbing into bed with me. Harlan Reed had been pacing around on his cell phone, but apparently he was ready to rehearse now.

"Gotta go, Max." I hung up and leaned over to kiss Harlan on both cheeks. It was a little weird to be doing that in bed while wearing only a leotard, but he didn't seem to care, so I pretended not to, either.

"Tell me, darling, what kind of list has 'no naked pictures' on it?" he said, one eyebrow raised in his trademark flirty expression.

I laughed. "My Don't Do list. All the stupid things that celebrity teens have done to ruin their careers, in one long list. If you don't do that stuff, you'll stay famous, and that's my plan."

"Hmm." Harlan leaned back against the pillows of the huge four-post bed in the soundstage set of my room. "Sounds like a plan for a boring life. Behaving is overrated. The trick is not to get caught."

"You are a bad influence," I told him.

"I am." Harlan's smile was more intoxicating in person than on screen—and that was saying something—but I knew better than to fall for it. The vibe he gave off was strange, not straight but not quite gay. More like he'd sleep with me in a heartbeat, but he'd also probably sleep with Max in a heartbeat. Or with both of us. Or with the lighting guy who was experimenting with the equipment over our heads right now. Or the production assistant currently barking into her headset about how Matthew Greengold was wanted on set. Harlan's sexual appetite was all about Harlan. He wanted attention, and he got it. Didn't matter who else was involved.

"Matthew's on his way," the PA said. "He says sorry he's late."

I shrugged. I was the only one who'd been on time this morning, and that was mostly because I was so bored that I'd wanted to do anything to get out of my hotel room. Sure, the hotel was the most luxurious place I'd ever been in, and I'd spent all my free time for the past three days just enjoying it. But the eight-hundred-thread-count sheets didn't matter if there was nobody else to see them. I definitely missed Max, but I'd have been happy to see pretty much anyone from LA. So far my London adventure was just me and a bunch of assistant directors running lines and learning marks. I needed someone to share the fun.

"I've never seen a call sheet that had me reporting to a bed before," I told Harlan.

"Those are the best kind," he said with a wink. "We can begin without Matthew, if you like."

"What, you mean run some lines?" I asked innocently.

"Can you two face each other?" the lighting guy called down.

Harlan rolled toward me, and I moved toward him. The lights changed yet again, and one of the prop people adjusted the sheets, making notes. Harlan yawned.

"Are you staying at the Four Seasons with me?" I asked.

"I have a townhouse," he said. "I'm here for longer than you, and I need my privacy."

Before I could say anything else, Matthew Greengold appeared, looking tanner than ever, even though the sun in London was about one-tenth as strong as in Los Angeles.

"Morning, kids," Matthew said, sitting right down on the bed with us. "I see you're settled in?" He didn't wait for an answer. "Harley, you know me. Chloe, here's how it works. I go for the hardest things first. We get past the thorny parts and the rest is a bed of roses."

"Okay," I said. "I didn't think there were any hard parts to making a movie. Isn't it the dream job?"

They both chuckled. "Good girl, keep us grounded," Harlan said.

"You're right. The hard part comes *before* we start shooting. Once you've got a green light, the worst is over." Matthew studied my face. "Let's put it this way: I'd like to tackle the delicate parts first. You're sixteen?"

"Almost seventeen," I told him. "And I'm an old soul."

"I believe that." He drummed his fingers on his script. "So have you ever done a sex scene?"

"Not on camera," I joked. But neither of them laughed. "Listen, I'm emancipated. I'm allowed to do whatever you want."

"Well, we'll have a body double for the nudity, your agent was insistent about that, and rightfully so."

Funny, she never told me about that, I thought. The last time Nika and I talked about nudity was when I went ahead and took a role in a trashy horror flick and she didn't want me to. I would've done topless back then, but I was a minor so I couldn't. "I guess she thinks it would send the wrong idea,"

I said. "But I just know you wouldn't ask me to do anything gratuitous."

"They'll still need to shoot a lot of us two in bed," Harlan put in.

"Which is why you're here right now," Matthew said. "It's a trial by fire, so to speak."

Both of them were watching me carefully, as if they were afraid I might burst into tears or faint at the idea of sex. But if that were true, wouldn't I have freaked out the second Harlan showed up? "Fine with me," I told them.

Matthew's brow furrowed, and an image of Anne Lynch popped into my mind. If she were here, she wouldn't like that answer at all. She'd want something more "age-appropriate." I don't care about sex, it's just one more thing that you can use to get what you want. But I guess lots of girls my age are more squeamish.

"Alan, my acting coach, he always says I'm safe if I'm in character," I added quickly. "So even if it's kind of intense for Chloe, I think it will be fine for Anissa. She's in love."

Harlan smiled. "Exactly."

"Still, it can be hard to hold on to character in such an awkward situation. You're dressed now, but we'll need your shirt off when we actually shoot. I'll have a closed set, of course, but there will be people around, lights, cameras . . . It's not exactly natural," Matthew said.

Anything with lights and cameras pointed at me sounds

perfect, I thought. *And how hard can it be to make out with the most gorgeous movie star on the planet?* But out loud I said, "I'll be tryin' my best. I just hope y'all can be patient with me."

"Absolutely." Matthew stood up. "Okay. Let's get choreographing."

"Choreographing?" I murmured to Harlan, while Matthew headed over to confer with the Director of Photography.

"Every sigh, every moan, every kiss," he said. "We'll have to memorize it like a dance—your head tilts this way, my hand goes that way, put your elbow here, and I'll stick my tongue there. Hope you brought your breath mints."

"Wow. That's . . . unsexy," I said.

"There's nothing less erotic than a love scene, love. My advice? Get stoned beforehand."

I blinked in surprise.

"It'll relax you," he said. "Or is that on the Don't Do list, too?"

I laughed. "Can I tell you a secret? I'm not that nervous about this."

"Of course you're not," he said. "You trust me."

That's right. It's all about him, I thought. But I nodded. "I do. So I don't need drugs. Tell you what, though, I want to do *something*. I want to see London."

"No problem there. You'll come out with us." Harlan lazily looped his arm over my waist.

"Who's 'us'?" I asked.

"My friends," he said. "My entourage, the media would say."

"They travel with you?"

Harlan shrugged. "I'm all over the world, all the time. If I don't bring my life with me, I lose track of it."

"I can't even get my boyfriend to come visit," I said, making a face.

"Don't you worry," Harlan said. "We'll go out tonight and find you a new one."

"I'll settle for just going out," I said.

"Oh, darling. Never settle," Harlan told me.

STAR CENTRAL BLOG

Back in town: Our British friends tell us HARLAN REED is up to his old partying ways, hitting the Funky Buddha Lounge last night in Londontown. You may remember that the last time he was there, a rumored bar fight with Jude Law took place over the attentions of a cocktail waitress.

Harlan's keeping better company these days, though. Sources put him with CHLOE GAMBLE, the costar of his new movie, *Frontier*. No underage scandals for Harlan, though— Chloe spent the whole night in deep, ahem, conversation with HENRY NORWICH, minor member of the royal family and major playboy.

"Chloe, I've only got a minute to talk. Matthew says you're shooting the sex scene tomorrow." Nika sounded distracted, but that was okay since I was distracted, too. The wardrobe girl was fitting me into some skin-colored thing that seemed like a cross between Spanx and a G-string. It was to make me look naked even though I wasn't actually naked.

"Yeah, and I cannot wait to be done with it," I told my agent. "Everybody just keeps fussing all over me, trying to make sure I'm comfortable. Jesus, I'd rather just take it all off and hop into bed with him for real."

"That would make you a porn actress," Marc's voice answered me. *Guess I'm on speaker,* I thought. Nika used to tell me things like that to make sure I didn't say something wrong. She really must be in a rush.

"Well, I'm no porn star, but I'm no china doll either," I said. "Matthew's all worried because I don't have my mama here with me for the shooting, to make me feel safe. Can you imagine my mama? She'd be busy trying to hump Harlan's body double!"

"Tone it down, Clo, they expect you to act your age." Nika sounded irritated. "You might find that when you're actually topless in bed with a camera rolling, you feel vulnerable."

"I don't do vulnerable," I told her. "When's Travis getting here? I don't like being alone."

"In ten days," she said. "Jude arrives next week."

"Any news from my loser of a daddy?" I asked.

Both of them were quiet for a second, which told me everything I needed to know. Daddy was up to no good, as usual. But Nika just said, "I'm not up-to-date on that. I'll put a call in to Sean."

"Anyway, here's what you need to worry about," Marc jumped in. "I want you to stay away from the London paparazzi. They're brutal, nothing like Los Angeles. The things they put in their magazines there would shock even you, Ms. Jaded Texan."

"So I have to behave myself, you mean?" I asked. "That's no fun."

"You're there to work, not to have fun," Nika said. "Call me after you wrap tomorrow so I know it went okay."

"Sure thing," I said, and hung up. She didn't care if I called, I could tell. Nika knew I wasn't the type to get neurotic about a little public make-out session. She just wanted to look like the caring agent to the kid actress. I'd have to make sure Matthew Greengold saw me calling to check in with her at the shoot tomorrow, so he'd keep having a good impression of us both.

Nika was wrong about one thing, though—I wasn't just here to work. I wanted to have fun, too. There was no way I could sit around my hotel room all by myself, or go get a massage, or make sure I got enough sleep so I'd be ready to shoot tomorrow. Maybe if Trav or Jude were here now, I could hang out and try to relax. But without anyone to talk to, I'd go crazy. I'd never realized it before, but when I was alone, I couldn't stand the silence. I'd even welcome my mama's whining right about now.

Luckily, Harlan didn't like to be alone, either.

"You about done with that?" I asked the wardrobe girl. "I got plans."

"I know he said the club wasn't local, but I kind of thought we'd stay in the same country," I joked as the limo swept us through a tunnel on our way into Paris. The Eiffel Tower was right there, so close I could practically touch it. I wished I had Travis here to see it with me.

"Harlan will take any excuse to fuel up the jet," the British guy next to me replied. "He likes to spend money, that one."

True. I hadn't spent a dime since I'd started hanging with Harlan and his friends. I hadn't seen anyone else pay for a thing, either, but maybe places just billed him, or maybe there was some secret business manager following us around and paying for the bottles of Cristal, the crackers and caviar, the free-flowing food and drink and company. I didn't know, and I didn't care. The man was made of money, so why should I worry about how much our partying cost?

"More champagne, ducky?" the guy asked. He didn't wait for me to answer before pouring. He was drinking whiskey, though.

"What was your name again?" I asked. Harlan had told me when we got on the private plane in London, but he'd had some redheaded extra attached to his mouth at the time, so I hadn't quite understood what he was saying.

"Callum. Callum Gardner." The guy peered at me for a second, as if I was supposed to react.

"Okay, Callum. Thanks." I raised my glass to him, then took a sip. It was just a little awkward in here, because Harlan and the redhead were practically having sex in the corner. Harlan's two assistants—who were really his best friends, apparently—had been on their cells since we landed, calling everyone they knew in Paris to come meet us. That left me and my new friend, Callum, who had shown up tonight for the first time.

"You don't know me?" he asked.

"Sorry," I said. "Friend of Harlan, right? He told me he takes his friends everywhere."

"Well, yeah, Harley's all right. But I'm not a little poodle that travels around in his purse." Callum shot a glance at the assistants—Jason and Ethan—to show what he thought of them. "But he and I got arrested together a while back, and that makes us friends for life."

"Arrested?" I said doubtfully. That would've been front-page news, with Harlan Reed's mugshot on the cover of every tabloid in the world.

"Absolutely. But Harley talked his way out of it, you know how he does. A sparkly smile, a few winks, some photo ops with the local sheriffs. That's all they wanted, really. But me, they would've left to rot. Harlan got me out with him, and for that reason I will always be at his beck and call, at least when he wants to go drinking in Paris."

I couldn't figure this guy out. He had wild eyes and the kind of English accent that I'd always thought was fake—sort of a cross between Simon Cowell and Captain Jack—but he didn't seem to be kidding. Or if he was, he was good at it. And everything he said about Harlan sounded almost like he was making fun of the biggest movie star on the planet. How could he get away with that? Was I supposed to take him seriously?

"So what were you arrested for?" I asked.

"Would you believe public indecency?" he said.

"From Harlan, no. From you . . ." I said.

He nodded. "Good girl! You're on to me: I'm a naughty, terrible man. But in fact we were hauled in for trespassing. And a bit of breaking and entering."

"Right," I said. "Because Harlan needs to steal things."

"It wasn't like that. We were doing this film, a sort of violent, modern Shakespearean thing, you see, and Harlan had one big soliloquy that sold the whole story. I'd always pictured it in a particular room, a place I'd seen once in an old manor house that'd been turned into an S-and-M museum. But damned if I could get permits to shoot in the place. So I took a camera, and Harley, and we just went in the window one night to get our footage. Nobody hurt but a few bureaucrats who didn't get their permit fees."

"Wait. You're a director?" I asked, surprised. The guy seemed more like a musician, or a cameraman. Basically, something more scruffy than a director. His hair was too long, and he hadn't shaved in at least a week. He was still kind of hot, though if he hadn't had that English accent he would've seemed like just another smelly biker type. But if he was a filmmaker, maybe I'd have to pay more attention.

"A director, yeah." Callum smirked. "The name was *Callum Gardner*, ducky."

"I guess I should know who you are, I'm sorry," I said. "You probably make those cool indie films everyone's always talking about at the Sundance festival, right? I always wish I could see movies like that, but all they ever play at the multiplex in Spurlock, Texas, are huge blockbuster movies with things blowing up all over the place."

Callum choked on his drink. "I suppose I should put a few explosions in my indie films, and finally get to Texas."

"Did I say something wrong?" I did my best cute-and-innocent gasp, the kind you use to cover up any blunders you make in answering a beauty pageant judge's question.

"No, you pegged me exactly. I make cool films that everyone talks about and no one sees." Callum laughed. "Sometimes I get hold of a prize like Harley over there, and then I stand a chance at winning an award or two for my movie."

"We're here! I need my escargot fix *now*." Harlan peeled the girl off of him and threw open the limo door. Ethan and Jason piled out after them, and I followed. I don't know what I'd been expecting from Paris—a glowing neon nightclub or some kind of bordello-like bar—but this was not it.

We were in a tiny alleyway, barely big enough to fit the car, and the road was paved with cobblestones.

"Ah, France. It smells like urine," Callum said, climbing out of the limo behind me.

"But it will taste like heaven." Harlan flung one arm over Callum's shoulders, one over mine. "We're going into the catacombs, my lovelies! I had them shut the place down for tonight, just us and our friends."

"What catacombs?" I asked.

"Tunnels under the Parisian cemeteries, ducky, very ancient and haunted," Callum said.

"And popular with the punk crowd," Jason put in.

"But I have a friend whose restaurant connects to the tunnels through his basement. So the VIP room's in the catacombs; it's fabulous," Harlan said. "We'll sit in a crypt and eat truffles!" He led us through a dark, unmarked door into a tiny, cramped kitchen. It was warm, and two skinny guys in white coats were busy cooking. We went through the kitchen and down a stone stairway into the lounge, or maybe it was a restaurant, it was too dark to see. Either way, it didn't feel any more like a crypt than any other darkened lounge I'd been to. Still, if Harlan Reed said it was cool, that meant it was cool.

There were several low tables and a bunch of velvet couches, and about twenty people lying around, most of whom jumped up and started kissing Harlan hello.

"Is this really some old tunnel?" I asked Callum.

"It's the tail end of a minor underground passageway, but it's also the most exclusive restaurant in Paris," he said. "Do you know, I tried to eat here once and they turned me away? Wouldn't even take my reservation. I'm not posh enough for them."

"And who are all these people?" I glanced around as I dropped down onto one of the couches. There were six-foot-tall blond women, a few superskinny French guys, one or two people who looked familiar, like maybe I'd seen them on one of Travis's soccer posters, and a bunch of beautiful types wearing black and smoking.

"Nobody, ducky. Harlan and his mates collect them like dolls. They're all quite full of themselves because they get to be here, but they're just warm bodies to him." Callum was sitting next to me, his arm thrown over the back of the couch. But he wasn't hitting on me, he was just amused at the parade of wannabes in front of us.

And so was I, I decided.

Because I wasn't here as a warm body, and I didn't have to scam an invite. I was here *with* Harlan, and I didn't have to sleep with him to get an invite, the way most of these girls—and guys—obviously did. I was here with him because we worked together, because I was an actor like him, because I was *not* a wannabe.

"Now that is a lovely sight." Callum gazed at my face. "A shit-eating grin, we'd call it."

"That's what we call it in Texas, too," I said. "This is really the most exclusive place in Paris?"

He nodded. "Most expensive, too."

"Then I'm going to have the most expensive food on the menu," I said. "And you and I are gonna get wasted on the most expensive champagne—"

"Careful, love, don't get yourself sick." Harlan threw himself down on the lounge next to me. "We've got our big scene tomorrow, and I don't want to be vomited on."

"Ugh!" The redhead rolled her eyes.

But Callum chuckled. "Now, that would be *my* kind of sex scene—two drunken sots going at it until someone hurls."

"Maybe I don't want to see your movies after all," I told him.

Harlan pulled out a joint and lit up, taking a long drag. "I told Chloe she needs to relax before we shoot, but she won't."

"I don't do relaxation, if that's what you want to call it," I said. "I don't want to lose my edge."

"Why not?" the redhead asked, taking the joint from Harlan.

I shrugged. "I like to be in control. My mama's drunk all the time, and she is not in control of herself."

Callum reached for the joint. "Control is overrated. You'll never be a truly great actor until you learn to let go of it."

"Yeah, look at me. I'm baked all the time and I'm a living

legend in the film world." Harlan began laughing as soon as the words left his mouth, and Callum laughed along with him.

"You don't really smoke while you're acting, do you?" I asked as they passed the joint around again. He'd been kidding—well, sort of—but the man *was* a living legend. He hadn't won an Oscar yet, but he'd been nominated for a couple, and he won lots of other awards. And besides, everyone in the world loved him.

"Sometimes," he told me. "Depends on the scene, depends on the character. Depends on my mood."

"You Americans are so down on drugs," Callum said. "But they're mind-expanding."

"And addictive," I pointed out.

"Yes. Well and good," he said. "Not everyone can handle them. All I'm saying is, sometimes it's best to let your psychological walls come down. If you want to let your character in, I mean. Who's going to be bedding this beautiful man tomorrow, hmm? Chloe Gamble?"

"No," I said. "Anissa. My character."

"Is she there? Is she in you yet?" Callum asked. "This Anissa, she's in love with him, yes? Desperately, passionately, all that?"

"Yes," I said. "She wouldn't be sleeping with him otherwise. It was the 1900s. Sex was a big taboo."

"Do you feel it? The passion?" Callum took another drag of the joint while he spoke.

Harlan had his eyes closed while the girl stroked his hair. He'd checked out of this conversation. But Callum sat leaning forward, his eyes on mine, his expression serious. He was a director, after all. He knew about acting, and actors. That was his job.

"I know what desperation feels like, and passion," I said. "That's how I feel about being famous. I'm desperate for it."

"Ah, but can you focus that on someone else?" he asked. "Your character, she's losing herself in this man. Can you do that, Chloe? Can you lose yourself?"

I didn't answer. The last thing on earth I'd ever try to do is lose myself. *Myself* was the only thing I could count on, especially now that Travis wasn't with me.

"See, ducky? You need to relax." Callum leaned back against the couch cushions. "Let Chloe loosen up so that Anissa can come through."

His eyes were glazing over now, like Harlan's, and they both had smiles on their lips. There was music playing, and a few people had started to dance. There was champagne everywhere, and the smell of the food from the kitchen was mouthwatering.

These people had been making movies since I was Miss Junior Sunflower Queen back in Bumfuck, Texas. They knew what they were talking about.

"Okay. I'll relax," I said, reaching for the joint.

Nika Mays's Manuscript Notes: Rising Star

"Something you want to tell me?" Sean asked when I pulled up in front of his house.

"Oh, you mean this?" I grinned, running my hand over the leather seat of the gleaming blue Bentley coupe I was driving. "You know my Mini was too small."

Sean shook his head, climbing into the passenger seat. "You did not spend your entire raise to lease a Bentley?"

"Nope. It's in addition!" I hit the gas and roared out into traffic. "Daniel said I could lease a company car, whatever kind I wanted."

"So Virtuoso is paying for you to drive a hundred-thousand-dollar car? That's kind of obscene."

"You think I should've asked them to get me a Volkswagen?" I asked. "This makes me look powerful."

"You *act* powerful, you don't have to use props," he muttered. "No wonder you offered to drive tonight."

"Damn straight. I want to take my car out and show it off," I said. "Why do you think we're having dinner at Nobu? Everyone will see us!"

Sean gazed out his window, not amused. I decided

not to pay attention to his mood. He'd gotten a hefty raise, too, all because of our Chloe Gamble/ EdisonCorp/Matthew Greengold deal. Before it had even hit the trades the next day, we were both in huge new offices with huge new salaries. Sean had no reason to be acting all sour.

"Hal hasn't spoken to me since the meeting," I said. "But I think he noticed the new car."

"He's old-fashioned. You broke the rules," Sean told me. "He probably wants you to apologize."

"Never going to happen. You and I just made some new rules." I reached for his hand and laced my fingers through his. "Daniel invited me to a meeting this morning with Brad Pitt! Hal wasn't even there."

"They brought me along to a meeting with Pacino's people today," Sean said. "Not quite as glamorous as Brad, but still."

"See? It's just like we said. We're legends." I did a little shimmy dance in my seat. "Thank you, Chloe Gamble!"

"Have you told her about Lonnie yet?" he asked.

"She's got enough on her plate. Matthew Greengold is starting her off with her big sex scene; he says it's a good way to force her past her inhibitions so she's completely in character. He's *that* kind of director."

Sean snorted. "She doesn't have any inhibitions to begin with."

"I didn't tell Matthew that," I said. "Anyway, Chloe's fine. She's far away from her father and she's hanging out with movie stars. Let her have some fun."

"Fine, but you and I need to deal with it. Lonnie's motion has legs," Sean said. "We did the emancipation in a sketchy way, remember. Their mother didn't even sign the petition for emancipation, we just argued that her abandonment equaled agreement."

"Chloe and Travis are both earning huge paychecks and handling themselves like adults," I said. "No judge is going to overturn it."

"I think you're underestimating Lonnie," Sean started. I pulled my hand out of his.

"We're on a date here, Sean," I said. "Can we not spend the whole time talking about the Gamble family?"

"Fine," he grumbled. "We'll just talk about your new car."

I didn't answer. There was nothing to say.

* * *

Travis Gamble was in my office when I arrived at eight-thirty in the morning.

"Wow, Trav, I didn't think teenage boys were physically capable of getting up this early," I joked. "Morning, Coop."

"Morning," Trav's best friend mumbled. He lay splayed on my couch, looking like crap.

"We never really went to bed last night," Travis admitted. "We were at an after-hours party, and I figured I would swing by before we head home. You never seem to have time to talk on the phone."

Guilt from the Gambles, I thought. "My schedule has been insane since I got promoted," I told him. "Hasn't my assistant been taking care of you?"

"Yeah, I have all the travel info for England. I leave the day after tomorrow," Travis said. "But we need to do something about my daddy before then. The judge set a date for a hearing, and that sounds pretty official to me."

I sighed. "Travis, I can't help you with your family issues. I know how you and Chloe feel about your father, and as your friend I sympathize. But you're an emancipated minor. You're in charge of your own destiny. Part of being an adult means learning to deal with things like this."

"But Travis says you're supposed to handle his

career problems," Coop piped up. "And his daddy is out to ruin his career."

"What do you mean?" The light on my phone was flashing, which meant my assistant had a call waiting for me. I needed to get to work.

"The lawyer told us that Trav's emancipation might get overturned," Coop said.

I felt a surge of annoyance. Why was Sean going around saying things like that? It was only a remote possibility, hearing date or not.

"If it gets overturned, I won't be allowed to sign any contracts myself. My daddy will have to decide if I'm allowed to work or not," Travis said. "And Sean said he could void the contracts I already have. He could say I'm not allowed to do that scene in *Frontier*."

My blood ran cold at the thought of that. If Lonnie got what he wanted, he certainly could torpedo the job in Matthew Greengold's movie— for Travis, but worse, for Chloe. Maybe Sean was right. I should pay more attention to Lonnie Gamble.

"My mama is freaking out, Nika, she calls about five times a day all worried about Daddy," Trav said. "And I'm starting to lose it, too."

"Okay. Let's meet and make a plan," I told him.

"But I really have to take this call."

"I'm leaving in two days. It has to be tomorrow," Travis said. "Sean said he has time around noon. And my mama wants to come."

"Good. Noon at Sean's office." I hastily scribbled it on a Post-it. "Try not to worry, Trav. I won't let anything stand in the way of your movie role."

Trav nodded, heading for the door. Coop followed, veering over toward me at the last second.

"Listen, ma'am, you don't know Mr. Gamble. He fights dirty," Coop murmured, shooting a glance at Travis, who was now flirting with my assistant. "Chloe can handle him a little, but not Travis. Trav's a good guy, and Clo . . ."

"I know what Chloe is," I said, smiling. "But it'll be fine, Coop. This is Hollywood. We all fight dirty here."

Before I could even get to my phone, Daniel Shapiro appeared in the doorway. "Nika, got a minute?"

"Of course." I shot a look at my assistant, telling her to take a message. Nobody was more important than my boss. He loved me right now, and I had to capitalize on that before things went south, because things always go south eventually. The more Daniel liked me, the better my long-term prospects were here at the Virtuoso Agency.

He came in and closed the door, which meant this was something big. I perched on the edge of my gigantic desk, while Daniel settled himself in one of my guest chairs.

"Ty Boswell," he said.

"I heard he's being considered for the lead in the new James Cameron movie," I said. Ty Boswell was twenty-three, with an ever-so-slightly nerdy air to his good looks, and his acting was phenomenal. Of all the guys in town who were being called "the next big thing," Ty had the best shot of actually getting there. He'd already been in one of the highest-grossing films of all time, not that he carried it. It was a blockbuster action flick with an explosion every five minutes and a couple of truly incredible robots. Still, Ty was a star because of it. "He can pretty much write his own ticket now."

"He can," Daniel agreed. "But he's not happy with his agent."

My mouth dropped open. "Are you kidding me? Who would be stupid enough to lose Ty Boswell at this point in his career? He's poised to be huge!"

"Apparently he feels a bit . . . stifled." Daniel could barely contain his glee. "He's been with the same agency for four years and he feels that they still think of him as a newbie—"

"Instead of as the big star he is," I finished for him. "Have you been meeting with him?"

"Of course. Who do you think put the idea in his head?" Daniel smiled. "But listen. Ty thinks he represents a new generation of actors. He sees himself as an Everyman. Not the slick leading-man type like Harlan Reed, but more of a scruffy, relatable type."

"Sure, the secretly gorgeous semi-loser who can still save the world," I said. "He's cute, and he can act, and he's got a cocky, charming presence. It's more fun to watch someone like that than just another handsome face. You feel like Ty is the guy next door, except he can kick ass. He *is* the next generation of movie star."

"Exactly. Which is why I need you to land him." Daniel let his gaze travel up and down my body. "He thinks I'm old, even if he doesn't admit it. You're more his style."

"I'm not *that* young," I said.

"But you'll be able to convince him that we're legit. We truly believe in his vision of himself, and we can sell him accordingly." Daniel stood up. "You know how to deal with the up-and-comers, Nika. Look at Chloe Gamble. Ty is just the male version."

"Well, he's much bigger than Chloe," I said. "He's already a household name."

"You can get him," Daniel said confidently.

"Of course I can." I grinned. "I'll put in a call right now."

"No need. He's coming in tomorrow at eleven-thirty. It'll be just the three of us," Daniel said. "He leaves for Tokyo right after. I want him to spend the whole long flight thinking about what a perfect fit we are."

"Got it."

"One thing," Daniel added, his voice casual. "Peter Bryant is going after him, too."

He wandered out of my office, leaving me to think about that last bit. Peter Bryant was a hot agent at a big firm. He was still young—in his thirties—and he was practically good-looking enough to be an actor himself. He had just married a reality TV star, and he owned a popular bar in Venice Beach. He was friends with everyone in Hollywood—which meant, basically, that he'd managed to make a bunch of really big name actors think they were his pals instead of his meal ticket. His client roster included several megawatt stars, and his personal contact list included several more.

Landing Ty Boswell would be a cakewalk for him.

Peter could just invite him out to play poker with Matt Damon and Harlan Reed and Brad Pitt, and Ty would think Peter was the greatest thing ever.

So that's my competition, I thought, staring out the window at my fantastic view of Beverly Hills. Daniel was putting me up against the hottest young agent in town to see how I did. If I failed, well, maybe I could spin it. Peter Bryant was ten years older than me, he had way more experience. I wouldn't lose my job over it, but I'd definitely lose face. But if I won—if I signed Ty Boswell— then *I* would be the hottest young agent in town.

"I need every piece of film on Ty Boswell. Clear my schedule for today, and no calls," I told my assistant. Then I closed the door.

I had some serious homework to do, Chloe-style. That girl never went to a meeting without researching every single thing about the other person. It was a good strategy. I'd watch every movie, every guest spot, every talk show interview. I'd read all Ty's press. Hell, I'd check out where he went to high school and what it said next to his yearbook picture. By this time tomorrow, I would know Ty Boswell better than he knew himself.

And I would know how to lure him in.

I took a deep breath, not bothering to wipe

the grin off my face. Even the thought of going head-to-head with Peter Bryant couldn't dim my good mood. Ty Boswell! A gigantic star, and Daniel wanted *me* to land him! I knew I could do it, and once I signed him, once I brought his $25 million paychecks to Virtuoso, I would be Daniel's go-to girl for sure. I would be untouchable.

This is my first test, I thought. Until now, I hadn't been on my own swimming with the big fish. I'd always had Hal to fall back on. I might not have wanted him, but he was there, lecturing me, berating me, mocking me . . . teaching me. He'd helped out with Chloe more than I liked to admit. And even when I went around Hal, like with the Snap network blowups, I wasn't alone. I had Sean.

This time I was going to do it with no help at all. Just me, Nika, in charge of my own destiny.

My BlackBerry buzzed to tell me I had a message. I reached over and turned the whole thing off. Nothing mattered today except making a plan for tomorrow's lunch. It wasn't just a social get-together, it was a full-out performance, sales pitch, and seduction all mashed together. I had to script it perfectly.

The Post-it on my desk said "Gambles, noon tomorrow, Sean's office."

I stared at it for a long moment, thinking it through. I couldn't do both meetings. Chloe had made me a success. And Lonnie Gamble was a Chloe problem—a *potential* Chloe problem, anyway. But Ty Boswell was a bigger fish. He was my future.

And anyway, Sean could handle it.

IM

CHLOE: Trav, OMG, you will not believe this!!

GAMBLEGOAL: What time is it there? Are you at work?

CHLOE: Ten in the morning, not shooting today, not at the studio, not even in England!

GAMBLEGOAL: ???

CHLOE: I'm in Spain! Ibiza!

GAMBLEGOAL: With Harlan?

CHLOE: No, his friend Callum. Harlan let us take his private jet. So fun.

CHLOE: But guess who's here? Sasha Powell! Bitch tried to pretend she didn't see me but we're on a yacht with only 15 other people. She's still avoiding me.

GAMBLEGOAL: What???

CHLOE: Got here last night, this Greek shipping heir comes up to me at a club and is my biggest fan. He's having a yacht party today, so Callum & I decided to come. Guess Sasha was invited too.

CHLOE: Want me to push her off the boat 4 U?

GAMBLEGOAL: No. Be nice. Say hi for me.

CHLOE: Srsly? Wuss.

GAMBLEGOAL: One a.m. here. I'm at Avalon, ran into your best friend.

CHLOE: Who?

GAMBLEGOAL: Kimber Reeve. I'm not throwing a drink on her for you.

CHLOE: Are you in the VIP room? With Kimber?

GAMBLEGOAL: No, she's dancing. She hit on me, like I wouldn't know she was just doing it to fuck w/ you. So I handed her off to Coop.

CHLOE: You gonna let her screw Coop? Poor Coop!

GAMBLEGOAL: Yeah, 'cause she's really hideous.

CHLOE: Sasha won't take her bikini top off, FYI. Everyone else here is topless. She a prude?

GAMBLEGOAL: Put your top on, Clo. Number 14 on the list, ain't it?

CHLOE: But it's Spain. Nude sunbathing is normal here, so the list doesn't count.

GAMBLEGOAL: Can you call me? Need to tell you about a Daddy meeting tomorrow.

CHLOE: Forgot to say Lars Svedman is here, too. (That Swedish guy who produced all 5 of last year's top albums) He's a legend. And he knows who I am! He loves my music.

GAMBLEGOAL: That's cool. Clo, the Daddy thing is trouble.

CHLOE: He wants to remix "Lucky Bitch," but Max produced that one. Think he'd be mad? He would, right?

GAMBLEGOAL: I'm heading outside where I can hear better. Call me.

CHLOE: No Daddy talk. I don't care. And I'm too wasted anyhow. Give Kimber a kiss for me!

"You ever seen my sister wasted?" I asked Coop on the way to Sean's office.

"Nope." He took the exit toward Culver City, where the law firm was based. He always drove now—it made him feel less like a leech. Keeping me sane in this fucking insane town didn't seem to count as worthwhile in Coop's book, and besides, his parents were pissed that he came to LA after he graduated instead of going straight to college.

"Chloe said it was ten in the morning and she was naked on a yacht and wasted," I told him.

Coop's ears turned red. He'd always had a thing for Chloe, but we all pretended he didn't. "Well, topless," I said. "And wasted at ten a.m."

"Weird," he agreed. "But you have to focus on your father. You'll see Chloe soon enough."

"Yeah." Maybe I'd see Sasha, too. If she was in Europe at the same time as me, it could happen. Famous people hung out in the same places—and Chloe was pretty damn famous now. I couldn't even buy groceries without seeing my sister's face on all the magazines near the checkout.

"I can't believe I come to LA and you take off to England," Coop muttered.

"It's only for a week. If you'd gotten off your ass and got your passport on time, you could've come with," I told him.

"You kidding? I barely got my mama to let me come to California." Coop pulled up to the valet in front of the office building.

"Besides, someone's got to pick up your dry cleaning and shit while you're gone. That fancy house don't take care of itself."

I grinned. As of tomorrow, Coop was my official personal assistant. Most actors had one, so why not me? It gave me an excuse to pay him, and it gave his parents the illusion that he was working hard. Win-win.

"You coming to this meeting?" I asked.

Coop shook his head. "That's family business." I knew what he meant—he didn't want anything to do with my daddy and all our fighting. Coop and me had been friends since I was in first grade and he was in second, which was plenty long enough that he'd seen a million Gamble family battles. I figured he was bored with it by now.

"What are you gonna do?"

"Head over to Prada and pick you up some pricey luggage," he said. "I called this morning and said it was for you and they promised me free stuff."

I got out of the Escalade, laughing. He already had the Hollywood assistant thing down, and I knew he'd be keeping some of that free stuff for himself.

Upstairs, Sean was waiting for me in his office.

And so was my daddy.

"What the hell?" I said, astonished.

"He says Early invited him," Sean told me, looking seriously pissed off.

"Your mama came to her senses and decided we should all sit

down and have ourselves a nice family meeting," Daddy said. He leaned back on the leather couch and crossed his cowboy-boot-covered feet, his usual self-satisfied grin on his face. "Trav, you remember Sylvia, my lawyer?"

I didn't even acknowledge the fake-blond, fake-tanned, fake-friendly woman on the couch next to him. At least she had a shirt on this time.

"I would've appreciated a heads-up," Sean said.

"I didn't know he was coming," I protested. "I don't want to be anywhere near him. Where's Nika?"

"Late." Sean glanced at his cell. "I left her two messages already, but her phone must be off."

"This Hollywood glamour has made y'all soft." Daddy chuckled. "Sylvia and me were the only ones on time for this little shindig."

"Do you want to reschedule?" Sean asked me, ignoring my daddy and definitely ignoring his lawyer. "I can have security escort these two out."

"I'm leaving tomorrow," I reminded him.

"Right, off to shoot your big movie scene," Daddy cut in. "I read all about it in that paper. What's it called, sugar?"

"*Variety*," Sylvia said.

"Yeah. That rag keeps me up on everything my children are doing," my daddy said. "'Course, I can read about Chloe anywhere these days. Seems to be having herself a real good time over there."

The words were mild, but I knew what my daddy meant. Chloe popped up in lots of gossip blogs these days, always out at some club in Paris or London or Madrid, or seen hanging out with socialites and British royals. They called her a party girl, but Daddy was saying that she was something worse.

"Who the hell is that piece of trash?" my mama's voice announced her presence before she'd even stepped into the office. "I told you to come alone, Lonnie."

"Y'all got your lawyer, I got mine," Daddy replied. "I ain't about to show up unprotected."

"I'm calling Alex and tell him to come." Mama pulled out her cell, but I took it from her.

"Mama, you want to explain what Daddy's doing here?" I demanded. "This was supposed to be me and Nika and Sean. I said *you* could come just so you'd stop freaking out."

"Now don't be mad at me, darlin'," she said. "I knew you wouldn't agree to letting your daddy come, and nobody wants him here less than me." She shot Daddy a nasty look. "But he ain't going away, and we need to talk frank before it turns into some big court case."

"You need to talk without Chloe here, you mean," I said. My mama and daddy both knew I couldn't stand up to them the way my sister could. We might be twins, but she got more backbone than me. She said I got more regular decency, but she never meant that as a compliment.

"I don't think I understand what it is your client wishes to discuss," Sean said, turning to Sylvia. "We have a court date on the books. We'll see you there."

"Mr. Gamble thinks it would be in the best interests of his

children if this matter were kept out of the courtroom," Sylvia said. "A long legal battle would only cause stress and embarrassment to the minor children."

"*Emancipated* minors," I cut in, but nobody even looked at me.

"I don't expect a long battle," Sean said. "Or any battle at all. Any idiot can file paperwork. That doesn't mean a judge is going to pay attention to it."

"I never agreed to no emancipation," my daddy said. "Nobody even asked me."

"That's because we hadn't seen you in months," I said.

"My lawyer tells me the parents have to say it's okay," Daddy went on, ignoring me like always. "You tryin' to say she's wrong?"

"No." Sean was getting angrier by the second, I could tell. He glanced at his watch, then at his phone. I knew he was wondering about Nika. She should be here for this fight. Chloe, too.

I pulled out my cell and and hit speed dial for Chloe, but it went straight to voicemail. It was nine at night in Spain, if that's where she still was. She was probably out at some club with her phone off. Either way, she couldn't really help. I was on my own here.

"Nobody asked me, either," my mama piped up. "I got back from a trip and the judge had already signed off."

"That doesn't sound entirely . . . typical," Sylvia said. Maybe she was taking lessons from my daddy, because she didn't mean it wasn't *typical*. She meant it wasn't *legit*. And the thing was, she was right. Sean had argued that Mama being gone meant that she thought we could manage on our own—that we were adults. Far as I can remember, none of us gave a single thought to Daddy.

I felt bile rise up in me at the thought that Lonnie Gamble could ever be in charge of my life again. That man was a selfish cockroach who'd made our lives miserable. And if he got control of Chloe's career, well, there's nothing she wouldn't do to destroy him. I shot Sean a panicked look, but he was cool. He didn't even blink.

"There's no need to ask permission of absentee parents. Both of you had, in effect, abandoned Chloe and Travis. Therefore, your permission was assumed by the court." Sean sounded snobby for the first time since I'd known him, like he was rich and smart and he thought my folks were poor and dumb. Like he was better than them. Like they were fighting out of their weight class.

I wasn't insulted. I just hoped he was right.

"Mr. Gamble certainly did not abandon his children," Sylvia gasped. "His family left him."

"Because he was sleeping around with every little slut he could find!" my mama snapped.

"That's immaterial," Sean cut in, before it could get out of hand. "It had been months. It was perfectly clear where Chloe and Travis were living, and he made no attempt to contact them. Judge Gutierrez knew that, and she'll remember it."

Sylvia didn't answer that one. "Trying to reverse the emancipation is nothing more than a crass, greedy ploy to get your hands on your children's money," Sean said, turning to Daddy.

"Anyone with eyes can see that. And trying to scare Travis into making some kind of settlement with you is even worse."

"You'd never pull this crap if Chloe was here," I agreed. My daddy narrowed his eyes at me and shook his head. All my life he'd been telling me I was no kind of man, and that's what he wanted me to know now, too.

"And you, Earlene," Sean turned to my mama. "I'm not *your* lawyer. I don't know what you think you're doing here, taking Lonnie's side."

"She just thinks he's gonna win," I said. "She always thinks he'll win."

"Well, he won't. So pick a side, Early," Sean said. "Because we all know that once Chloe finds out about this, your percentage of her salary will stop coming."

Mama's face paled. In another world, maybe it would've been interesting to watch her try to decide whether she was more scared of my daddy or of Chloe. But this was my world, and it just sucked. My mama didn't give a crap about how I felt, or how my sister felt. She wanted to figure out where her best chance of getting rich was.

"I'm on Chloe's side," she finally said. "I brought her out to LA, didn't I? I helped her get her start in Hollywood."

Mama had really just come along for the ride, but I didn't say that. Why bother?

"I guess we're done here." Daddy stood up and grabbed his cowboy hat, putting it on in his usual cocky way. "But you tell

Chloe to be careful, you hear?" He pulled a folded-up magazine page out of his pocket and tossed it down on Sean's coffee table. It was a paparazzi photo of Chloe on the beach. Topless. "Maybe that just bothers me 'cause she's my little girl. You Hollywood types have a different way of life than we did back home." Daddy gave us a wink. "We'll be seeing y'all at that hearing with Judge Gutierrez."

Once he was gone, my mama started to cry. That's what she always does when she thinks somebody is mad at her—you can't yell at a crying woman, it's mean. That never stopped my sister, but I could see that Sean wasn't going to be the jerk to take on Mama, and I never had the stomach for it, either. Coop and me had a theory that the rules are different for girls. They can be nastier than we can.

"I know y'all think I'm crazy for bringing him here, but that man is dangerous," Mama blubbered. "He ain't gonna stop until he gets what he wants."

"Chloe told you she won't cut Daddy in on her money," I said. "Same goes for me. Why should we give him something he didn't earn?"

"So he don't go and ruin us all, darlin'," Mama said. She pulled out her compact and fixed her makeup, now that she'd gotten away from a lecture. "You think you're so high and mighty, the two of you, with your expensive lawyer. But Lonnie don't scare easy."

"Earlene, I don't want any more stunts." Sean sounded tired. "If you're worried about your ex-husband, get your own attorney and divorce him. Don't drag Travis into it."

Mama didn't answer. She just blew me a kiss and headed for the door. Her porn guy was probably waiting downstairs.

I wished Coop had come up here with me. I wished Chloe had. Anyone to take the pressure off. Because Sean was looking at me with a strange expression on his face, and I could tell he had his doubts about me. Truth was, the emancipation thing never bothered me because I always figured it would be me and Clo taking care of ourselves together. But with her in Europe and me here alone, it didn't seem so easy.

"Nika's here," Sean's assistant buzzed in.

Sean rolled his eyes. Nika rushed in, all electric. "I'm so sorry I'm late!" She gave me a quick kiss. "Let's get started."

"You missed the whole thing," I told her. "My mama and daddy just left. Where the hell were you?"

"Your daddy?" Nika shot Sean a look.

"Yeah. It was a party." Sean said sarcastically. "He and Early double-teamed us to get a settlement."

"For what?" Nika cried. "He doesn't stand a chance!"

"Don't stand there all indignant about it when you couldn't be bothered to show up," Sean snapped. "You know as well as I do that we got them emancipated in a questionable manner. It's entirely possible that the judge will reverse it, especially if you keep letting Chloe act this way." He tossed the magazine picture at her.

Nika seemed a little shocked to see it, but she just went back to arguing with Sean. "Look, I had an important meeting and I got here as soon as I could. This isn't my department anyway. You're the lawyer."

"I'm an entertainment lawyer. Not a family lawyer." Sean's face had turned red and he was all but yelling. "You can't just dump the Gambles on me!"

"Both of you shut it!" I cried, jumping up. "Y'all are talking like I'm not even here. I seen enough of my parents screaming at each other about me and Clo. I don't need to see you."

"Sorry, Trav." Nika ran her hand through her hair. "I had no idea your father would be here. And I think I just landed a really big client." She was apologizing, but her voice was filled with excitement, not regret. "I would've been here sooner if I could've."

"Who?" Sean frowned.

"Ty Boswell!" Nika practically did a dance. "He's thinking it over, but I know I got to him. And when I sign him, I'll be untouchable at Virtuoso!"

"Guess that means it don't matter if my daddy gets his hands on our money," I muttered.

Nika's smile vanished. "Of course it matters, Trav. But it won't happen. We won't let it, right, Sean?"

He sighed. "No."

"You know what? I think I'll come with you to London tomorrow," Nika told me. "It's about time I paid Chloe a visit, and it'll be good for you to have company for your first big movie role."

I stared at her. "You think that's gonna placate me?"

"No." Nika's eyebrows drew together. "We're friends, Travis, I don't have to placate you."

I shook my head. "You don't have the time to be friends these days."

"Trav . . ." Nika sounded shocked.

"I get it," I said. "It's business. You don't want to be my babysitter anymore, or Clo's. You're busy being a superagent. But you can't keep thinking that we're all friends and nothing's changed. You gonna be *friends* with Ty Boswell, too?"

She just stared at me.

"I'm an adult now, right?" I said. "That means I'm on my own— for the good stuff *and* the bad stuff. And so is Chloe."

chapter five

From Nika Mays's Manuscript Notes: Flying High

Success. Everyone wants it. But the thing nobody tells you about success is that you can't really enjoy it. Most people have this idea that you strive to reach a goal, and when you achieve it, you're happy. End of story. But that's not how it works, at least not in Hollywood. I'd been obsessed with the idea of being an agent since the day I graduated from Stanford. First, I was determined to get a job—*any* job—in the Business. It took a while, but I finally landed a receptionist job at the Hal Turman Agency. Success! And did it make me happy?

Hell no.

I had friends who answered phones at bigger, more important agencies. I had friends who had real jobs in other industries, jobs that didn't require them to do things like make hair-frosting appointments for the boss's wife. And I had friends in my agency who got promoted faster than I did. Basically, I was jealous of everyone else, all the time. I was *not* happy.

So I became obsessed with getting the next job in the Business: as assistant instead of receptionist. And when I got that, I wanted to be a junior agent. And when I got that, I wanted to be an actual agent. And when I got that, I wanted to be an agent at a bigger agency. And now that I had that, I wanted . . . more.

Yes, my name was in the trades a lot. Yes, my star client was shooting a movie with the biggest director on earth. Yes, my agency was one of the best in town. But I was still only an agent. I wanted to be a superagent, just like Travis Gamble said.

Maybe then I would be happy.

"I can't believe they're flying me across the world just to film one scene," Travis said from the seat next to me on the plane. "It's not even two pages long."

"The length isn't important, the acting is," I replied. Greengold's company had booked Trav in business class, but I got him bumped up to first with me. Virtuoso would have to pick up the tab, but it was worth it. Travis wasn't the most satisfied client right now, so I wanted to spoil him a little.

"I don't know anything about acting." His perfect forehead wrinkled as he studied the script for *Frontier.* "I should've gone to see Chloe's coach."

"Alan couldn't help you with this scene, you're a natural," I told him. "It's you and your sister saying good-bye. Just imagine you were heading off somewhere dangerous and you didn't know if you'd ever see Chloe again."

Travis grabbed his outrageously expensive first-class beer and took a swig. "I don't even want to imagine that. Me and Clo stick together, and we always will."

I rested my head against the smooth leather of the seat and stretched my legs out, just because I could. When I'd told Daniel Shapiro I was going to England, he said that first class was the only way to fly to Europe. He hadn't even asked me why I wanted to go, or how I planned to juggle the rest of my clients, or any of the questions Hal

Turman would've asked. The rule is that when your client is on location, you go visit. Every agent knows that, and Hal was the one who'd taught it to me. But he still would have grilled me about the details, and he would've made me fly coach.

When we got to London, it was the middle of the night—and Chloe was not in her hotel room.

"Ms. Gatsby left a message for you," the desk clerk at the Four Seasons told Travis. When I'd suggested that Chloe register under a fake name to avoid stalkers, she'd picked "Jay Gatsby" instantaneously. The clerk handed over a folded piece of paper, and Trav opened it to find "Dragon Bar" scrawled in Chloe's handwriting.

I'm as much of a partyer as anyone else—it's the best way to network in Los Angeles. But I was jet-lagged and cranky, and I knew that Chloe's call time was at eight in the morning. Still, I plastered on a smile, put on some more lip gloss, and headed out clubbing with Travis.

Chloe was in the VIP lounge, of course, along with Harlan Reed and Callum Gardner, a bad-boy British director I'd met at Sundance one year. He'd hit on me, I'd ignored him, and that was that. If he remembered it now, he didn't let on and neither did I.

"Trav!" Chloe flung her arms around her brother and held on tight, while I went over to say hello to Harlan.

"The luscious Nika Mays," he purred, kissing my hand. "Chloe didn't mention you were coming."

"Chloe didn't know," Chloe chimed in, still hugging Trav.

"I thought I'd make sure her brother was delivered safely," I told Harlan.

"Very nice of you, darling. Have a drink." He leaned forward to pour me some Cristal himself, and I hid my surprise. We'd never actually spoken before, and that was because Harlan Reed famously hates agents. But it was late, my skirt was short, and he was obviously wasted. Still, he was also one of the most beautiful men on the planet, so I sat down next to him on the couch and took the glass of champagne.

"Clo, where's Jude?" Travis asked. "How come she's not here?" Jude had arrived in London three days earlier, I knew. And she had definitely flown coach. But if she was hanging out with Chloe in places like this, she was probably getting more than enough freebies to make up for it.

"She's off dancing with some French girl," Chloe said.

"A French girl she stole from me," Callum Gardner put in. "Shameless hussy."

"Nika, did you know Anne Lynch is starting tomorrow?" Chloe asked, throwing herself onto the lounge opposite us. "She sent me flowers today to say she can't wait to do our first scene. It was just so sweet."

"She's a class act, that Anne," Harlan murmured. I shot a look at him. He wasn't just drunk; his eyes were glassy and his smile was of the vague, dumb type that the potheads back in my high school used to wear.

Almost like he knew what I was thinking, Callum pulled out a joint and lit up. I sipped my drink and glanced around the room. There were a bunch of hot girls in skimpy outfits lounging on the sofas. They were clearly stoned. And so was Callum. And so was Harlan.

And so was Chloe.

"What the hell?" Travis asked, saving me the trouble.

"It's all right, ducky, Harley's got private security standing guard," Callum said. He offered the joint to Travis, and even I had to laugh at the expression on Trav's face.

"My brother is an athlete. He's got to keep

his lungs pristine." Chloe plucked the joint from Callum's fingers and took a drag.

"Don't you think you should be clear-headed for your scene with Anne tomorrow?" I asked.

"I will be." Chloe shrugged. "I'll be relaxed. I've never found a way to do that before—it's fantastic for my work."

I studied her face. She did look happier than usual, more peaceful. I'd never given it much thought, but "Chloe" and "relaxed" were not two words I would ever have put in the same sentence. She was the type who considered sleep to be a waste of time.

"It's a little trick I learned before we shot our big sex scene, right, Harley?" Chloe said with a smile.

"Mmm." Harlan took a drag and held it out to me.

"Not my thing," I told him. "I'm sorry I wasn't here for that, Chloe. I hope you didn't feel too overexposed."

Callum snorted, and Chloe rolled her eyes. "Acting is acting," she said. "Don't matter if I have my shirt on or not."

"*Dude!*" Travis cried, embarrassed.

"Oh, hush up," Chloe said. "I'm happy. I want to dance and have fun and not talk about work."

Travis frowned. "Who are you and what did you do with my sister?"

She laughed. "Come on and dance with me."

But Travis shook his head and stood up. "Know what? I'm beat. I'm going back to the hotel. You coming?"

"No." Chloe pouted a little, but Travis didn't seem to care. He glanced at me and I shook my head. I was here to see Chloe, and I wanted her to know we were still friends, no matter what Trav thought.

"Fine. Later." Travis headed out without a backward glance.

Before I could say anything to Chloe, my BlackBerry buzzed, making me jump. I grabbed it and saw a new e-mail.

From Ty Boswell.

I turned my back on Chloe and her friends and bent over the phone to read. Ty was in Toyko, and I hadn't heard from him since we'd said good-bye at the office the day before. Daniel Shapiro had wanted Ty thinking about me during his long flight to Japan, and it looked like that's exactly what happened.

Ty's message was funny, and thoughtful . . . and flirty. There were one or two questions about the career strategy I'd laid out for him at lunch the day before, which proved he was mulling it over. But mostly it was the kind of stuff I would expect from a guy who was trying to pick me up over drinks.

I sat back against the silk cushions on the couch, my mind whirling and my heart beating fast. I'd gone after Ty Boswell the way that Peter Bryant would—by making friends instead of talking business. I'd let Daniel do all the schmoozy our-agency-rocks talk, while I'd focused on Ty's dreams and ambitions, his likes and dislikes, everything from who his idols were to where his favorite pizza place was. And I'd been charming, sure. But . . .

"More, love?" Harlan Reed asked, letting his hand rest on my thigh as he reached over to refill my glass. "Where are you staying?"

"At Chloe's hotel," I said.

"All alone?" he murmured.

"I'm afraid so." I leaned in closer to him. "I'm here for business, not fun."

"Shame," he replied, blatantly running his gaze up and down my body.

It was Harlan Reed. He was possibly the most perfect male specimen I'd ever seen in my life, and he was also outrageously wealthy and powerful. But I wasn't interested in sleeping with him. Instead, what I found interesting was the idea that he wanted me to. I know I'm hot. But movie stars can get a hot girl any day of the week, a girl ten times hotter than me. It hadn't really occurred to me that any megawatt star would be attracted to *me*. But if Harlan wanted me, maybe Ty did, too.

Maybe I had something to offer Ty that Peter Bryant didn't. Not that I would do anything really unprofessional . . . and not that I wanted to be a tease. But if Ty was attracted to me, he'd think about me. He'd listen to me. He'd chase me a little bit. And he'd hire me to be his agent. It would be fun to have an agent relationship with a bit of sexual tension, and Ty liked fun. I didn't need to just be his *friend*. I could be something more interesting.

I was a decade younger than Peter Bryant, and I had a better rack. I was going to be a superagent before he knew what hit him.

"Hey, Chloe," I said. "Let's dance!"

"Just what the hell do you think you're doing in London?" Hal Turman's voice bellowed through the phone the next day. "I walk into your office to find out you're off on some boondoggle—"

"Hal, I'm here to see Chloe," I interrupted. I got up from my directors chair—well, it said "Chloe Gamble" on the back—and headed for the soundstage exit. "You know perfectly well that I'm supposed to visit the client and make her feel like I'm paying attention."

"I didn't sign off on this," he retorted. "It just so happens that I would've come with you. Chloe is a rising star, she should get visits from the big fish."

I bit my lip to keep from blurting out something really insulting. The idea that I was still supposed to ask his permission for anything just took my breath away. Plus, if Hal thought he was the big fish in Chloe's life, he was dead wrong. I was the one who'd gotten her here—I was the big fish. Even Daniel Shapiro thought so. I'd barely even seen Hal since that meeting at EdisonCorp, and now he wanted back in on Chloe?

"She's in good hands, don't worry," I said as nicely as I could. "Chloe doesn't need anyone to kiss her ass."

"Every actor in Hollywood needs their ass kissed on a daily basis, and don't you forget it."

Hal sounded disgusted. "Don't take your eyes off the prize just because you're getting some press, Nika."

"Thanks for the advice," I snapped. "Chloe's shooting with Anne Lynch. I have to go." I hung up before he could say another condescending, infuriating word.

When I got back to the video village, where everyone gathered behind the director to watch the video feed from the cameras, I found Travis hanging out with an older guy. He looked familiar, but it still took me a minute to place him.

Joe Handelman. One of the old guard agents, a guy who'd been kicking around the Business forever—started in the William Morris mail room with my boss, Daniel. Moved through the ranks at CAA back in the day. Represented the kind of movie stars who were always called "actors" instead of "stars." Serious, talented, iconic people . . . like Anne Lynch.

I put on a smile and strode over with my hand out. "Joe, hi," I said brightly. "Nika Mays."

"Of course." Joe shook my hand and nodded toward the monitor, where Chloe and Anne were running lines between takes. "Your girl's doing great."

"She always does," I said. "So you've met Travis?"

Joe grinned and clapped Trav on the back. "We're talking soccer. My kid's starting high school next year, and it turns out Travis here played on the school team."

"St. Paul's," Trav told me, as if I wouldn't remember the elite prep school he and Chloe had attended for all of half a year, before they both got so successful that they just stopped going. I used to nag Chloe about the importance of staying in school, but now that she was a full-fledged star, there was no point. I made a mental note to make sure she got her GED at least.

"Trav didn't just *play*, he was a star," I said. "It runs in the family."

"Mmm. She's fearless, going toe-to-toe with Anne at her age. Not to mention Harlan Reed." Joe studied Chloe while he spoke.

"Chloe always says age don't matter," Travis put in. "Guts matter more."

"A wise woman," Joe agreed.

"Quiet on set!" one of the PAs called, and everybody stopped talking. Matthew Greengold took his place behind the camera and called action, and Chloe turned into Anissa right before our eyes, a naive young lady learning to properly serve tea from her mother. Of course Anne Lynch disappeared into her role as the matron. She disappeared into every role, she was a genius. But I'd never seen Chloe do it before. Playing Lucie Blayne on *Cover Band* didn't require much stretching—the character was basically a more cutesy version of Chloe. And nothing else Chloe had done in her short career involved much in the way of acting, either. I'd always known she was fantastic, because Chloe's whole personality changed every time she had a new audience to please. To her, every meeting and every press interview was an acting gig. Sometimes I wondered if even she knew the difference between her true self and the façades she wore.

But even I hadn't expected this kind of performance from her. It was riveting. *She* was riveting.

Joe Handelman leaned forward in his chair, gazing at the monitor with a laser-sharp focus, shaking his head a little as if he were in awe. He'd been Anne Lynch's agent for twenty years. You'd think he would be used to seeing her brilliance up close.

He's watching Chloe, not Anne. I don't know why it had taken me so long to realize the truth. Joe was here with Anne, doing the client visit like he was supposed to. But he was also here to see Chloe Gamble, hot young up-and-comer in her first meaty role. She wasn't a teen TV star anymore, she was an actress in a Matthew Greengold film. Maybe she wanted new representation—people who didn't think of her as that kid whose career they started, but rather as a serious actress. The minute Joe got Chloe alone, he'd plant that idea in her head the same way Daniel had convinced Ty Boswell that his current agents didn't understand him.

I sat back in my director's chair and watched the powerful agent as he watched my client. Joe was so pleasant, chatting with me, talking sports with Trav. He was a big fish. He had been for years.

Hal knew there would be other people here to see Chloe, I realized, feeling stupid. It's why the on-set client visits were so important—I wasn't here to coddle Chloe, I was here to defend my turf. That's why Hal wanted to come. He always went to meetings when other people of his stature were going to be there. He probably figured Joe—or some other agent—would show up, sniffing around Chloe. And maybe he figured they'd back off once they saw that she had a big-fish agent, too.

Well, I was a big fish now. I would keep Chloe—and Travis—on my own.

When filming wrapped for the day, I headed straight for Anne Lynch.

"I just wanted to say hello. Chloe's told me how gracious and generous you've been to her," I said, shaking the hand of the legend.

"She's more than repaid me," Anne said. "Little Chloe has true talent."

"She does," I said, and meant it. "She's a star, just like she always told me."

Anne pursed her lips. "Let her be an artist, not a star. It's a much healthier road to walk."

I smiled and nodded, and kept my thoughts to myself. Chloe could definitely act, and she even seemed to like her sessions with her acting coach. But what she wanted went beyond acting, and beyond singing and songwriting. As far as I could tell, Chloe Gamble was after world domination. And I was going to be her agent the whole way.

"Annie!" Joe Handelman came right over when he saw me with his client. I wasn't much of a threat to him—he'd been representing Anne Lynch back when I was in middle school. But it's just common sense not to leave your client alone with another agent. Which is why I immediately said good-bye and hustled my two clients out of there and away from him.

"I don't think I can do this," Travis said the second we got to Chloe's trailer. "Clo, that was real acting back there. You were incredible!"

"I know, wasn't I?" Chloe laughed, tugging at her clothes. "But this corset is killing me."

One of the wardrobe assistants began unbuttoning Chloe's long dress, while a makeup girl removed the wig that turned her long blond hair into a complicated updo.

"Anne says the uncomfortable costume helps you find the character," Chloe went on. "Because poor Anissa had to dress like this every day of her life, can you imagine?"

"Can you get me one of them corsets?" Travis muttered.

"Trav, you'll be fine," I said. "You don't need help from the wardrobe when you've got your Oscar-caliber sister right there in the scene with you."

"Ain't that the truth." Chloe checked her cell while she spoke. "We're going to Amsterdam tonight, did I tell you? Harlan has some friends there."

"No way," Travis said. "How long will that take?"

"He said it's an hour-and-a-half flight, but there'll be plenty of champagne on board." Chloe shrugged.

"Travis has rehearsals tomorrow," I pointed out. "He can't be out partying all night."

"You can sleep on the plane back," Chloe said. "It's Amsterdam, Trav! So much fun."

"Clo, I'm jet-lagged. And I gotta make a good impression on Matthew Greengold tomorrow. He only hired me because of you, and this movie is way out of my league."

I watched Chloe's face as she tried to think of a way to talk him into doing what she wanted. Travis had a point. He was a great-looking kid with a nice presence on-screen, but *he* was no artist. He'd never taken an acting class. He'd never been faced with this kind of role before. He might not be able to do it even well-rested and focused, but he'd never pull it off hungover.

And Chloe knew it. She got herself all worked up to cajole him, she put on one of her beauty-queen smiles . . . and then a sad little girl pout . . . and then she just stopped. All her fake attitudes disappeared, and she simply looked at her twin brother. I knew she didn't want to hurt his chances.

"Oh, all right." She sighed. "I guess we can skip one night of fun."

"We can still have fun," I said. I took out my BlackBerry and texted my assistant to find us the most expensive restaurant in London and reserve the best table. Time to spend some quality time with my clients. My friends.

When it came to entertaining, my company credit card didn't have a limit.

I never even heard my BlackBerry ring. When I got back to the hotel at midnight—early, by Chloe standards—I noticed a voicemail waiting. It was Sean.

"Holy crap, babe, call me back!" he crowed. "You won't believe what happened today. Dave Quinn wants to meet with me, and it's not about Chloe—he wants to offer me a job. He's looking for a right-hand man on the features side, now that we convinced him to get into the film biz. And he wants *me*! Says he was so impressed with the way we handled the Gamble v. Snap thing that he wants a creative thinker like me on his team. Nika, seriously, call back. Quinn is trying to poach me!"

I hit delete and stared at my phone for a minute. Sean was my boyfriend. My partner. And he was about to become a major Hollywood player, all because of Chloe Gamble. I should want to call him

and jump around shrieking with glee. I should be
thrilled for him.

But all I felt was jealous.

STAR CENTRAL BLOG

Everyone's favorite Texas rodeo dad, LONNIE GAMBLE, showed
up at a Pro Bull Riding event at the Staples Center last night.
(That's right, hipsters, there are rodeos in LA!) Lonnie talked
roping calves and riding bulls, but he soon switched to his
favorite subject: his daughter, CHLOE GAMBLE.

"I just plain think it's wrong to put a girl her age in a nude
scene," Lonnie pontificated. "My Chloe was as innocent as
an angel last time I saw her, she wouldn't ever have done a
picture in the buff. I don't know what kind of advisors she's
got around her, but I think they're out for themselves. They
convinced my girl to get herself emancipated and they want
to treat her like an adult. But she's still only sixteen. Ain't
nobody thinking about the harm that could come from it,
nobody except me."

Our sources tell us Chloe has a body double for the MATTHEW
GREENGOLD pic *Frontier*, but Lonnie says no. "I never heard
that," he said. "I never heard about any such thing."

THE NEXT STEP

"Amsterdam tonight?" I asked as our driver headed for the
Four Seasons at the end of the day. "Callum can't come this
time but Harlan wants to go again. Or else he says we can go
to Paris."

"Paris," Jude said, slumping in the seat next to me. "After a nap. I stayed out too late last night."

"I kinda thought I'd see London while I was in London," Trav said. "Y'all ever go anywhere without Harlan these days?"

"Why would I? I ain't got my own private jet," I said. "And besides, his assistants always have good pot."

Travis rolled his eyes like I knew he would.

"I'm just joking," I said.

"Are not," Jude mumbled. She put her head on my shoulder and closed her eyes.

"We can stay local if you want," I told Trav. "I got tickets to a private Stella McCartney show tonight. Front row. Maybe we can hook you up with a supermodel to get your mind off Sasha Powell."

"I don't know. Don't you ever get tired of it?" Trav said. "All we're doing is blocking scenes and rehearsing, but I'm wiped. We don't need to go out *every* night."

"You've only been here three days and you're tired already?" I teased him. "I actually have to shoot tomorrow, you know."

"Even more reason to stay home. You're a serious actress now, don't you have to meditate or something to prepare yourself?"

I almost laughed. If I ever tried to meditate, I'd probably get a brain clot. Far as I could tell, you just sat there and tried not to think. But telling my mind not to think was like telling a cat not to purr. My brother wasn't wrong, though, I did need to prepare. I was shooting another scene with Anne Lynch in the morning, and those were grueling. The woman changed something in every single take, and I had to pay superclose attention just to keep up with her.

I'll call Harlan's assistant and get him to send over a joint for before bed, I decided. Travis didn't want to hear it, but the truth was that I liked the marijuana. Callum had been right—it relaxed me. It didn't quite turn off my mind, but it made me think about dumb things like how pretty a flower was or how delicious a strawberry was. And I'd already written most of a song just because I was letting my imagination wander. Callum called it relaxing, and Harlan called it giving his restless soul a break. I didn't have a name for it, I just knew it helped me stop *thinking* long enough to do a good job *acting*.

"Let's just order room service and watch TV," Travis said. "We still need to talk about the Daddy situation."

"There is no situation," I said. "You and me are adults now and he can't touch us. Let him go crying to *TMZ* about how we don't love him, I don't give a crap."

"He's taking us to court—" Trav started.

"And that's why we got Sean." I shook Jude awake and opened my own door as soon as the car stopped in the hotel driveway. Usually I waited for the doormen to do it, because they shielded me from the photographers who camped out there waiting to get a shot. But Travis was making me feel antsy.

"Chloe, love, over here!" one of the paparazzi yelled.

"Chloe, how's Henry Norwich?" another called, trying to get a rise out of me.

"Haven't seen him lately," I replied. "But get a shot of me and my twin!" I grabbed Travis as he climbed out behind me, and we smiled for the cameras.

"I hate that," he said once we got into the lobby.

"Try being the invisible friend," Jude said. "Sometimes they literally shove me out of the picture."

"Get used to it, Trav, you're famous," I said. "If you make nice with them, they'll be nice to you."

"I don't think they're nice to anybody," he said. "Marc's starting to worry about your party girl image. It don't play well to the *Cover Band* demographic."

"So what? I'm no role model," I said. "I'm allowed to live my life like I want."

"Daddy talks to the press about how it makes you look like a slut," Travis said.

That stopped me, but only for a second. I was no slut, and if I liked to go out dancing and partying, it didn't make me anything but a normal girl. "If Max would've just come with me, there'd be no problem," I said.

"You're dreaming if you think Harlan and his buds would be taking you all over Europe with your boyfriend," Jude said. "Seriously, if we're going out later, I have to sleep."

She yawned and headed for the elevators. The production

company had booked a room for her at some crappy hotel way across town, but I'd taken one look at it and brought her to stay with me. I had a suite, anyway, and with Jude there I never had to be alone. Travis was only here for another few days, but Jude would stay until I was done shooting.

Trav and me followed her. "I'm staying in," he decided.

"I'm going to that fashion show," I said. "Lars Svedman will be there, he's the one who sent me the tickets."

Travis whistled softly. "Max know you're hanging out with famous music producers?"

"Sure he does," I lied. "Besides, it's just business. Lars knows everyone in the music industry, and that's a good contact for me. Once I get out of *Cover Band* I'll be able to do my own albums, and I might need some advice."

The first thing I noticed when I got to the fashion show was that I had worn the perfect dress. All the fashionistas were in black or gray, and I was in bright red. People are afraid to wear striking colors, but all it takes is confidence. So I had a ton of attention on the way in, and I made sure to hold hands with Jude while all the cameras were going. That way, she wouldn't get pushed out of the shot, and I would get some buzz on the gossip sites for holding hands with a girl.

The second thing I noticed was that Lars Svedman had not come alone. He had Shani with him. Tall, dusky, brilliant Shani—the best-selling female pop star in the world for the last two years running. And they both waved the second they saw me.

The third thing I noticed was Kimber Reeve.

"Incoming," Jude muttered, nodding toward Kimber, who was in a gray chiffon blouse and skinny jeans. Boring.

"Well, hey there, *Clo*," my former rival cooed, coming right up to me. "Hi, Jude."

Jude rolled her eyes.

"Don't you just look adorable in that dress. Like Red Riding Hood!" Kimber went on.

She was doing my bit, being overly sweet just to annoy me. I'd done it to her a hundred times, back when she was on a hot streak and I was nothing but a kids' TV star. But these days I was the hot one, and she was nothing. Her director boyfriend had dumped her, her NBC show had gotten cancelled, and she'd lost her juicy role in *Frontier*—to me.

"Kimber Reeve, what a surprise," I said. "What are you doing in London? I guess you have some free time to travel these days, hmm?"

"I'm here with Stan Moore. We're meeting with a potential finance partner for our film," Kimber said. "You know Stan, don't you? He and his wife won best film at Sundance last year."

"Can't say I've heard of him," I said. "Of course, I'm hanging with more of an Oscar crowd than a Sundance one."

Kimber narrowed her eyes, and I grinned.

"I've got to run. Lars and Shani are waiting for me." I gave her a little wave and headed off to sit with my two new A-list pals.

"I hope y'all don't mind, I brought my friend Jude," I said. "She's a fashion photographer."

She wasn't, not yet, but she was smart enough not to say so.

"Delighted," Lars said. He kissed me hello, and he kissed Jude, too. "Chloe, meet Shani, One of my most beloved collaborators."

I turned to Shani, and she grabbed me in a hug, her famous smile almost blinding me. "I'm so happy you could come tonight! I have been dying to meet you."

"You kidding? I wouldn't miss it," I said, thanking God I hadn't gone off somewhere with Harlan. "But nobody told me I'd get to meet my idol! I used to sing your songs in beauty pageants."

"Shut up, you did not." Shani laughed.

"And I always won," I told her. That wasn't because of her songs as much as my ability to win over every pageant judge in Texas, but I didn't mention that part. She'd been on top of the charts since I was ten, but she wasn't even that old, she was around Nika's age. Shani had come from nowhere, like me, busting out of a small town in Georgia and never looking back. She had a famous voice, a famous ass, and famous hair. And she had enough platinum records to fill a whole room.

She also had parents who supported her and helped her

every step of the way. It was a good bet that she'd never been taken to court by one of them.

I shook off thoughts of my loser daddy and sat down in the front row. Poor Jude got shoved over to the side, because Shani and Lars put me in between them, and they immediately launched into a discussion of how much they loved my last single, "Lucky Bitch." I couldn't help sneaking a glance over at Kimber, the lucky bitch I'd written it about. She was three rows back, sitting with some skinny guy whose beard looked like a bird's nest.

Not so lucky now, I thought happily.

" . . . sound was rough around the edges," Lars was saying.

"But that was perfect for what it was, an Internet hit," Shani put in. "Chloe, did you ever release that song on a label?"

"Nope. Just online," I replied.

"The Snap network thought "Lucky Bitch" was too 'mature' for her show's target audience," Jude put in. "As if Chloe's entire life isn't too mature for her target audience."

"I hear that," Shani said. "When I was younger, everyone wanted me to do girl-group kind of stuff. All innocent and sugary, you know?"

"But then you put out *Here I Am* and that all changed," I said. "That album was your coming of age, that's what all the blogs said."

"Yeah, and I was eighteen." Shani laughed. "I'd been writing those songs since I was fifteen. You don't have to be old to be an old soul. That's what Lars told me. He thought I could pull off mature songs and he was right, like he always is."

Lars bowed his head as if he was humbled by the praise. But I knew it was an act. As successful as Shani was, most everyone knew it was because of Lars. He'd produced albums for more megastars than anyone. She might be more famous— hell, even I was more famous than him—but in the Business, Lars was a bigger deal than both of us.

"I told you, I want to produce your 'Lucky Bitch' when you're ready to grow up," Lars said. "I already have it in my head."

I felt Jude watching me, but I didn't meet her eye. Instead, I focused on Lars.

"Wow," I said. "That is just so sweet of you. But my boyfriend, Max, is a musician, and he produced that song for me, and the next one I wrote, too. It's going to be released on the *Cover Band* soundtrack."

"Ah." Lars threw up his hands and smiled. "I cannot compete with love."

But as the lights went down and the thumping bass of the fashion show music filled the air, Shani leaned in close and whispered to me like we were best friends.

"Love won't get you as far as you deserve, Chloe. When a legend wants to work with you, say yes."

"Another late night?" Anne Lynch asked disapprovingly up on the hotel roof deck. Jude had gone to bed as soon as we got home, but I felt restless. Still, the last person I'd expected to run into at three in the morning was Anne.

"You're up," I pointed out.

"It's hardly the same thing. I have insomnia," she told me. "You have youth."

"I got home an hour ago, I just can't sleep," I said. I'd meant to get myself a joint, but I forgot. If I'd smoked, I would've gone straight off to dreamland.

"Maybe you should give your body a break, go to bed at ten one of these nights." Anne sipped her drink—Scotch, I figured—and shook her head. Then she caught me watching and laughed. "There I go again, sounding like your mother! I can't get out of character."

"You don't sound like *my* mama," I said. "She'd be tagging along to every club I went to, making a sloppy scene every time."

Anne didn't answer. She closed her eyes and took a deep breath. "I love the air in London. Always foggy. It's like a giant, smelly humidifier."

"You're weird," I said before I could stop myself.

"When you've been in this business as long as I have, you're allowed to be weird. That's the reward for living through all the madness. I may look like a typical old dame, but it's just one more act. There is nothing normal about being me." She opened her eyes and smiled. "So what adventures kept you out until midnight?"

"A fashion show, and the after-party," I told her. "I was there with a big-time music producer."

"Exciting. Do you know, little Chloe, Matthew and I were talking about the theme song for the movie. *You* should sing it. Write a ballad and give it to Matthew. That will be a much more productive use of your time than fashion shows."

"I don't do ballads," I said. "They're too sappy."

"Then channel Anissa and write it as her," Anne said, like it was the most obvious thing in the world.

I chewed on my lip, thinking. "Movie songs win Oscars," I said.

Anne chuckled. "There. I've given you a project, so you can stop behaving like that dissipated old scoundrel, Harley. He's a lazy man who's lucky enough to be beautiful. You're different. You need to be doing something new all the time."

"Let's see: yacht in Spain, tunnels in Paris, hash dens in Amsterdam, croquet at a castle in Scotland, hot springs in Germany . . ." I grinned. "I have been doing a lot of new things since I've been here!"

Anne waved her hand as if none of that stuff mattered. "I'm talking about work. The rest is just a distraction." She sat up suddenly and leaned toward me. "It's a dangerous thing, to be where you are, little Chloe."

I frowned. "I am right where I want to be. Where I've wanted to be my whole life."

"Exactly," Anne said. "So what are you going to do with all your energy now? Do you even know how to sit still?"

I shrugged. I'd given up trying to figure out how she knew me so well. "There's always a next step—a bigger role in a bigger movie. I'll put my energy toward that."

"I suppose," Anne said in a tone of voice that meant she thought I was an idiot. Well, it was hard to imagine a bigger movie than *Frontier*. Just being in this cast had landed me in every celebrity magazine in the world, far as I could tell. Not a day went by when I didn't find a hundred new Google entries when I searched my name. Even if I was the star of my next movie, the fame wouldn't feel much different.

"I could release an album of my own," I said. "I could tour."

"Whatever it is, figure it out," Anne told me. "Hot springs and nightclubs might feel nice for a few hours, but they'll rot your soul."

"You sound like my old agent, Hal Turman."

"Hal Turman wrote the book." Anne downed the rest of her drink and stood up. "You scrambled up the Hollywood ladder mighty fast, Chloe Gamble. You're going to have to find another ladder."

She kissed me on the top of my head and wandered off toward the elevator. Her penthouse suite was only one floor down, and it had three bedrooms and an office. I could work toward that kind of power, a whole giant apartment to stay in for only two weeks of filming.

But it wasn't the same. My own suite was already pretty damn nice. A nicer hotel room just didn't seem that exciting, not the way my first movie role had, or my own TV show, or my first viral video.

I pulled my cell from my pocket and stared at it for a minute. Lars and Shani had both programmed their private numbers into it.

I dialed Max.

"Clo?" his voice sounded warm and close, even though he was a million miles away. "What's up?"

"Just missing you," I said. "It's lonely here."

"You've got Travis and Jude," he said. "And it's only for another couple of weeks."

"Can't you come for the weekend?" I asked.

"Sorry, Clo." Somebody else was talking to Max in the background, a girl, and I could tell he wasn't paying much attention to me. "Listen, we're setting up for our gig at the Troubadour. Can I call you later?"

"You hanging out with any groupies while I'm gone?" I asked.

"Like there's a groupie in the world who compares to you," he said. "Bye, babe."

I hung up and looked around the roof deck. You needed a special key to come up here, and it was late. Nobody would see me. I slipped off my top and unhooked my four-hundred-dollar bra, and then I lay myself down on an overstuffed lounge chair. I held the phone up over myself and snapped a photo.

"Something to think about while you're playing tonight," I typed into the picture mail message to Max. Then I hit send.

I didn't even put my shirt back on before I called Lars.

"Sorry it's so late," I told him. "I can't stop thinking about what you said."

"I don't sleep," he said. "I hope you're calling to say yes."

"Yes," I said. "I want you to remix 'Lucky Bitch.'"

"Who will protect us?" Chloe asked. "Once you've gone?"

I looked into her eyes and saw fear, confusion, even love. But I didn't see Chloe. "I'm sorry," I said. "Sorry, Clo."

Matthew Greengold called cut and my sister threw up her hands. "That's three takes, Trav!"

"You're freaking me out," I said. "I feel like I'm talking to a stranger."

"It's called acting," she said. "I'm Anissa."

"Everything okay, you two?" Matthew asked, coming over with a bottle of water. He handed it to me.

"Thanks," I said. "Gets hot in this suit."

"Thick wool. I'm a sucker for historical accuracy, but it's hell under the lights," he said.

"We're fine, ain't we, Trav?" Chloe said. "Just havin' a bumpy start, as our mama would say."

Our mama had never said that in her life, but Clo liked using cheesy expressions that made her sound like a sweet little Texas girl. Matthew nodded and clapped me on the back. "Take five and we'll go again."

As soon as he walked away, Chloe dropped her big smile and narrowed her eyes at me. "Get it together, Trav," she said, grabbing my arm. "We rehearsed this a ton of times."

"I know, I'm sorry." I reached up to touch my hair, but I stopped when I remembered it would take ten minutes for the hair girl to fix it. "I'm nervous. It's the real thing now, there's all these people watching and it's such a big movie."

Chloe sighed. She hates insecurity, mostly 'cause she can't understand it. Far as she's concerned, it's a sign of weakness. That's the one thing she ever agreed with our daddy about. I wasn't too thrilled about it, either. Put me on a soccer field and I knew for sure that every move I made was the right one. But this was different. I was dressed in a costume, pretending to be some old-timey dude while a hundred people watched, and the whole thing was costing millions of dollars. I felt stupid, and I didn't care if Chloe thought that made me weak.

"It all comes down to this, Trav," my sister said, taking my hand. "This is your shot. Do good now and you're in. You're a movie actor."

I nodded.

"Look, I'm still me. I'm being Anissa but I'm still Chloe," she said gently. "And you're my brother. It's just us, same as always. You and me against the world."

"Okay," I said, squeezing her hand. "Thanks for being cool. I'll get my head in the game."

"Damn right you will. I told Matthew you'd be perfect for this role," Chloe said, grinning. "I know you ain't gonna make me look bad."

Chloe was owning this role. Nothing could make her look bad. But she wanted me to step up, so I would.

When Matthew called for action, I ignored the cameramen and the crew the same way I always ignored the crowds at soccer games. I focused on Chloe and nothing else.

"Who will protect us?" Chloe asked. "Once you've gone?"

This time, when I looked in her eyes, I saw my sister. Didn't matter if she was Chloe or Anissa. She was my sister, and it was me and her against the world.

IM

COOPERMAN: Trav, you are all over the blogs today! Marc is loving it. Greengold thinks you're great and keeps blabbing about it to everyone. What'd you do, blow him?

GAMBLEGOAL: Bite me.

GAMBLEGOAL: I filmed my scene with Clo and we rocked it. Greengold was psyched.

COOPERMAN: Nice. Nika keeps calling me with new meetings for you. Busy week when you get back.

COOPERMAN: You're lucky you have a kick-ass assistant to keep track of your calendar.

GAMBLEGOAL: You're lucky you have a famous genius actor for a best friend.

GAMBLEGOAL: Are these meetings for acting? Not model stuff?

COOPERMAN: Two for modeling, most for acting. What, you too good for posing in your jockstrap these days?

GAMBLEGOAL: I said bite me.

COOPERMAN: Remember you're seeing the Vivienne Westwood people tomorrow before you go to the airport.

GAMBLEGOAL: Got it. You're a nag.

COOPERMAN: That's what you pay me for. Best job ever. Working at the DQ never got me laid this much.

GAMBLEGOAL: HA!

COOPERMAN: Speaking of my excellent assistanting, you're confirmed to host a party at The Vanguard Saturday when you get back. It's $10K, and we need to be there for two hours.

GAMBLEGOAL: My plane doesn't land until seven that night.

COOPERMAN: You want to cancel?

GAMBLEGOAL: I guess not, just make sure you bring lots of Red Bull.

COOPERMAN: Anyone you want to invite? I got a list of the girls we usually hang with. What about that Kimber chick?

GAMBLEGOAL: Up to you. Just don't tell Clo.

GAMBLEGOAL: Hey, invite Chloe's boyfriend. Max Tyrell. He must be getting lonely.

COOPERMAN: Your mother keeps calling. Can't remember when you're getting back.

GAMBLEGOAL: Typical.

COOPERMAN: You bummed about coming back?

GAMBLEGOAL: No way. It's not my scene here. Chloe doesn't even seem like Chloe anymore.

COOPERMAN: She getting a swelled head?

GAMBLEGOAL: It's not her fault. Everywhere we go, people kiss her ass so much that she's starting to buy it.

COOPERMAN: Don't you worry, loser, I will never let that happen to you.

chapter six

H METER BLOG

BUZZING UP: KIMBER REEVE, set to star in *Forget Me Not*, penned by quirky indie duo STAN MOORE & LUCE BRODY. The married pair directed and produced last year's festival-circuit fave, *Life*, and sources say they hand-picked Kimber to headline the movie. Not a huge film, but after her recent PR nightmares, there's nowhere to go but up!

BUZZING DOWN: Our insiders say HAL TURMAN can't catch a break. Since selling his boutique agency to Virtuoso, the old-timer has been sidelined. Virtuoso just snatched TY BOSWELL away from his agents, and Hal's former sidekick NIKA MAYS made the deal. When asked for a comment, poor old Hal didn't even know it had happened! Time to retire, Hal?

BUZZING UP: Guess it's in the genes—TRAVIS GAMBLE is the name on everyone's lips this week. After shooting a bit part in the MATTHEW GREENGOLD film *Frontier*, Travis is the uber-director's favorite cause. Greengold has instructed the TV arm of his company to find a place for Gamble—stat. He must've done a damn good job on *Frontier*. You go, Travis!

A LOVE SUPREME

"I thought you couldn't come!" I cried, throwing my arms around Max the second he walked through the door of my suite. Max held me tight. "Travis thinks you need more normal stuff around you," he said. "And if you *need* me—"

"I do!" I cut him off with a kiss. "I need a date for the benefit tonight. We're going to the British Museum or something. We can sneak out the back door and meet up with Harley afterward."

Max groaned. "I don't want to go out," he said, kissing my neck. "I'm only here for the weekend. Do we have to?"

I closed my eyes and enjoyed it for a moment. But the idea of spending the entire night in the hotel made me feel claustrophobic, even if I was spending it with Max. "We could skip the benefit and go to a music party," I said. "It's a birthday party for Lars Svedman. It'll be perfect for you! Bono's gonna be there, and Shani said Sir Paul might show up."

"Paul McCartney?" Max said, his eyebrows shooting up.

"I know, he's ancient, but it's still a big deal, right?"

"Wait, since when do you know Shani?" Max asked.

I bit my lip. Truth was, I probably shouldn't take Max to this party. I hadn't told him about my agreement with Lars, and I had no idea how he'd react. But everyone there would be in the music biz, and that had to be good for my musician boyfriend, right? If I hooked him up with some famous friends, he couldn't be mad at me for using another producer.

"I met her at a fashion show. Remember I told you how Callum and I went to Ibiza that weekend? Well, Lars was at this yacht party with us and he was so, so sweet. He's the one who introduced me to Shani."

Max had stopped even hugging me. He just stood there frowning.

"What?" I said.

"You. Look at you, hanging out with all these heavy hitters, Miss Texas Teen Supreme." He shook his head.

"Don't laugh, I held almost that exact title," I told him. I reached out and ran my hand down his chest. "We should go to the party. Think how good it would be for your career."

"It would," he said. "But I'd rather stay here with you. I missed you, Chloe." He pulled me into his arms and kissed me, and I felt a stab of guilt. I was glad to see Max, and I wouldn't mind a quickie before we left, but I still wanted to get away from the hotel.

"Tell you what. Let's go take a shower and get ready to go out," I said. "Together."

"I'm not gonna say no to *that*," Max said. And I knew that afterward, he wouldn't say no to anything else I wanted to do, either.

*   *   *

"Is this where he lives?" Max asked as we walked into the manor house. The place looked like the set of some old movie about British kings and queens. It had a name, too, something like Bartleton House or Bradenson House. I hadn't really been listening when Lars told me about it, and anyway he just called it his "country place." One of the PAs had gotten the details and given them to my driver, so all I had to do was get in the car looking fantastic. I was starting to think I had to get an assistant of my own, to do the stuff Coop was doing for my brother, like keeping track of parties and cataloging all the couture that designers kept sending me.

"He uses it as his retreat. He also has a place in London," I said. "And I think he records here. But he still lives in Sweden most of the time."

"Nice life." Max gazed around at the oil paintings on the wall, the Oriental rugs on the floor. I was more interested in the noise coming from the drawing room, where the doorman was leading us. Music and voices and laughter. The sounds of a party.

There were maybe fifty people, and each and every one of them was famous. Right away I spotted Justin Timberlake and that short guy from Radiohead, and all the members of Coldplay. There were some old guys near the bar who looked familiar, and Fergie was practically hanging on them so I knew they must be old-time rock gods.

"Holy crap, it's Jack White," Max said, starstruck.

"And one of the Jonas Brothers," I replied. "Most bizarre party ever."

He squeezed my hand. "You don't even look impressed. You used to this already?"

"Not really. I'm just a good actor," I said. "Let's go find Shani."

She was sitting on an actual bearskin rug near the biggest fireplace I'd ever seen, a glass of wine in her hand.

"Chloe Gamble!" she cried, jumping up to hug me. "I thought you weren't coming."

I shrugged. "That art benefit sounded boring. I'll just send them some money." I pulled Max closer. "Meet my boyfriend, Max."

"From the The Ruffians," the guy next to Shani said. I didn't know his face, but I knew her boyfriend was a rapper-turned-manager named Chill, so I figured that was him.

"Yeah." Max reached out to do the stupid fist bump–handshake thing that guys do. "I didn't think anyone knew about us."

"LA's my territory, I know about everyone," Chill said. "You guys are good. You gotta dump the bassist, but otherwise it's solid."

"Come say hi to Lars," Shani said, pulling me away. "The boys can talk business."

"This party is so much less prissy than a club party," I said as we snaked through the crowd toward the birthday boy. "It feels more like Texas than Hollywood."

"It's rock and roll, babydoll," Shani joked. "Invite-only from Lars's friends. No posers allowed."

When we got to Lars, enthroned on a giant lounge, he was in deep conversation with Sting and Bono.

"I am not interrupting that," Shani said. "Those guys are way too serious."

"Good. Let's dance," I said. "Do you have any pot? I'm too uptight without it."

She shook her head. "But my backup singers might. Go check the bathroom."

By the time I got to the loo, as they all called it here, I'd met five more people who I'd only ever seen on MTV, and they all knew who I was. Kath Cruzer, the hot British singer, hung onto the belt loop of my Rock & Republic jeans as we made our way through the crowded hallway and into the bathroom.

"Thank fucking God," Kath said. "I need to pee." She ran for a stall, which was really an entire little bathroom of its own tucked into this big lounge area. "Who's got weed?" Kath called from behind her door.

"I do," a girl with purple hair said, leaning in to check her eyeliner in the mirror.

"Are you sharing?" I asked.

"I always bring enough for everyone." She winked at me.

"I guess I should find my own dealer," I said. "I hate to be the girl who bums all the time."

"Don't be ridiculous," Kath said, coming out of the stall still yanking up her leather pants. "You're the talent. You're there to take. Other people will give."

The purple-haired girl was pulling things out of her bag. "I have coke, too."

"Ooh, that!" Kath cried. "I'm in the studio in the morning."

"So?" I asked.

"Pot makes me sleepy the next day. Coke doesn't." She shrugged. "You've never tried it?"

I shook my head.

"A line for Chloe Gamble," she commanded. "And two for me!"

Unbelievable. I was used to being the most brazen girl in the room, it was kind of my thing, but at a music party, I wasn't even close.

"You just stick with me, blondie, I'll show you how," Kath said. "You'll love it. You can dance all night and not get even a bit tired."

"Can you stop that?" Max asked in the elevator at the Four Seasons. He nodded at my fingers, drumming against my Ferragamo purse. "You're too bouncy for four o'clock in the morning."

"Nothing wrong with bouncy," I said. "Let's stay up all

night—my call time is at seven anyway." I pinned him against the wall and kissed him. "I'll make it worth your while."

"Are you kidding me?" The doors pinged open and Max pulled me out into the hallway. "Why didn't you tell me you were shooting tomorrow?"

"I feel great. Totally focused," I said. Truth. Maybe it wasn't as relaxing as pot, but the coke had given me a giant burst of energy.

"Chloe, what the hell?" he said. "You're going to crash just when you need to work."

I pulled out my key card and stuck it in the door of the suite. Jude had cleared out for the weekend so me and Max could be alone, but I was wishing she was here now. Max was a buzz kill.

"It's an easy shoot. Anne gets to chew scenery and I just have to sit there and cry," I said.

"So you're working with an acting legend and you're going to show up exhausted and strung out," Max said. "That's real professional, Clo."

"What is your problem?" I snapped. "It's not like you were begging to leave that party."

"I didn't even want to go in the first place," he said.

I tossed my bag on the couch and stalked off toward the bedroom. Max had spent the whole night talking to producers and promoters and rock stars. He should be thanking me, not lecturing me.

"You think I'm an idiot?" he said, following me. "I know you're on something."

"So what? I ain't hiding it," I said.

"No, you're hiding other things instead." Max sounded bitter.

"Excuse me?"

"Shani told me about Lars," he said. "About how you're going to record with him once shooting's done."

"Oh." All the energy drained right out of me like he'd punched a hole in my gut. I'd been so happy at the party, dancing and having fun. Max and me didn't spend much time together, but somehow I'd forgotten about the whole Lars situation. Of course Shani told him. She didn't know she wasn't supposed to.

"Were you even going to mention it?" Max asked.

"I didn't want to make you mad," I said.

"So you figured you'd just lie about it and that wouldn't make me mad?"

"I didn't lie," I said. "I just didn't tell you. You don't get to know everything I do."

"I'm supposed to be your boyfriend."

"Well, right now you sound more like a jealous little boy," I said. "I'm so sorry if I get to have more of a music career than you. I tried to help by taking you to meet people, but I guess that wasn't good enough."

"What the hell are you talking about?" Max exploded. "It's Lars Svedman, he's the best producer in history. Of course you should work with him. You think I'm jealous? I'm freakin' *proud* of you."

"Okay," I said, confused. "So . . . you're not mad?"

"Not about that," Max said. "I'm mad that you didn't tell me. I'm on your side. Why would you lie to me?"

Why? I didn't even know. It hadn't occurred to me to tell him the truth, because I was screwing him over and we both knew it. When you do that to someone, they stop liking you. They don't stay on your side. "I didn't want to lose you," I said. "I thought you wouldn't forgive me."

Max shoved his dreadlocks back off his face. "What is there to forgive? You're taking care of your career. We never said I was your producer for the rest of your life. And it's new stuff, right? We still have the songs we did together."

"Right. I won't let him touch our songs," I lied. Max was being so unexpectedly cool about this that I didn't want to tell him it was "Lucky Bitch" that Lars wanted to change. I wasn't working with Lars for awhile. I had time to make it right—I'd write a new song, even better than that one, and tell Lars that "Lucky Bitch" was off the table. Or something. Right now I just wanted Max to think it was all okay. "Thank you for understanding," I said, taking his hand. I pulled him toward the bed.

"Stop it," he snapped, yanking his hand away.

"You said you weren't mad," I cried.

"Chloe. You lied to me. That's the issue here." Max frowned. "You've never been a liar before."

Not true. I could lie before I could talk, my mama used to say. Only I never thought of it like a bad thing. Far as I could see, lying was just the way to get what you needed in life. Tell people what they want to hear, and they'll give you whatever you ask for. But Max had one thing right—I didn't usually lie to the people I liked.

"I haven't seen you in weeks," I said. "I feel like it's a whole different world over here, and the stuff that happened in Los Angeles doesn't count anymore."

"You mean, our relationship doesn't count?" he asked. "'Cause I can read, Chloe. I know you're out all the time with Henry Norwich and Harlan Reed and—"

"Know what? I met Henry Norwich exactly one time," I cut him off. "And yeah, I'm out all the time because it's fun. I'm doing great at work. Matthew Greengold loves me. Anne Lynch loves me. Why shouldn't I have a good time?"

"Does having a boyfriend back home cut into your fun?" he asked. "Because that's fine with me, I'll clear out and let you have your freedom. But don't pretend that everything's okay between us when it isn't."

I stared at him, shocked. "Are you dumping me?"

"No. You're dumping me," Max said. "You're turning into some party girl I don't even recognize, and you're lying to me and doing drugs—"

"Oh, don't be such a prude," I snapped.

"You're the one with the Don't Do list," Max said. "You're supposed to be the prude."

"I get to do what I want. That's the reward for living through the madness," I said. "That's what Anne Lynch told me."

"Whatever, Chloe." Max sighed. "I know you're lonely over here, and if you want to go out, I don't blame you. But you have to be honest with me."

"Okay. I will be," I said.

"So are we together or not?"

I gazed at him, his gorgeous green eyes and his strong shoulders. I adored Max. He'd always been real with me, and he knew me from before I was famous. I trusted him as much as I'd ever trusted anyone besides Travis. And maybe I was cheating on him musically, a little, but I hadn't cheated on him at all with any other guy. Besides, I'd go home to LA soon enough, and then I wouldn't want to go out every night like I did here. I'd have my friends again, and my brother. I wouldn't need the constant stimulation.

And I didn't want to lose him.

"We're together," I said.

But later, while Max slept, I stayed awake and watched the sun come up. Alone.

STAR CENTRAL BLOG

Twin power, celebrate! CHLOE and TRAVIS GAMBLE, the blond and beautiful acting pair, are turning seventeen today, according to devoted dad LONNIE GAMBLE. Our reporter found Lonnie camped outside the Hollywood Hills house where the twins live, even though no one was home. We smell a publicity stunt!

"I'll wait as long as it takes," Lonnie told us. "I plan to wish my kids a happy birthday if it kills me. This is the first year I ain't been with them for the big day."

So why is he sitting outside all by himself?

"Chloe and Travis got people around them who won't let me anywhere near them," Lonnie says. "And my wife does all she can to keep us apart—ever since she took the kids, she's been filling their heads with lies about me."

While Lonnie wouldn't elaborate on exactly what those lies are, he did say that his estranged wife, EARLENE GAMBLE, doesn't live with their children, so it's hard to know how she could be talking too much trash.

With Chloe still in London shooting *Frontier* and Travis probably out partying hard, Lonnie's chances seem pretty slim.

"They've got to come home sometime," Lonnie said. "I'm a patient man."

IM

GAMBLEGOAL: Hey, Clo! Happy Birthday!

GAMBLEGOAL: We're 17! Long way since our 16th back in Abilene, TX, huh?

GAMBLEGOAL: Chloe? You there? I keep getting voicemail.

GAMBLEGOAL: Whatevs. Call me later.

"The party on Saturday was fine, because nobody saw you drinking," Marc said to me while I downed my Pomegranate Red Mango yogurt. "But cancel the Playboy Mansion on Thursday night."

"Why?" Coop asked.

"Because it's the Playboy Mansion," Marc said.

"But Travis ain't even hosting that one," Coop said. "Come on, he can go as a guest!"

"Travis is barely seventeen. He's a clean-cut, athletic good boy," Marc said. "And good boys don't go to bad places, no matter how much their best friends want them to."

"I don't care," I told Coop. "It's just a party, it's not like there's Playmates posing naked everywhere."

"Really?" Coop shook his head. "What a waste."

"Honey, if we can keep the Travis train rolling for another few years, you will have plenty of time at the Mansion," Marc said. "Be patient."

"I got to go back to Texas in a month. I got no time to be patient!" Coop said.

"You could stay and be my permanent assistant," I said.

"My folks ain't like yours. They'd kill me if I didn't go to college," Coop said. "They almost killed me for putting if off for this one semester."

I didn't answer, but I didn't have to. We all knew it was true—my mama and daddy didn't give a crap about college. Far as I knew, they'd never even heard the word before. They thought finishing high school was optional, and maybe they were right, since neither me or Chloe had.

"But I like it around here," Coop said. The yogurt place was in the middle of Westwood, which was right next to the UCLA campus. "I go to college in LA, I can still live with you and be your assistant."

"Hey, Coop, find out what I got to do to graduate," I said. "Nika told me there was some test I could take once I was emancipated. I'd get a real high school diploma, not a G.E.D."

"Speaking of Nika, she said to remind you about the meeting with ABC tomorrow. It's not an audition, just a meeting," Marc said. He stared at me as if I was supposed to be psyched.

"What?" I asked.

"Right, I'm talking to the clueless Gamble," he sighed. "Trav, you need to learn the rules of the game. It's ABC. They want you for a part and they're not even making you read for it. That means you're big-time."

"Oh. Cool," I said.

"Because Matthew Greengold told everyone you walk on water," Marc added.

"Okay," I said. "Am I supposed to send him a thank-you note?"

"Only if you get the part," Marc said. "Remember what we practiced for Kimmel tonight—your stories about shooting with Greengold? Say the same stuff in the meeting tomorrow."

"Seriously?" I asked. "Won't that be boring?"

"Boring is good. Boring is safe," he told me. "And nobody's hiring you for your conversational skills, anyway."

"We got to boogie if you want to work out, Trav," Coop put in. "You have to be there in two hours for Kimmel."

I nodded and downed the rest of my yogurt. The gym was

right next door, which is why I'd made Marc have our meeting here. Though he didn't seem to mind—he'd been openly staring at the guy behind the counter for the last five minutes.

"Do you mind?" I teased him. "I'm trying to conduct business here and you're checking out the yogurt pusher."

"Excuse me, I do not drool all over every cute boy I see," Marc said. "But I'll let your gay slur slide because you're a Texas rube." He dropped his voice. "I'm looking at the *other* guy."

"Dude. He's got no ear!" Coop sounded disgusted.

"What?" I spun around to look at the Red Mango guy.

"You'd think in a city with five plastic surgeons on every street, he could have that thing fixed," Marc said, pushing away his yogurt. "Makes me lose my appetite."

"Are you coming with us to the studio later?" Coop asked, standing up.

"Of course. I'm not going to let Travis show up at his first talk show without his publicist," Marc replied.

But I wasn't really listening to him anymore. I'd barely even glanced at the guy with the mangled ear who was cleaning the counter. I was too busy staring at my mama—and her high heels and her short skirt, and her porno boyfriend's hand on her ass.

"Mama," I called. "What are you doing here?"

My mama jumped in surprise, then clapped her hands. "Well, hey there, sugar! Alex, look who's here!" She toddled over and flung her arms around my neck, and I could smell the wine on her breath.

"Mama, you have a liquid lunch again today?" I asked.

"I am having a probiotic tea for lunch," she said. "It's Alex's favorite."

I glanced over at the porn king, who was busy ordering tea from the dude with the scars where his ear should be. Marc was flipping through *Star* magazine and Coop was checking my phone messages, acting all Hollywood assistant–like.

"Jesus, my life has gotten strange," I muttered.

"Maybe, but it's a damn sight better'n Texas," Mama said. "Now, darlin', tell me if you seen your daddy. 'Cause Clo's check didn't come yet this month, and I think maybe he put a lien on my wages. That's what Alex said."

"Daddy's been laying low," I said. "Sean got the court date moved back since he can't represent us anymore."

"Why not?" Mama frowned.

"He left to work for . . ." I suddenly remembered my mama's disastrous affair with Dave Quinn. "Um, for EdisonCorp."

"Travis, I am a grown woman, you can say the name of my ex," Mama said. "So Sean's moving up in the world? Nice of him to make this mess for you and Clo and then desert you."

"He didn't desert us. He found another lawyer to handle our case, an actual family lawyer," I said. "I'm supposed to meet him tomorrow."

I wanted to wait until Chloe got back from England, but it didn't really matter. I couldn't get her to talk about the Daddy situation for two seconds. I was never going to convince her to take a meeting with some strange new lawyer. I wasn't even sure

Chloe had realized that it wouldn't be Sean taking care of us anymore. She was so wrapped up in her movie and partying with her new friends that she barely answered texts these days.

"Here you go, baby," Alex said, coming over with a cup for my mama. "Hi, Trav."

"*Travis*," I corrected him. "What are you doing skulking around UCLA? Looking for talent among the college girls?"

"Well, not all of them are prissy like you," Mama said.

"Forget it, I don't even want to know," I muttered.

But Alex laughed. "Even adult entertainment professionals don't stay in the Valley all the time, Travis," he said. "Much as you might want us to."

I rolled my eyes. "Coop! Let's get out of here," I called.

"You sending me tickets to your show later?" Mama asked.

"How do you even know about that?" I said. I hadn't seen my mama in more than a week, and I definitely didn't tell her anything about work.

"Darlin', you are my child," Mama said, pouting. "I keep up on what you're doing just like any mama would."

"Right. How else will you know if you're getting a cut of the money?" I said. "But you did manage to forget our birthday two days ago."

My mama's mouth dropped open in surprise.

"Real nice, Mama." I said. "Happy birthday to me."

As we headed to the gym, Coop clapped me on the back. "I'll send her a couple tickets," he said.

"No, just one. I can't let anyone know there's a porn producer connected to me and Clo," I said. "Mama can leave her sleazebag at home."

Marc might think I didn't understand the game, but I understood it well enough for that.

STAR CENTRAL BLOG

CHLOE GAMBLE took time out from her busy shooting (and club-hopping!) schedule to make a YouTube video for her twin brother, TRAVIS. The fierce twin set turned seventeen last Sunday, and it seems that someone forgot the big day. Judging from Chloe's hilarious intro song, she flaked on the date because she was so intent on staying in character for her movie, *Frontier*. But what better way to say "I'm Sorry" than to pull together a band of friends with names like SHANI, TAYLOR SWIFT, and SIR ELTON JOHN, and get them to sing an all-star Happy Birthday to Travis.

If you want to see the video, do it fast. Time Warner, who owns the rights to "Happy Birthday," will be sure to yank it as soon as they catch on. Let's just hope Travis Gamble saw it first!

"Can I get you anything?" Nika's assistant asked me. "Water? Diet Coke?"

"No thanks," I said.

"I'll take a Coke," Coop put in.

"Absolutely." She shot me a smile. "Happy birthday! I saw Chloe's thing online."

"Thanks."

"You should've had a party," she said. "We can still go out and celebrate." She went off to get Coop's soda, and we both checked out her ass.

"She hot for you?" Coop said.

"Nah, she's just doing the Hollywood thing," I said. "Though usually she ignores me while I try to hit on her."

"Well, you're the shit now. I bet she wants you bad." Coop wiggled his eyebrows like an idiot and I laughed.

"I am the shit," I told him.

"Happy birthday, Trav," Nika said, opening her office door. "Come on in." She was smiling, but her eyes looked serious. I figured I'd skip the small talk.

"What did ABC say?" I asked. "Is it bad?"

"What? No. It's fantastic!" Nika said. "It's for Legacy, a four-episode guest stint. Did they tell you about it in the meeting?"

"Yeah, I'd be playing the long-lost half brother," I said. "And nobody is sure if I'm a good guy or a con man."

"Sounds like fun, doesn't it?" Nika said. "They're offering top of show, which is TV-speak for a bucket of money, and this is for sweeps so it'll get a lot of attention."

I was already wondering how much I could hide from my mama. "Hey, those details don't go in the trades, do they? My daddy won't find out how much money I'm making?""It's never a well-kept secret," Nika said. "If Lonnie wants to find out, he can probably pay somebody off."

I sighed and sat back in my chair. "I wish we were eighteen instead of seventeen."

"No judge is going to overturn your emancipation, not with the money you're making," Nika said. "Besides, that's why we have lawyers on the team."

"But not Sean."

"No." Her expression turned serious again, and now I got it. She had boyfriend issues.

"When does he start the new gig?" I asked.

"Monday." Nika stood up, signaling for me to leave. Didn't matter to me. If she didn't want to talk relationships, that was just fine. She and Sean had always seemed like the perfect power couple, but what did I know?

"So I'll call the showrunners and tell them it's a yes?" Nika said. "I'm sorry to run you out of here, I have a big meeting in five minutes."

"It's cool. Hey, can you make them put Coop in my contract? So he gets paid?"

"I don't know about that," she said. But she must've noticed me frowning, because she immediately changed her tune. "But I'll see what I can do. Sound good?"

"Sounds great." Nika might not be kissing my ass like she did with Chloe, but it was definitely a big change since the days when she booked me modeling jobs as a favor. "I'll call you later. I have to run." She kissed me on the cheek and took off for her meeting.

Coop was hanging out with the assistant. "Well?" he said as soon as Nika left.

"I'm on the show. Four episodes!" I still couldn't wrap my brain around it. Legacy was one of those shows that everyone in America watched, huge ratings, the whole thing. And now I was going to be on it, with twenty million people staring at me for an hour every Tuesday night at ten.

"Holy crap," Coop said.

"I know," I agreed.

"So, listen, Travis . . ." Nika's assistant looked a little nervous. "There's someone who wants to see you, in the screening room. Do you have a few minutes?"

"Who is it?" I asked.

"I can't say." She looked back and forth between me and Coop. "But it's worth it."

"Okay. Lead the way."

She jumped up and started off down the hallway, so we followed. "You think it's a surprise party?" Coop asked me.

"God, I hope not. I don't even know any of these people." We passed the conference room, where Nika was sitting down at a table full of guys in suits. "Where's Hal?" I asked.

"Hal Turman?" Nika's assistant sounded surprised. "He's in his office, probably. Did you want to say hello?"

"No. I just figured he'd be in that meeting," I said.

"It's about a new client. No need for Hal." She stopped in front of a closed door. "Here we are."

Coop reached for the doorknob, but she grabbed his arm. "Travis only. You're stuck with me."

"I can handle that," Coop said.

I opened the door and went in, letting it click shut behind me.

Sasha Powell sat in one of the big leather chairs. "Hey, Trav," she said.

"Sasha," I said, surprised. My heart started to pound. It was strange to see her, considering how we'd left things. We hadn't spoken at all since the day she walked out of my house, the day my daddy showed up in town. But before that we'd been like a couple of rabbits, going at it every night. "I thought you were in New York."

She shrugged, patting the chair next to her. "I have a meeting with Spielberg. And New York was no fun without you."

"Sorry," I said, staying where I was. "Spain must've been okay, though, right?"

Sasha actually blushed. "I guess Chloe told you I saw her?"

"Of course she did," I said.

"I was only there for a few days. That would've been better with you, too." Sasha pouted a little with her famous plump lips. Didn't matter if she'd dumped me, she was still the hottest girl on earth. I didn't make a move for the chair, though.

"So what are you doing here?" I asked.

"I was with my agent, and I heard you were coming in to see Nika, so I thought I'd wait," she said. "We share an agency now."

"Does that matter?" I asked.

"It means we have to play nice." Sasha stood up and walked over to me, sliding her hand up my chest. "And we know how to do that."

She gave me a little push, and I sat down in the chair. Sasha straddled me, sitting on my lap. "I missed you," she whispered.

"Um, we're in the middle of an office," I pointed out.

"So what?" She leaned in and kissed me, moving my hands around her body until I was holding her ass. "Don't you want to?"

I definitely wanted to. But Coop was ten feet away, just outside the door. And so was Nika's assistant . . . and every other employee of the Virtuoso Agency.

But Sasha Powell was a superstar. She was used to getting what she wanted, and she wanted me. Right now. Right here.

"Yeah," I said, pulling her closer. "I want to."

Nika Mays's Manuscript Notes: Business vs. Love

Hal Turman had a theory about why he'd managed to stay married to the same woman for thirty-five years. He said it was because she stayed out of the Business. All Mrs. Turman cared about was her house and her rose bushes and her charities, and she didn't give a rat's ass about Hollywood. Hal always rolled his eyes whenever some celebrity couple got married. He said that two show-biz careers in one relationship was disaster waiting to happen. Because the Business gets in the way of the couple, and the couple gets in the way of the Business. That's why his wife stayed out of it.

I always figured it was just his typical sexist bullshit.

But after Sean took the job at EdisonCorp, I started to understand. It wasn't the Business that got in our way, it was the competition. We'd started out together, both of us nobodies. We'd put our minds and our skills together and pulled off some truly amazing deals. And we'd advanced because of it—Sean up his legal ladder and me up my agenting ladder.

Now, though, he was ahead. He'd jumped right off his ladder and on to a bigger one. Did he need to know the law to run EdisonCorp's movie arm? I doubted it. He barely even knew the movie business, that's what killed me. He was an entertainment lawyer. He understood contracts and lawsuits. Not the actual facts about how a feature film gets produced.

So why had Dave Quinn poached Sean, and not me?

Sean didn't want to hear me whine about it. He said I never wanted to run a studio, I wanted to be an agent, and everyone knew that. It wasn't because I was a woman, or because I was black, or anything like that.

The thing was, I didn't really want Sean's new job. I just thought Quinn should have offered it to me. But that's not the sort of thing you're supposed to say to your boyfriend. So instead I just spent all my time feeling annoyed and pretending it had nothing to do with our careers.

"You mind not checking your e-mail *again*?" I asked Sean over steaks at Musso & Frank. "We're supposed to be having dinner."

"Sorry, I'm waiting on a draft of that presentation for tomorrow," he replied.

"Sean. This is literally the first time I've seen you all week," I said. "Turn off your BlackBerry."

"Is yours off?" he asked.

It wasn't, and we both knew it. Ty Boswell's lawyers were going over our contract with a fine-tooth comb, and I had to be on call in case they had any questions.

"Look, it's a brand-new job. I have to be on top of things," Sean said. "Give me a month or two and I won't be so busy all the time."

"What are you even doing? You have exactly one movie in the works, and you're not actually producers," I said. "You're just the money."

"Quinn is thinking of buying a smaller production company. They've got a couple of interesting properties in development," Sean said. "I can't tell you who, though, sorry."

I shoved a piece of meat into my mouth to give myself time to think before I answered him—before I yelled at him, more like. We always told each other everything, even if we weren't supposed to. That's why we were such a good team.

"And they're pulling me in on another deal," Sean went on. "The Snap network is on the block. We've got a serious offer to buy the entire thing, but it's mostly for *Cover Band*."

"You mean for Chloe," I said, almost choking in surprise. "EdisonCorp wants to sell her contract."

"Yeah. It's not movie-related, but I obviously know all the players, so Quinn's asked me to step in," Sean said.

"You're not serious, are you?" I said. "Why would you sell your hottest property?"

"It's a lot of money," he replied.

"That's ridiculous. Spend the money yourselves and increase Chloe's success, don't sell her on the way up," I said. "Give it a year or two and she'll be worth three times as much."

"Maybe, but Quinn wants to be in the movie

business, not television. Snap was an experiment for the company, and frankly, it's been a disaster. The network has no viable shows right now. Without *Cover Band*, they've got nothing to build on." Sean checked his e-mail again, while I stared at him and thought about what an idiot he was being.

"So make a *Cover Band* movie," I said slowly, as if I was talking to a five-year-old. "It would be dirt cheap, you can do it as soon as *Frontier* wraps, and then you go right into production on the show. You've got a hit movie, which translates into new viewers for the network's fresh episodes, and you're in Quinn's precious movie business without having to dump a successful property."

Sean frowned, thinking about it. "Honestly, without Chloe, we don't have anything to build a features company with, either," he said. "We've got her under contract for two more years, it only makes sense to use her as much as possible."

"Now you're thinking," I said sarcastically.

He smiled. "We're a good team."

No. I'm good, I thought. *I'm better at your job than you are.*

"Speaking of Chloe," he said, "you need to get on top of this Lonnie Gamble situation."

"What?" I said. "They've got a court date next week when Chloe gets back. You said the lawyer you found was good."

"I meant the PR," Sean said. "Lonnie's got a way with the gossips. He's charming, and they all think he's funny. And he's talking a lot of shit about how this movie is exploiting her. Greengold's people are even making noises about it. What is Marc doing?"

I thought frantically, trying to figure out what he meant. To be honest, I'd been paying more attention to Ty Boswell lately than to the Gambles. Chloe was off shooting, and anyway I couldn't put her up for any more jobs because her contract with EdisonCorp kept her locked up for too long. And Travis had fallen into that guest stint on the ABC show, so he was set for the moment.

Ty needed more hand-holding. He wanted to talk every night. He wanted to run all his new ideas by me. He wanted to get together for drinks, and for coffee, and to flirt. It took up all my time, which was fine since Sean was always working.

"Lonnie won't shut up in the press. I can't believe you don't know that," Sean said incredulously. "Don't you see why? He's setting it up so that if he wins in court, he can yank permission for Chloe to do *Frontier*."

"And hold it over your heads until you cough up more money," I finished for him.

"Or whatever else he wants," Sean said. "He could tie up the film in legal wrangling for months."

I sighed. "Marc left me a message yesterday about Lonnie, but I didn't have time to get back to him. We'll have to come up with a strategy."

"I don't think Lonnie will convince the judge to overturn the emancipation," he said. "But it is possible. I just want to be prepared."

Sean reached across the table and took my hand, but it sort of annoyed me, given how he'd seemed to think I was incompetent thirty seconds earlier. And given how incompetent I thought he was sometimes.

My BlackBerry buzzed with a text message. I let go of Sean's hand and pulled the phone out to check. It was from Ty.

TIEBO: We're official! Lawyers just sent my signed papers to your office.

NIKAMAYS: So you're finally mine?

TIEBO: All yours. Be gentle with me.

I smiled, and Sean cleared his throat. "Can't that wait until after dinner?" he asked.

"It's Ty Boswell," I said. "So, no."

"You can't complain about me being a workaholic when you're the same way," Sean said.

My phone rang. I grabbed it and hit talk.

"Nika, I want to celebrate," Ty's voice murmured in my ear. "You're my agent now, you have to come when I call, right?"

"That's not entirely true," I said, as Sean rolled his eyes. He pulled out his own BlackBerry and started to work.

"Which part isn't true?" Ty asked.

"I don't *have* to come," I said.

"But you want to," he said.

I did want to. Ty Boswell was young, hot, and famous . . . and he was seriously into me. Sean was, well, boring. He might be a shark, and cute, and my partner in all my most kick-ass professional moves. But he was also a guy I'd been sleeping with for months, who had a job that I should have, and who had no time for me.

"Where are you?" I asked.

"My place," Ty said. "You coming over?"

"I'll be there in twenty," I said. When I hung up, Sean was already signaling for the check.

"What's that all about?" he asked.

"There's some glitch with Ty's agency papers,"

I lied. "I have to go to the office for a bit. Sorry."

He shrugged. "Work comes first."

When I got to Ty's humongous house in Beverly Hills, I got out of the Bentley and just stood there in the driveway. I shouldn't be here, not at night, not when there was absolutely no professional reason to see my client.

"Come on in, superagent," Ty called, opening the door. "I've got Stoli on ice."

What could I do, now that I was there? I had to have a drink with him. One drink, and then over to Sean's house.

"So are we going places?" Ty asked as soon as I stepped into the house. "You're going to make me huge?"

"I am," I promised.

"Then let's celebrate," he said, reaching for me.

My heart gave a huge thump, and I let him pull me into his arms. His lips were on my neck, his hands under my shirt. I had to stop him . . . but how could I? I'd never been with anyone like Ty before. Six months ago, I wouldn't be on the radar of a guy like this—so famous, so rich, so hot. And now I was in his house and he was pulling me toward the bedroom.

He was something new for me, a flavor of ice cream I'd never tried. And I wanted to. I wanted him.

"Let's celebrate," I said.

My BlackBerry woke me up in the morning. I rolled over and grabbed it before I even remembered where I was. The caller ID said Hal Turman. I hit ignore and sat up in Ty's California king bed. He was still asleep, and snoring. I ran a hand through my hair. My head was pounding. All the intoxicating magic of the night before was gone, and the only thing left was cold reality.

It was almost nine. I should be at the office, where everyone expected me to behave like a grown-up, like a responsible, intelligent agent who understood that there are boundaries that professionals simply don't cross.

Hal had never taught me that agents can't sleep with their clients. He didn't have to. It was obvious. Sex complicates everything, and a complicated relationship is an insecure relationship. Clients leave over things like sex. And agents get fired for losing clients that way.

I knew better. I'd wanted to use the sexual tension between us to land Ty. I hadn't planned to actually give in to it. I'd worked for years to get where I was, and I was poised to become huge. Signing Ty Boswell put me solidly at the top of the pool of agents I worked with. Daniel Shapiro's go-to girl. Serious competition for Peter Bryant. I was there . . . and I'd risked it all just for one night in the sack with a hot actor.

It's because of Sean, I thought. I'd been mad at him last night. We hadn't been spending enough time together lately, and I hadn't been truthful with him about his job, about the way I felt—jealous and competitive. I knew Sean would hear me out and he'd probably even understand exactly how I felt, but I still hadn't wanted to say anything to him. It was embarrassing that I felt so envious. It meant I was petty, and selfish, and all kinds of things I didn't want to be.

I'd let it all get bottled up inside me so that I was so angry at Sean that I wanted to hurt him. That's why I slept with Ty.

It's pathetic, I thought. *I couldn't face being honest with my boyfriend, so I put my whole career in jeopardy.*

I got out of bed as quietly as I could and grabbed my clothes off the floor. I didn't even glance back at Ty as I headed out, getting dressed on the way to the front door. If I was lucky, Ty would never even mention this. Movie stars could sleep with anyone they wanted, any time they wanted. It was a big deal to me, but maybe not to him. Maybe he didn't even realize that his agent wasn't supposed to know what he looked like naked.

Maybe I could still save my career.

I knew what I had to do, and I did it as soon as I got into the Bentley. I hit Sean's number on my phone and waited for him to pick up.

"We need to break up," I told him. "This relationship is getting in the way of my business."

chapter seven

HOME SWEET HOME

"Chloe! Over here!" one of the photographers shouted.

"Smile, Chloe!"

I ignored them, pretending I couldn't hear because of the earbuds in my ears. The iPod clipped to the strap of my tank top was off, but the paparazzi didn't know that. I peered through the crowd for Max, who had promised to meet me at the airport. It would've made more sense to take a car service and hire security, which is what Nika and Marc had wanted. But Max offered to pick me up, and things between us had been weird ever since his visit to London. I figured I could make him feel important by coming to meet me like an old-fashioned gentleman, or at least like a guy in the movies. It would get him in the tabloids and help his band, and it would show everyone that I was a good girl who still had the same boyfriend as when I'd left.

"What are you listening to, Chloe?" someone yelled. He was right in my face, pointing to the earbuds, so I couldn't pretend I'd forgotten about them.

I pulled them out and gave him a wink. "I'm listening to myself, of course. A new single I've been working on."

"Happy to be home?" someone else yelled, now that I was trapped into a Q&A.

"You know it!" I replied, putting on a girl-next-door smile. "Y'all can't even believe how foggy it is in England! I need my fix of the California sun."

"Where's your suitcase, Chloe? Didn't you buy anything in London?"

"'Course I did!" I said. "I bought so much that I had to ship it all back! The world doesn't have enough suitcases."

"This way, Chloe!"

I turned, still smiling, and gazed out over the flashes. Where was Max? I'd been on the plane for hours, and I wanted to get home.

"Have you spoken to your dad yet, Chloe?"

The smile dropped right off of my face. "What?" I said

"Your dad. Lonnie," the paparazzo called. They all pressed in a little closer, like sharks that smell blood in the water. "He's been hoping to spend some time with you now that you're back."

"Well, I guess he'll see me in court," I snapped.

"Lonnie says you're partying too much, Chloe," someone said. "Do you have a reply to that?"

"Chloe!" Max shoved his way through the crowd, and just in time, too. I was not about to let my ass of a daddy go around talking trash about me. But Marc would not be happy if I spoke my mind to the photographers, 'cause it would be up on *TMZ* before I even got back to my house.

"Thank God." I hugged Max tight and tried to ignore all the cameras capturing the moment. "I am just about done with the attention here."

He grabbed my hand and pulled me past the paparazzi—well, the airport security guys helped, too—and outside to his SUV. Some of the photogs got into cars and followed us, snapping pictures right up until Max turned into traffic.

"Okay, so Nika was right," he said. "You should've taken a car."

I nodded. "Marc says security ain't an option anymore, it's necessary. I didn't believe him until they started asking about my daddy."

"They were just trying to get a reaction from you. They'll make more money from a picture of you yelling than one of you smiling." Max sighed. "They know it's a story. Your father won't stop talking to them. He pays them off, tells them where he's gonna be, when he's going to his lawyer's office, all that. The paps have even been following Travis lately."

"He didn't tell me that," I said.

"You're not so easy to get a hold of these days." Max wasn't just talking about Trav anymore, but I ignored that.

"Well, I'm back now, so everyone can talk to me as much as they want, except my loser of a daddy." I unclipped my iPod and stuck it into the dock, since Max's wasn't there. "Listen to this, it's the new song I'm working on with Lars. We spent last weekend in the studio."

Max listened for a few seconds, then started talking again. "Coop said if you landed past noon, we'd have to go straight to the courthouse, and it's twelve-thirty. Sorry."

"Coop? Since when's he calling the shots?" I asked.

"Since he became Trav's assistant. Turns out, he's really good at it." Max laughed. "He keeps your brother's schedule, so he figured he'd keep yours, too. At least for this court date."

"I want to go home first," I said. "Daddy can wait."

"But the judge can't," Max said.

"Oh, I'll just sweet-talk him," I said. "I don't see why I got to be there, anyway. Isn't that what the lawyer's for?"

"You have to be there to prove that you're a responsible adult," Max said. "Showing up late won't help with that."

I rolled my eyes. When did Max get so boring? There was no judge on the planet who would take my daddy's side over mine. I was a damn movie star, making buttloads of money. And Daddy was a loser who just wanted to sponge off me. I don't care how he tried to spin it, I would always spin it better, because I was younger and hotter than him. "Just take me home first," I said.

He shook his head, annoyed.

"What are *you* so mad at? You haven't even listened to a word of this song," I snapped.

"Really, Clo? You think I should pay close attention to the music you're doing for somebody else?" he said.

"You told me it was fine, you said I'd be an idiot not to work with Lars," I said.

"That doesn't mean you have to rub my face in it," he said.

"I wanted your opinion because I trust you," I said. "But fine, if you want to be a baby about it, don't listen." I hit the forward button in the iPod to skip to something else.

The intro chords to "Lucky Bitch" filled the car, and I swear my heart actually stopped for a second. Fast as I could, I hit the forward button again, but it was too late.

"What was that?" Max asked.

"Nothing. You don't want to hear my stuff, remember?" I reached over to take the iPod out of the dock, but Max stopped me.

"That was 'Lucky Bitch,'" he said.

"So?" My heart was pounding fast, but I'm used to covering up my feelings. He was being all passive-aggressive and I was pissed off about it. I kept my mind on that, and my voice came out bitchy just like I needed it to.

"It sounded different," Max said. "Play it."

I didn't move. I didn't speak. Usually if you just stay still and quiet for more than a couple seconds, people back down. Silence freaks everyone out.

Not Max. He glanced at the iPod and hit the back button. "Lucky Bitch" started up again, the same chords me and him had laid down in that studio in the Valley . . . but with a completely different backup harmony. A different beat. A different producer.

Max listened to the whole song. I didn't say anything.

When it was over, he pulled my iPod out of the dock and handed it to me.

"I didn't mean to play that one for you," I said.

"You told me Lars was only doing your new stuff. You said the songs we did together were off limits."

I tried to ignore the hurt in his voice. "Lars just had this remix in his head, and he wanted to do it," I said. "It's not like we ever released that song, not officially, so—"

"I barely even recognize it," Max cut me off. "He changed everything. The whole point of 'Lucky Bitch' was that it's raw—"

"Lars doesn't think so. He says it wants to be lush," I argued.

"Well, he's wrong. And you said you wouldn't let him touch my stuff."

"It's *my* stuff," I pointed out.

"Right." Max's voice was clipped. "Nice job of not lying

to me again, Chloe. Do you even realize you're doing it, or do you just not care?"

"Can we not have a big relationship talk in the car, please?" I said, disgusted.

Max turned off the 405 freeway, but it wasn't my exit. He didn't say a word. He didn't have to.

"I said to take me home first," I told him.

"You're due in court. And I'm not a taxi service."

He didn't look at me for the rest of the drive to the courthouse. I didn't look at him, either. It was his loss. Who dumps a movie star? I'd be able to get a new boyfriend by tonight, but Max would never get anyone like me again. If he wanted to be with somebody successful, somebody who could help him, then he should've known that there would be compromises.

The sick feeling in my stomach wasn't worth paying attention to. It was just shock or something. Nobody had ever broken up with me before, I'm the one who does that. Anyway, the feeling would go away soon enough.

"Good luck at the hearing," Max said, pulling to a stop at the entrance to the parking lot.

"There's paparazzi everywhere," I said, gazing out over the sea of cars, vans, and photographers. "Can't you drive me up to the door?"

"You know what? They're here for you. I don't want the attention," Max said.

I laughed under my breath. "No worries there," I told him.

I grabbed my purse, stuffed my iPod into it, and climbed out of the SUV. I kicked the door shut behind me and walked off toward the damn courthouse. No good-byes. What would be the point?

The parking lot was gray and ugly, just like everything else had been since the plane landed at LAX. I'd spent my whole life dying to get to Los Angeles, but now it just looked dirty and tired. In Europe, I could pretend none of the Gamble family craziness existed. But there was no way to escape it in LA.

I pulled out my cell and texted Trav to tell him I was out here. But the paparazzi spotted me before the guards from the courthouse could make it outside.

Twenty feet from the front door, I couldn't take a single step more. There had to be forty people surrounding me, pressing in close, shutters clicking away. Their voices yelling my name all blended together into a strange kind of white noise, like the sounds of the crowd cheering at a beauty pageant or a rodeo.

"What do you think your chances are today, Chloe?"

"Chloe, where's Max?"

"Do you think your dad will regain custody, Chloe?"

These weren't the kinds of questions I was used to. The paparazzi liked to talk to me about my clothes and my music and whether or not I liked the other actors I worked with. They joked around with me about being a beauty queen and about how strange Hollywood seemed to a small-town girl like me. But this was uglier, and there was a nasty undercurrent that reminded me of my mama's sleaze of a boyfriend. Everything he did felt dirty, and right now the paparazzi felt dirty in that same way.

"Move back. Move back *now!*" voices yelled. I couldn't see a thing over the heads of the photographers. They were taller than me, and there were so many of them that it was like staring at a wall. Some knelt, some stood behind them, just shooting away as if I was doing anything interesting at all. The court security was still shouting at them to move, but the paps ignored them.

"Hey, now! Step off, y'all, that ain't right." The voice cut through the white noise like a chainsaw. Instantly, the photographers spun to shoot my daddy, and they sure as hell cleared a path for *him*.

"There's my girl!" he said with a shit-eating grin. He came right up to me and hugged me tight like we were actual family and he was used to hugging me. Far as I could remember, that man had never so much as patted me on the head before, but now he was all mushy and misty-eyed and I had to stand there and take it, because a hundred cameras were on us.

"You told them we were coming to court today?" I hissed into his ear as he held me.

"You ain't the only one knows how to make a scene," my daddy replied.

I pulled away as soon as I could without looking like a complete bitch, though Daddy tried to hang on longer.

"C'mon, y'all, step back and let us through now," he called, waving off the photographers. They actually listened to him, not that they stopped shooting. They just started moving backwards toward the courthouse doors, letting me and him walk forward.

I held my purse in front of me with both hands so I wouldn't have to touch him, but my daddy kept an arm around my back like he was protecting me, ushering me safely forward.

Three guards were there now, and they did hold the photographers away. It wasn't easy—they all but grabbed my daddy's arm and mine and hauled us through the throng of reporters and inside the glass doors.

Travis, Coop, Nika and Marc and my mama all stood inside with some bald guy in a suit, who had to be our new lawyer. There were a row of metal detectors between me and them, but that didn't stop me from seeing the furious expression on my twin brother's face. Trav probably wanted to punch Daddy right about now, and I didn't blame him.

I glanced over my shoulder and saw that the guards had moved a couple screens in front of the door, and they weren't letting anyone in. The photographers couldn't see us anymore.

"Get your damn hands off me, you lying sack of shit," I snarled, shoving my daddy away.

"Whoa there, Clo!" he cried, laughing. "What kind of way is that to talk to your loving daddy? Why, you might be back under my roof in just a couple hours."

"It's *my* roof, Daddy, I'm the one who actually earns in this family," I told him. "And you'll be dead before you ever see a dime of my money. That's a promise."

Hearings on TV are always kinda short and exciting, but I was just about ready to stretch out on the bench in the courtroom before our lawyer, Martin Lesher, was even done talking. He was no Sean. Sean was cool. This dude was old, bald, and the most boring person I'd ever seen besides the librarian back in Spurlock, Texas.

"Stop yawning, Trav," Chloe said. "Look mature."

Judge Gutierrez shot a look over at us and I felt like a kid who just got caught whispering in class.

"They about done with this?" I murmured. "How long does it take to see what an ass hat Daddy is?"

"The judge is a woman, and Daddy's Daddy," Clo pointed out.

Great. That meant Daddy would have her bent over the table in her chambers in another five minutes.

"I'd like to review the lease, please," Judge Gutierrez said.

Martin went up to her desk and handed over the paperwork for our place in the Hills. My name wasn't on that lease, only Chloe's. She'd been the one with all the money when we rented it, and besides, we share everything. Always have, always will. But did that make me look like a baby? Like I couldn't even sign a lease? The last time I saw Sean, when he introduced me to Martin, I got the feeling Sean was worried about me. He kept saying how

I should call him if I needed anything, and giving me his new card. When I told Chloe, she said it was 'cause he wants to stay in good with us since he's a movie executive now. I thought it was 'cause Sean figured I needed taking care of. He hadn't seen Clo since she left for England, but he sure saw a lot of me. And I think he had doubts now about the emancipation, like maybe I wasn't ready to take care of myself.

I was, though. If I had to, I'd take care of me and Chloe both. But I wouldn't have to. Now that she was back, we'd be fine. No more partying with forty-year-old movie stars for her, no more hiding from Daddy for me.

"Sugar, do you think I'm gonna have to testify?" my mama asked, leaning forward from the bench behind us. "I fell asleep there for a second! Why'd your yummy lawyer stick you with this guy?"

"Sean said Martin's the best family lawyer in town," I told her. I was talking to Chloe, too, since she'd never paid even a bit of attention to any of the legal stuff once she left for Europe. I wasn't sure she even knew we had a new lawyer until she got here.

"Who cares? We could send a monkey up there and it would be fine. Daddy don't stand a chance," Chloe said.

But when I glanced over at my daddy, he was looking right back, like he knew what we were saying. He shook his head at me, and I turned away.

"It's the skank's turn," Mama muttered. Martin seemed to

be done talking, 'cause he was back with us now and Sylvia was getting up to speak to the judge.

"That judge looks even more annoyed than I am," Chloe said, grinning.

"That's 'cause she's a classy woman who knows a quack slut lawyer when she sees one," Mama replied.

"Says the porn mogul's girlfriend," Chloe said.

I was listening to Sylvia, though. Martin had been telling our side of the story, and I knew that. Sylvia was talking all about Daddy, and his side, and how we'd abandoned him and he'd been worried sick and now his family had been illegally taken out of his hands and we'd denied him his parental rights under the law. My mama was wrong about this chick—Sylvia might be a slut, but she was no quack. She sounded good, like a big-word-using lawyer from the movies. Like Sean.

By the time she sat down, I was holding on to Chloe's arm to make sure she didn't jump up and start screaming. My sister pretended she didn't care about this hearing, and that Daddy was no threat. But she was scared shitless that he'd actually win and get put back in charge of us. I knew she was, because I was, too.

Judge Gutierrez cleared her throat. "Okay, I've heard everybody out. Now let me be as brief as possible for all our sakes. Mr. Gamble, your motion to reverse emancipation of the minors Chloe Gamble and Travis Gamble is denied."

I felt a rush of relief, and Chloe relaxed beside me.

"Whatever irregularities you think occurred in the granting

of the emancipation, it was a decision made presuming parental approval since neither parent was even in the same state with the minors," the judge went on. "As far as I can see, Mr. Gamble, you did not attempt to protect, support, or even contact your children for months, and only did appear when they were on comfortable financial footing. That does not make you a fit father."

"Oh, *snap*," Chloe whispered, grinning.

"Chloe and Travis are earning more than enough to support themselves, they have a roof over their heads, they have competent representation, both legal and professional—although I do want to see a financial planner in the mix, please, Mr. Lesher."

Martin nodded and made a note on his laptop.

"All in all, this hearing is a waste of the court's time. Chloe and Travis can take care of themselves, and you, Mr. Gamble, can now stop trying this case in the media."

Wow. I'd never heard such a slam from any grown-up. Coop's folks disapproved of my mama and daddy, I could tell 'cause they were always so nice to me. And lots of our teachers over the years had been annoyed with our parents. But nobody ever said an honest word about it before, they just acted all polite while they obviously thought our folks were trash. But this judge, she was hating on Daddy, and I kind of loved her for it.

I couldn't help myself—I looked over at him.

He was smiling.

Daddy stared right at me, and winked.

"What the hell is he so happy about?" Chloe asked, like she

read my mind. "He ought to be scurrying off to hide like the rat he is."

After the judge left, Martin ushered us toward the door. Nika and Coop came up from the back of the room, and Nika hugged us both. "I have a car out back, and I called the LAPD to send a few guys to make sure you get out of here without being hassled."

"That's right, y'all run out the back and enjoy your freedom," my daddy interrupted, walking right up to us. "I'm goin' out the front like a real man."

"You just got reamed by the judge. You ain't no real man," Mama sneered.

"Not like your boyfriend, Early?" Daddy asked, still smiling. "He's a real man, ain't he? With a bona fide respectable job."

"You lost, Daddy, 'cause you're a loser," Chloe said. "Go on and slink back to Texas."

"I will, sweetpea, I'll head right on down to Texas," Daddy agreed. "And I'll file suit there. Ain't no Texas court gonna hold up this Hollywood emancipation bullshit. Y'all are from Texas, and that's where your daddy lives. It's Texas law you got to abide by, not Hollywood."

Daddy slung his arm around Sylvia's shoulders and sauntered off toward the courthouse doors where the paparazzi waited. I took Chloe's hand.

"I told y'all," Mama said. "That man's not goin' away. He ain't never gonna stop coming after you, Clo, long as there's a breath in his body and money in your pocket."

"You sure you can't come over tonight, Travis?" I could practically hear Sasha pouting, even over the phone.

"You should come out with us," I told her. "We're going to The Ivar. Chloe wants to party."

"That's not my scene," Sasha said. She didn't bother to add that it shouldn't be my scene, either, but I knew that's what she meant. "You're flying tomorrow. You need your sleep," she added.

"If I go to your house, I won't get any sleep anyhow," I said.

She laughed, her famous sexy laugh. "Is that so bad?"

"No. But it's my sister's first night back, and our daddy got schooled today. We have a lot to celebrate. And I'm going to be in New York for next two weeks. Chloe and I hardly have any time at all."

"Fine," Sasha sniffed. "I guess I'll see you when I get back to New York."

"You know it. I'll call you before I get on the plane tomorrow," I said. I figured that was the best I would get out of her, anyway. Sasha hated my sister, and the feeling was mutual. If they both came out tonight, something bad was bound to happen. What is it with girls and their feuds?

Legacy shot in New York, which Nika said was because the showrunner was powerful enough to insist on it. I guess he was from New York and he didn't want to have to move to California, but most people just go where the networks tell them to. This show had been on the air for four seasons and was a huge hit, so the guy in charge always got his way.

Fine with me. New York was where Sasha mostly lived, and it was far away from my mama and my daddy. I'd miss Chloe, and Coop wasn't going to come with me for the whole time. But still, New York City!

"Sasha says not to drink too much because I have to fly tomorrow," I told Chloe and Coop in the VIP room a few hours later. "She says it will dehydrate me."

"That's crazy. You can stay up all night drinking, because you have the plane ride to sleep tomorrow," Chloe said. "Or send somebody to get pot. That's not dehydrating." Coop stared at her in shock. I forgot he hadn't seen Chloe in London. He was used to the regular, no-drugs-allowed Chloe. This was the first time he was meeting Chloe 2.0.

"I'm not you, Clo, I need to concentrate when I'm acting," I said. "I fly in, I start on my guest spot the next day. I want to read the script on the plane, and I want to be awake to see New York."

Chloe yawned. "This place is dead. We should just go to Vegas."

"For the night?" Coop's eyes were bugging out of his head.

"We don't have a private plane, sorry," I said. "You'll have to get used to living like a regular human again."

"Dude, if you think *you* live like a regular human, you've lost your mind," Coop teased me.

"I bet I can get somebody to fly us to Vegas," Chloe said. "Or we can take a limo."

"No way, that's a long drive. I won't make it back for my flight tomorrow," I said. "Jeez, Clo, just go dance or something. You're tweaking."

"I wish Jude was back," Chloe said. "If nobody interesting shows up, I'm gonna have to call Jonas Beck."

"I wouldn't do that. He's been out of work ever since you torpedoed *Cover Band*," I said.

Chloe pulled out her phone. "Then I'll definitely call him. Nika says I have to get back into Snap head. Now that Sean's in charge, they want to do a big concert with the band, and he actually called to see if I would pretend to date Jonas again."

"Wait, you were only pretending to date him?" Coop asked. "I thought you and Jonas Beck were the real deal."

Chloe shrugged. "We're friends."

"He's gay, Coop," I said, shattering my buddy's worldview, which did not involve the kids we grew up watching on TV turning out to be gay.

"I might as well do it now that Max and me are through," Chloe said, texting Jonas on her BlackBerry.

"On the house," the hot waitress said, appearing with a bottle of vodka and some glasses—and two dudes carrying trays of tapas, which is what people called snack food here in La-La land. "And my shift is over at midnight, if you want to hang out."

"Thanks, but I'm taken," I told her.

"I'm not," Coop put in.

The girl looked at him, considering it. "Who are you?" she asked.

"Travis's best friend," he said.

"Oh." She frowned. "Maybe some other time."

She wasn't even out of the VIP room before Chloe began laughing. "You'll get more play if you're his assistant."

"Shut up," Coop grumbled. "I'm not on the clock."

"Oh my God, my prayers have been answered," Chloe said, jumping up from the couch. "It's Kimber Reeve."

"I thought she hated Kimber," Coop said to me.

"She does." I shrugged. "But I guess that's more fun than sitting around not smoking pot with her brother who's not a movie star. She got spoiled hanging with Harlan Reed."

"Hey there, Kimmy!" Chloe called. "It's so nice that they let you into the VIP lounge!"

Kimber put on a smile even faker than my sister's. Her friends piled onto another one of the posh sofas, but Kimber came over to talk. "Clo! What are you doing here? Did Matthew kick you off his movie?"

"Nope, that only happens to you," Chloe said.

I laughed, and Kimber glanced over at me and Coop. "Hey, Kimber!" Coop called cheerfully.

Kimber froze, busted. She looked back and forth between Chloe and Coop, trying to suss out the situation.

"Oh, right, you hooked up with my buddy Cooper," Chloe said sweetly. "That was real charitable of you, Coop."

"Chloe . . . ," Coop began.

"You know, it's so funny running into you here, Chloe," Kimber said. "I went to see The Ruffians tonight and I figured you might be there. But Max said he dumped you."

Chloe hesitated for a tiny second, and I knew Kimber had gotten to her. Kimber knew it, too.

"Anyway, Max said maybe he'd meet up with me later for drinks. I'll just text him and tell him where we are," Kimber went on.

Chloe laughed. "You think I care? Max is a buzz kill. Hey, Jojo!"

Jonas Beck walked in looking like crap. Dude isn't even that much older than me, but he was all skinny and pale and he looked like a forty-year-old.

Kimber gave him an up-and-down glance, and I could tell she was thinking the same thing.

"Clo." Jonas kissed my sister hello and reached out to shake my hand.

"Jonas, this is Coop," I told him.

"And this is Kimber," Chloe added. "She used to be an actress."

Jonas nodded at Kimber, but she didn't even take the bait. She just spun around and headed back to her posse.

"What's with him?" Coop murmured. "He didn't look like that on Chloe's show."

"I don't know," I said. Jonas had been a TV star since he was a little kid, and he played Chloe's love interest on *Cover Band*.

He was a good guy, but he used to be kind of a junkie, that's what Sasha had told me. "He's been out of work since Chloe shut down *Cover Band*," I said. "Maybe he's been partying."

Jonas flopped down on the couch with us. "Hey, Trav, I heard you got the brother on *Legacy*. Good for you," he said. "I read for that a couple weeks ago, but they wanted someone less recognizable."

"Damn. Sorry," I said.

"No, it's not you. They just said people remember me as a kid and they won't see me as the mysterious stranger." Jonas shrugged. "My agent doesn't care if I have to play nice guys for the rest of my life."

"No work talk. I want to dance," Chloe cut in. "Jonas, did you bring any pot?"

"No. I have some X," he said. "But I thought you didn't do that shit, Miss Texas?"

"Changed my mind," Chloe said. "Can I have some?"

"Yeah, sure."

"Know what? I'm out of here," I said, standing up. "I got a flight in the morning."

I'd missed Chloe when she was in Europe, and since we only had one day together before I took off for New York, I'd figured we would spend it together. But she didn't care, she was more interested in having fun.

"See you later, Trav," my sister said, heading off to do some X and dance all night.

"You going to go to Sasha's after all?" Coop asked. "'Cause I bet I could get Kimber to take pity on me again."

"Nah, I'm going home," I said. "Guess I'm just not in the mood for famous girls tonight."

STAR CENTRAL BLOG

Everybody knows that CHLOE GAMBLE and her hot twin, TRAVIS, are emancipated minors—because their father won't shut up about it! LONNIE GAMBLE is determined to be a part of his kids' lives again. We caught up with Lonnie at the Lakers game yesterday (in other words, he cornered us while we were trying to talk to Leo DiCaprio).

Lonnie was there with his ever-present lawyer, Sylvia Ray, and his ~~date~~ ~~friend~~ sugar mama, Darlene Glenn, the ex-wife of cosmetics giant Stu Glenn. Lonnie didn't want to discuss his kids this time, though, he wanted to talk marriage.

"Thing is, me and the wife got hitched real young. Too young. We were still kids ourselves and we didn't have a clue how to raise Chloe and Travis," the philosopher told us. "I ain't saying I was an angel, but their mama told them all kinds of terrible things about me that just ain't true. She poisoned them against me. That's why they take her calls and not mine."

In spite of this, and in spite of the TWO WOMEN with him, Lonnie claims to love his wife and wants the family back together.

"Earlene never should've let them get emancipated. They're just kids and they don't know what's best," he says. "We need to get ourselves back to normal, two parents and our kids living under one roof and loving each other. God willing, it'll happen soon."

Last time we checked, EARLENE GAMBLE was dating adult film producer ALEX BOBROV, so don't hold your breath, Lonnie!

Nika Mays's Manuscript Notes: Marketing

Hal Turman always rolled his eyes whenever somebody said the word "merchandising." He didn't consider it a real word, he said it was a term that soulless money-men created. But what would a blockbuster movie be without the toys in a McDonald's Happy Meal? Or tie-in books on Amazon, dolls in Toys R Us, Halloween costumes of the characters—and don't even get me started on the video games. The movie is just the advertisement for the stuff. The merchandise.

Hal hated it. I'm not sure why. He used to talk about some magical time before they did such things, back when a movie stood on its own and it was all about writing and acting and directing. As if people went to the movies to see art. It was revisionist history, if you ask me. The big studios always treated their actors as if they were products to be sold. They used to make up names and histories for people, and tell them how to dress and who to date. At least now we were all honest about what was going on—we wanted people to spend as much money as possible, and that meant paying to see the movie, and then paying for all the posters, games, books, clothes, backpacks, and whatever else we could think of.

Frontier wasn't exactly merchandise-friendly. There couldn't be a tie-in book, because the movie was based on a book to begin with. But the publisher would definitely be reissuing it with a new cover, and Chloe's face might be on that cover. And since it was a period piece, there weren't any robot or alien toy possibilities. There were angry Native Americans, though, and a lot of action scenes involving guns and boats and horses. So there could be some toys, and there could definitely be a video game. The question was, how much of Chloe would be in these things?

My assistant invited Hal to all the meetings involving Chloe—he'd gotten so offended when I left him out that I decided to throw him a bone and let him feel like he was still attached to the money train that was Chloe Gamble. Whenever he said things I disagreed with, I ignored him. But I had to admit that it was kind of fun to see Hal drag his old butt into the merchandising sessions, because I knew how much he despised it.

That was the only fun thing about it, though. "Why am I here again?" Marc whispered about halfway through the most boring meeting in history.

"To guard Chloe's public image," I replied. "We don't want her face ending up in inappropriate places."

Marc snorted. It was bullshit, and we both knew it. Marc was here to protect *me*—from Sean.

It was the first time we'd seen each other since I dumped him, and it was freaking me out. I figured dragging Marc along would give me somebody to focus on whenever I got tempted to stare at Sean's biceps or wonder if he was thinking about what I look like naked. Hal probably would have worked, too, but Marc was much more fun.

"That's all I've got for today," the guy from the bedding company said, putting away his swatches. Chloe's face wasn't going to be on sheets or anything, but it would be on the packaging for the Anissa line of upscale bedroom accessories. (As far as I knew, Anne Lynch's character didn't have a line of frilly floral bedspreads for old ladies, but anyway, that was her agent's headache.)

"Finally." Marc started to get up.

228   Ed Decter

"Do you have a minute?" Sean asked. "I figured we can talk *Cover Band* since we're all here."

I was so surprised that I actually looked him in the eye for the first time all morning. "Okay," I said. Was it an excuse to spend more time with me? Did he want me to send Marc and Hal off somewhere?

"We've decided to use the return of the show as a relaunch of sorts for the entire Snap network," Sean said. "Now that Leslie Scott is gone, we're starting over with a new president, a new slate of shows, and a whole new Chloe Gamble."

He hadn't gotten up from his seat, so he clearly wasn't trying to move the meeting to my office. And he was talking as much to Hal and Marc as to me.

"Your new president only started this week," Hal said. "You can't relaunch anytime soon."

I felt a stab of disappointment. Sean really was here to talk business. So far he hadn't shown any signs of awkwardness or even anger. Did he just not care that we'd broken up? I hated having to sit at a boardroom table with an ex, but it was even worse when the ex didn't seem to give a crap.

Marc slid his laptop toward me, showing me the *TMZ* page up on the screen. It was an item about

Ty Boswell, and how he'd been caught leaving some model's house at seven o'clock this morning. Rumor had it that he and the model were into threesomes with an underage TV starlet, but at least it wasn't Chloe.

"Thanks," I whispered to Marc.

It was good to remember where I stood, why I'd dumped Sean. My night with Ty had meant exactly nothing—nothing to him, that is. Everything to me. Not because I was in love with him or because I'd expected a movie star to suddenly be committed and monogamous. But because if I'd gotten caught leaving Ty's house after sleeping together, my credibility as an agent would've been shot. My career would've been over.

I had to focus on work and forget all about my love life. At least until I was solidly as established at Peter Bryant.

So the fact that it felt strange and lonely to be in a meeting with Sean where he was on the other side, where he wasn't my partner? I would just have to ignore that. And if Sean didn't seem to be upset by our breakup? I would have to ignore that, too. And my incredible guilt over having cheated on him? Well, I actually *wanted* to ignore that.

"First we'll focus on the concert, because we need time to get the script in shape," Sean was saying. "We'll start rehearsals, make all the arrangements, and be ready to shoot the concert as soon as Chloe gets back from Cannes in May."

"What script?" I asked, trying to shake off my thoughts.

"The movie script," Sean said, rolling his eyes. Actually rolling his eyes at me in a meeting! He knew I wasn't listening. But that didn't mean he could be rude, did it?

"A *Cover Band* movie?" I said. "So you decided to take my idea?"

Sean ignored that. "We're going to film the concert and offer it as a Pay-Per-View to gauge interest. We'll tease it on our website and our sister networks, and we'll do ticket giveaways to the target audience." He turned to Marc. "We'll need Chloe to do some TV promotion and we'll send her on the circuit to build awareness of the event. We want to do a large-scale concert, treat her like a rock star."

"She'll be singing as Chloe or as her character?" Hal asked.

"The entire band from the show will perform in character, then Chloe can do a solo encore, as long as she sticks to inoffensive material. Once we've got that in the can, we'll shoot the movie concurrently with the next season of the show. We haven't decided yet whether to release it preseason or postseason, so it'll have to be a stand-alone plot. The timing will depend on the network's broader strategy, which obviously I can't discuss."

"What if you can't sell the Pay-Per-View concert? Then the movie's off?" Hal asked.

"You'll be able to sell it," I said. "Chloe's blog is hugely popular with the tween set, and the 'Where's Lucie?' interstitials the network has been running have worked exactly as well as Chloe said they would."

"They're the only thing keeping the network alive," Marc snarked.

"If our main star hadn't bailed on us six months after launching the network, maybe we'd be in a better place," Sean replied, as if he hadn't been the guy behind the deal to let Chloe bail.

Marc shrugged. "So you want me to start teasing the concert on Chloe's blog."

"Yeah. Who writes that blog?" Sean asked.

"A forty-year-old gay man in New York," Marc replied.

"Make sure Chloe reads it before she does any press," Sean told me. "If the kids ask her anything about it, I want her to sound convincing. Same with her Twitter."

"Thanks for the advice," I said sarcastically. Sean had agreed to putting legal language in the EdisonCorp contract specifically banning Chloe herself from using any of the social networking sites, and he was probably patting himself on the back now that Chloe had started partying like an adult. The last thing we needed was a drunken tweet from some club in Vegas. Instead, Chloe's online presence was as sweet and innocent as that of her *Cover Band* character, Lucie Blayne.

"So you want her to promote the concert, go to Cannes, then shoot the concert, and then start shooting the show again immediately, *and* the movie at the same time," Hal said, his bushy eyebrows drawn together in a frown. "Busy schedule."

"We'll obviously give her whatever time she needs to promote *Frontier,* as well," Sean said.

"That's all grunt work, nothing glamorous except the Cannes festival. She won't like it," Hal said. "And if she doesn't like it, she won't do it."

All three of us stared at him.

"What are you talking about, Hal?" I said. "Of course she'll do it. It's her job. It's what she wanted, to backload the *Cover Band* stuff so that she could do *Frontier* first."

"Plus she starts off with music. She likes that," Marc added.

"What've you got to hold over her head?" Hal asked. "Nothing. You gave that girl everything she wanted."

I sighed. "Hal, that's exactly the point. What Chloe wants is an incredible career, and she's always known how to get that. So she lobbied for the movie, and now she'll have her TV show, too, only bigger than it used to be. Plus a rock concert."

Hal just looked at me for a long moment, and then he shook his head. He pushed back his chair and heaved himself up from the table.

"Good to see you, Sean." He offered Sean a handshake on the way out.

"Where are you going, Hal?" I called after him. "It looked like you wanted to give me a lecture."

"I used to lecture you back when you wanted to learn," Hal grumbled, waving me off. "Now you know everything."

"Well," I said. "He's right about that."

Marc laughed along with me. Sean didn't.

But so what? He was just another studio exec with a bunch of ideas he stole from somebody else, and I was done with him.

H METER BLOG

BUZZING UP: TRAVIS GAMBLE is shooting a juicy guest role on the über popular show *Legacy*, where he's romancing three generations of women! In real life, Travis is on-again with SASHA POWELL, and the pair are burning up Manhattan. *Caliente*, Travis!

BUZZING DOWN: JONAS BECK. Looks like reconciliation is in the air for the Gamble twins, since CHLOE GAMBLE is hanging with her ex, Jonas, *all the time*. Since splitting with The Ruffians' MAX TYRELL a few weeks ago, Chloe's been out and about looking gorgeous as always. But Jonas ain't as lucky in the looks department. People are whispering about an eating disorder or too many drugs for the former child star. Clean yourself up, Jojo!

BUZZING AWAY: HAL TURMAN, ancient agent to the youngest clients, has announced his retirement from monster agency Virtuoso Artists Agency. Nobody remembers when Hal started in the Biz, but he'll be missed when he's gone. Happy trails, Hal!

chapter eight

IM

CHLOE: Trav, you out?

GAMBLEGOAL: On our way home. Gaga concert. Rocked.

GAMBLEGOAL: Now time to sleep.

CHLOE: It's only 1 a.m. in NY! Y'all are lame.

CHLOE: Sasha got yoga in the morning or what?

GAMBLEGOAL: Don't be a bitch. I have an early call time on the show.

GAMBLEGOAL: I'm trying to be professional.

CHLOE: Lucky you. All I have is rehearsal with my stupid band.

GAMBLEGOAL: How's it going?

CHLOE: Who cares? It's a concert for a kiddie show.

CHLOE: Today I shot a teaser for it. So bad.

CHLOE: My character sounds like a 5-year-old.

GAMBLEGOAL: It ain't Frontier. It's a Snap show.

GAMBLEGOAL: At least it's easy, right?

CHLOE: It's BORING.

GAMBLEGOAL: What R U doing tonight?

CHLOE: Me & Jude & Coop seeing a band @ Spaceland, then
meeting Jonas.

CHLOE: Jude back with her old girlfriend from my show.

GAMBLEGOAL: Sexy.

CHLOE: Yawn.

CHLOE: Jonas is so wasted lately. He's no fun anymore.

CHLOE: Coop meeting some chick after Spaceland.

CHLOE: The girls from my band won't even go out. Babies.

GAMBLEGOAL: So it's just you & Jude & the gf? Sorry.

CHLOE: I might ditch them and find Harlan's asst. Jason.

CHLOE: He's back in town. Can't wait till Harley gets back so there's
someone fun.

GAMBLEGOAL: Or you could stay home.

CHLOE: I'll do that when I'm dead.

E-MAIL FROM TRAVIS GAMBLE

Hey, Coop! Sorry I missed your call—we're shooting all the time.
This schedule is intense. Thanks for jumping my mama's car. I guess
when you're passed out drunk in the front seat, your battery gets
drained. Nice asshole boyfriend she got, huh? Buys her a car and
then takes off for the weekend so she's on her own. She say where

he went? Maybe he's off testing some new so-called actresses. Loser.

Listen, text me when you get a chance and tell me if my sister's been home at all this week. I call her and she doesn't answer and then she leaves me messages at four in the morning like she totally forgot I'm in a different time zone. What's going on with her? Sasha says she heard Jonas Beck's parents made him go to rehab—but then who's Chloe out with every night? You?

She leaves for Cannes in a couple days, right? You still keeping on her about her schedule? Dude, we should give you a raise for being the Gamble wrangler. 'Cause that is a thankless job!

Anyway, we wrap my third episode at the end of the week and then I have a few days off. Me and Sasha are heading to Miami; she's borrowing Matt Damon's place right on the beach. You should come meet us. I'll tell my assistant to get you a plane ticket—HA!

I need the vacation, this show is majorly stressing me. Everyone's all nice, but there's something weird. Like, this character is supposed to be so important to the family on the show, but then they don't write me anything good to say. The regulars do all the hard work, the yelling and crying and whatever. I'm always just standing there and trying to look cool, and half the time I don't have my shirt on. I asked one of the writers how come I never say anything much, and he said it's because my character has mysterious origins and they want to keep people wondering. So I guess you can't talk and be mysterious?

I don't know, Coop. I have a lot of scenes and all, it's not like I'm an extra. It's more that they only give me the simple stuff, like I'm just reacting to what the other characters do. It's totally easy. But then all the actors and the directors keep saying I'm doing a great job. You know, I got it when Matthew Greengold said I did good on *Frontier*, because me and Chloe were in the zone on that scene. But here, I'm kinda lame and they're praising me.

Sasha says I worry too much. She hates TV, though, she could care less about doing a good job on a TV show.

I never did an audition for this part, and Jonas did, remember? I'm starting to think they only gave it to me because Matthew asked them to. His company produces this show. Do you think I'm paranoid?

Whatevs, man, I'm not putting up with it. I'm no Chloe, but I can act better than this.

Nika Mays's Manuscript Notes: Conventions

The Cannes Film Festival is the best party of the year. It's like Mardi Gras, the Oscars, and a porn movie all rolled into one. In the U.S., there are certain things that just aren't done, because we have puritan ideas about sex and drugs and parties. But Cannes is on the French Riviera, and the people there are absolutely *not* puritans. About anything.

So the parties are not to be believed.

Then there's the film. Any movie that stands a chance of being a hit shows at Cannes. Any star, writer, or director in those movies comes to Cannes. And so do their famous friends. And so do their fans. And so do the paparazzi. Any movie that hits big at Cannes is guaranteed to get a lot of attention. It doesn't always translate to a huge box office later on, but it definitely means huge early buzz.

And huge early buzz is like catnip to Hollywood. It's every agent's dream—buzz at Cannes for Chloe Gamble would mean I could secure three top-notch movies for her in the next year, before anyone even knew if her Cannes film made money. Of course, in Chloe's case none of that mattered, because EdisonCorp already owned her. She couldn't do a thing in the next two years unless she had their okay. Still, if she got the buzz at Cannes, I could try to convince Sean that *Cover Band* wasn't the best project for her. I could try to move her into one of the other films their new company had in development. I could insist that they renegotiate her contract again.

There was no downside for Chloe. She already had her next gig, and she had money in the bank. *Frontier* would screen for the first time at Cannes, and the buzz would launch her into the stratosphere. I didn't have to hustle to sell her, I just had to sit back and enjoy the ride.

I couldn't wait.

And neither could Chloe. She'd been moaning for weeks now about how much she hated the rehearsals for her *Cover Band* concert. She hated the teasers and other promos she had to film. She was bored playing Lucie Blayne, a sixteen-year-old, mystery-solving rock star. It cracked me up—less than a year ago, Chloe was beyond thrilled to be Lucie. She soaked up every second in front of the camera, whether she was filming a commercial, doing a publicity interview, or singing the theme song from the show. I knew Chloe would start enjoying it again once things got moving—when she was singing for an arena full of people, and when the show was actually on the air again, generating attention.

Chloe had never lived through this kind of in-between period before, where there was a lot of work and no real fame. Some actors loved it, because it meant they could go back to their real lives for a while. They weren't on talk shows, doing publicity tours, or visible at a theater near you. So the gossip-hungry people of America forgot about them, and the paparazzi left them alone.

That was not what Chloe Gamble wanted. She wanted to be front and center in everyone's minds, every second of the day.

She didn't have to worry. She was out every night at a different club, in a different outfit, generating her own publicity. It would be a relief to get her to Cannes, because there she could talk about *Frontier* all the time, and the whole world would be paying attention. Maybe then she could dial down on the partying. It was starting to give Marc headaches. Chloe hanging out with Travis and Coop was fine. Chloe hanging out with Paris Hilton, who was a decade older, was not. And forget about Harlan Reed and his entourage.

"Nika!" my assistant said as I blew by her on my way out the door. The car was waiting downstairs to take me to the airport. I was traveling alone to Cannes, and I planned to spend the entire time plotting a strategy to poach Grace Farrell from CAA. She was a huge star, and she was thirty years old. I needed an older actor on my client list to cement my reputation, or else I'd start being seen as an agent to the youngs. And I did *not* want to become the next Hal Turman. I wanted to be the next Peter Bryant.

"What? I'm late," I said.

"It's Hal's last day, you told me to remind you."

"Damn." I sighed. I'd been avoiding Hal ever

since the announcement. It said "retiring" but we all knew it meant "fired." Of course Daniel Shapiro had bought Hal out, given him a huge retirement package, and probably anything else Hal wanted. But at the end of the day, Daniel had fired him.

After Virtuoso acquired the Hal Turman Agency, they had the client list, and they had me. What did they need Hal for? He operated in old-fashioned ways, and the rest of the Business didn't.

I was hoping there'd be other people in there saying their farewells, but instead it was just Hal, behind his gigantic desk, with all his awards and mementos packed away in cartons. I didn't want to go in and face him. He looked so small in the emptiness, and I had no idea what to do with a small Hal Turman. He'd been larger than life to me for my entire career.

"I'm off to Cannes now, Hal," I said. "I wanted to stop by and say good-bye. I can't believe I'm going to miss your farewell dinner."

Hal just looked at me, and he didn't have to say a word. We both knew I could've taken a later flight. Nobody cared if you showed up on the first day at Cannes. Things didn't really get started until the weekend, anyway.

"Listen, Hal . . ." I perched on the edge of one of the guest chairs. "I'm sorry I couldn't warn you in advance about this whole retirement—"

"It's bullshit," he cut me off. "I should've stayed on my own and then nobody could tell me I was done when I'm not."

"I'm sorry," I said again. "I wasn't in the loop on this decision, probably because they knew I would've told you right away."

Hal waved me off, dismissive.

"You can still open up your own shop if that's what you really want," I said, but it wasn't strictly true. He could never be the Hal Turman Agency again, because Virtuoso owned that name now, and all the clients attached to it. And Hal had a non-compete clause that would prevent him from working as an agent for at least a year. "But, Hal, maybe it's not so bad. The industry has changed, you're always saying that."

Hal looked at me then, really looked at me for the first time in ages. "You're the industry now, Nika?" he said. "Sell your little company to a big one, steal clients by any means necessary, find loopholes in the legal language . . . anything to get ahead."

I felt a rush of blood to my face, as if Hal

was my disapproving father, telling me I'd been a bad girl.

"You taught me everything I know," I said, and it was true.

"Maybe." Hal sighed, and all the animation drained out of him. "Maybe I am too old. It's always been an ugly business, but I think it's more crass than it used to be."

"Then it's time to leave. You're not used to the Internet age," I said. "Things are different now."

He chuckled, shaking his head. "You tell yourself that all the time, sweetheart. Still, the one thing that never changes is good advice. You don't want to listen to me anymore, Nika. But you should. You'll see."

I stood up. "I've got a plane to catch. Good-bye, Hal."

"I was wondering who I'd see on the plane," Kimber Reeve said, dumping her Gucci purse onto the first-class seat next to mine. "Hi, Nika."

"Kimber. Hey." I held out my hand for a shake. We weren't on a kissing-hello basis, and I knew that Chloe would rather have me punch Kimber than shake her hand, but that's not good business.

"I can't wait for Cannes!" she said as she sat down. "I've never been, have you?"

"Nope, I'm a virgin," I admitted.

"Where's Chloe?" Kimber didn't even try to hide the disdain in her voice, which I kind of appreciated. They detested each other, we both knew it, and she wasn't going to try to play otherwise.

"She's coming on Friday. She has to finish up rehearsals with her band," I said. "The day we get back from France, her TV show goes into production. The concert is that weekend, and it's nonstop filming from then on."

"Hmm." Kimber didn't say anything more. I'd been bragging so I could tell Chloe that I did, and Kimber looked annoyed. My work was done.

I pulled out my iPad and called up my file on Grace Farrell.

"Nika, do you know Stan and Luce?" Kimber's voice broke into my thoughts five minutes later.

Glancing up, I saw the writer-director/husband-and-wife team piling their stuff onto the seats across the aisle from us. Kimber must have paid their way, because while they were critical darlings, their little indie films had never made a single dime.

Ed Decter

"Of course I do," I said, getting up to kiss them. "We met at Sundance a couple of years back."

"You've moved up since then," Luce told me, grinning. "I knew you'd get away from Hal eventually."

I nodded, ignoring the sadness that pulled at me when I remembered Hal's face. "You guys, too," I said. "Are you screening at Cannes?"

"World premiere," Stan replied. "Nothing like *Frontier*, but we're proud of it."

"You should come. We're at the Salle Debussy," Luce said. "Sunday."

"I definitely will," I told them. And I would. I'd absolutely loved the film they did the year before, and I was curious to see what Kimber could do. I'd never pegged her as an indie film kind of girl.

"It's a departure for you, huh?" I asked her as we all buckled in.

Kimber shrugged. "It's acting. My father always said if a door shuts in your face, you just have to find another way in."

"Good for you," I said. "It wasn't fair, what happened with your NBC show."

"I'm over it," Kimber told me. "TV sucks anyway. It must be driving Chloe insane, being stuck on that show."

And there it is, I thought, smiling. I was a

little relieved to see the Chloe-hate come out. Because Kimber had seemed almost cool there for a minute.

When I woke up several hours later, somewhere over the Atlantic, Kimber wasn't in her seat. And neither was Stan Moore. His wife was asleep, along with everyone else on the plane, as far as I could tell. I pretended to be sleeping when Kimber showed up again, from the back of the plane—the bathroom in coach, I figured. Stan appeared about two minutes later.

It's funny. If it had been Chloe in the bathroom banging her director, a married man twice her age, I would've been beyond furious. But I'd known Chloe when she was just a kid from Texas, and we were friends. I cared about her on a personal level. With Kimber, well, she was Chloe's age. But she didn't have Chloe's crappy family life or her need to escape from her past. She didn't have that strange combination of self-confidence and vulnerability that Chloe's upbringing gave her.

Besides, Kimber was just an actor to me, not a friend.

And every actor was a potential client. So Kimber's secret was safe with me.

STAR CENTRAL BLOG

We've all been missing Father of the Year LONNIE GAMBLE since he lost his bid to reverse the emancipation of his famous offspring, CHLOE and TRAVIS GAMBLE a couple of months back.

Turns out Lonnie's been busy since then—with not one, but two new court cases!

While CHLOE GAMBLE wings off to Cannes and TRAVIS GAMBLE parties it up in South Beach, their father LONNIE has been busy in the Lone Star State. Our legal snoop tells us that Lonnie has filed suit in Texas to have the emancipation of his minor children reversed. Lonnie's legal flack/gal pal Sylvia May claims that the kids and their mom were residents of Texas, not California, when the judge okayed their freedom. Seems they never changed their legal residence when they up and left Lonnie in the dust.

Apparently Texas isn't where Lonnie wants to take care of all his legal business, though—he chose California to file for divorce from wifey EARLENE GAMBLE. Makes sense—divorce her here, get half of her money.

Here's the BIG news, though: Lonnie wants the emancipation reversed AND he wants full custody of the kids. The reason? He says EARLENE is an unfit parent because of the company she keeps, namely porn producer ALEX BOBROV. As proof, Lonnie's posted pictures on his website from this week's Adult Film Convention, where Earlene has been spending some time. Is she in porn now? No, but she is wearing next to nothing and letting a couple of actual porn stars lick whipped cream off her cleavage. Doesn't exactly scream Good Mom!

Lonnie always says he "ain't quittin' till the kids are back under my roof." Seems like he might have found the way to do it!

FESTIVAL

"Welcome to Cannes," the clerk at the Carlton Hotel said, holding out the key card to my room. "Have fun."

"Done deal," I told her.

The bellhop started toward the elevator, but I didn't follow him. I headed straight for the front entrance, right across the wide, famous street, and on to the beach. Nobody was allowed into the hotel except for celebrities, far as I could tell. You needed to have a special badge from the film festival, so fans and photographers had to stay out. It was for security, but what's the point of being at Cannes if nobody sees you?

The paparazzi were lined up outside the doors just waiting for anyone to come through, and they glommed on to me like honeybees to a big, juicy flower. Half of them didn't speak English, but I didn't mind. "Chloe!" sounds the same in every language, and it was a rush to know these guys would be putting pictures of me in magazines in Japan and India and God knows where else.

International star, I thought happily as I slipped off my sandals at the edge of the sand. I left them there, along with my top and my skirt. Technically I was wearing lingerie and not a bikini, but when the fabric is that small, what's the difference?

I headed straight for the water of the Mediterranean, the photographers following me the entire time.

All my makeup was waterproof—I'd done it myself on the plane just so I'd be ready for this. There was an old story about some actress named Brigitte Bardot who stunned the world by prancing around on the beach at Cannes in a bikini in the 1950s. Lots of photographers still had the pictures hanging in their studios, and it made her famous. Nobody my age knew about it, so why shouldn't I steal the idea? It's amazing what a ten-minute search on Google will give you. If the other actresses wanted to be better than me, they should do their homework.

Times had changed since then, so I figured I'd go a little further and get myself wet. I dove straight into the water and made a show of flipping my hair back when I surfaced. Then I walked back out and sat on the sand.

"Chloe!" Nika appeared next to me, wearing actual clothes instead of a bathing suit. She looked like she wanted to throw a blanket around me. "What are you doing?" she murmured, sitting down next to me. "I thought we were meeting at the hotel."

"Hotel's right there," I said, nodding toward it. "I felt like being outside, making a splash."

"Ha-ha," Nika said. "You're half naked."

"It ain't see-through, don't worry," I said. "And I guarantee that every article about Cannes tomorrow will have my picture on it. Marc will thank me."

Nika sighed. "Not all publicity is good, that's a lie. You should be age-appropriate."

"You kidding? We're back in Europe now, nobody here gives a crap how old I am," I said. "Thank God."

"We have dinner tonight with Anne and Harlan and Matthew," Nika said. "Let's go get dressed."

"Is Amanda here yet?" I asked as we headed back up the beach. I'd thrown Mandy a bone and asked her to come along as my stylist. She still hadn't really forgiven me for losing her the *Cover Band* job. She'd given up a lot of private clients in order to take that gig, and then it had vanished as soon as I went off to film *Frontier*. But Amanda was doing wardrobe for the concert when we got back, and I figured a free trip to France ought to be enough to make her shut up about her troubles. Besides, Jude refused to come to Cannes with me, so I had to bring someone else. She'd said that she wanted to stay home and focus on her own life instead of being "Chloe's friend" in Europe again. Seemed kind of crazy to me. Being Chloe's friend meant living like a rock star, and how bad could that be?

"She's up in your suite putting all your clothes away," Nika said.

"What are we doing after dinner?" I asked. "A party or a club?"

"Neither. We're turning in early so you look perfect for the premiere tomorrow night," she told me.

"Oh, come on, Nika, it's Cannes! We can sleep in two weeks."

"*You* can't, you start work the second you land back in LA," she said.

I made a face. "Even more reason to party now," I said. "Once I'm stuck being cutesy Lucie again, all the fun is over."

"Cutesy Lucie pays the bills," Nika said.

I didn't bother arguing. Nika never listened anymore, like she was stuck in a time warp with me as the new kid in town, all wide-eyed and innocent. I'd never been that way, but we'd all acted like I was, because that's what people want to see in their TV good-girl actresses. Still, I'd gone beyond that now. My part in *Frontier* was serious adult acting, my songs were good enough to have Lars Svedman producing them, and I was officially an adult no matter what my pathetic daddy tried to do. I didn't need to pretend I was a naive kid anymore.

Nika just didn't get it. She didn't get *me*, not these days.

Luckily, she wasn't in charge. I was, and I would stay out as late as I wanted. Harlan would come with me. Or his assistants would. Or his friends. I knew them all, and they'd do whatever I wanted. Hell, total strangers would do whatever I wanted, just for the chance to hang out with me.

I didn't ask Amanda to come out partying. She was too old, and too heavy. But I had to hand it to her, she put together a damn good outfit for me. I'd stopped dressing myself ever since *Frontier* wrapped. I was good at it, but it wasn't worth my time. Designers sent me so much stuff, and it took too long to go through it all myself. If someone else did the work, I had more time for fun. Back in the day, I mocked the spoiled, rich pageant girls who had stylists, but this was different. I had a stylist because I needed one. Ain't no oil princess in Texas who *needs* a stylist.

Dinner was incredible: not just the food or the famous restaurant or the A-list people there . . . but the publicity! People thronged around us on the sidewalk and watched us through the windows and photographed us while we kissed one another hello. Paparazzi were everywhere, and all the other tables at the place were filled with other famous faces. It was like a huge party where only the most recognized people in the world were invited.

And I was one of them.

"Enjoying yourself, ducky?" a familiar voice cut through the mayhem during dessert.

"Callum!" I flung my arms around him, thrilled. I was drunk enough to make my mama proud. "I didn't know you were in Cannes."

"I never miss a party," he said. "Besides, I'm conducting business. I'm in production this time next month and damned if I know where the money's coming from."

"You're doing a movie that soon? You never told me," I said.

"It's not your style, I'm afraid. It's called *Roulette*. A sexy, drug-fueled romp through the seedy underbelly of Monaco's casino life." He twisted his face up like he just sucked a lemon. "At least that's what the business copy says. Me, I think it's a character study."

"Your tagline sounds more interesting than my life," I complained. "I've been bored out of my mind in Los Angeles. I miss you!"

"It's not me you're pining for, ducky, it's the life," Callum said. "Your real world is back in Hollywood, and this is your vacation spot. Of course you'd rather be here. You're all backward and twisted up, you crazy little thing."

I laughed. "I never actually know what you're talking about."

"Tell you what, you come star in my little film and I'll get all the money I want," Callum said. "Word on the street is that you're the hottest thing at Cannes this year. Of course I've been repeating that to anyone who's listening."

"You're the best," I told him.

He winked. "What are friends for?"

"Callum Gardner, come talk to me," Matthew Greengold called across the table.

"The master calls." Callum turned away, but I grabbed his hand.

"Where are we going tonight?" I asked. "I want to hear all about your movie."

"I knew it, you want to sign on and remove all my troubles," he said. "We're going out, Miss Gamble, and we're not going home again until we've hit every single party in Cannes."

IM

CHLOE: Travis! I just met George Clooney!

GAMBLEGOAL: Is he short?

CHLOE: You're taller.

GAMBLEGOAL: Score!

CHLOE: @ a party last night I borrowed Reese's hairbrush!

GAMBLEGOAL: You're so glam.

GAMBLEGOAL: And I am an awesome TV rock god, BTW.

CHLOE: ???

GAMBLEGOAL: On LEGACY.

GAMBLEGOAL: They only write me easy scenes so I knew they didn't trust my skills.

CHLOE: Idiot writers.

GAMBLEGOAL: So today I pulled a Chloe and tore the place up.

CHLOE: Tell me.

GAMBLEGOAL: My character was making a real lame threat—the line was boring.

GAMBLEGOAL: Then on take three I grabbed a vase and threw it at the wall.

CHLOE: You did not!

GAMBLEGOAL: Did. The other actors were horrified, and the director loved it.

GAMBLEGOAL: They had to get more vases for more takes.

GAMBLEGOAL: Showrunner said it was "gutsy."

CHLOE: Ballsy.

GAMBLEGOAL: Bad-ass.

CHLOE: Hard-core.

CHLOE: OMG, Angelina! Gotta go.

GAMBLEGOAL: Kiss her hello for me.

STAR CENTRAL BLOG

CHLOE CANNES DO ANYTHING!

If there were a Miss Cannes Film Festival award, this year's winner would definitely be former beauty queen CHLOE GAMBLE! The starlet, pictured here frolicking in the surf at the famous beach in La Croisette, has been the toast of the town all week.

Gamble's film, *Frontier*, screened on Saturday to a standing-room-only crowd and earned rave reviews for director Matthew Greengold, cinematographer GREG WELLIN, and all the actors—including luminaries HARLAN REED (Best Actor Oscar shoo-in!) and ANNE LYNCH. But the most glowing notices were for Chloe Gamble, this year's hot new ingénue. There seems little doubt that Chloe will win a jury prize for Best Supporting Actress, as even her costar—and competitor—Anne Lynch was overheard saying.

"I feel like I'm in a fairy tale," Gamble told reporters at a press conference yesterday. "I never thought anything could be more incredible than acting alongside my idols, Anne and Harlan. But to see this kind of outpouring for the film, well, it's beyond my wildest dreams."

*   *   *

"Picture it, ducky," Callum said, gazing up at me from the Persian carpet, where he was lying on his back. "It's like Bonnie and Clyde, they're besotted with each other, and they're junkies."

"Romantic," I said.

"So they're high as a kite, and they steal the money on a lark. But it turns out they've accidentally taken it from a terrifying fucking drug lord. Only they can't remember what they did with it."

"And they're on the run, trying to remember their drug trip and not get killed," I said. "It does sound like you, Callum." I took a hit of pot and held it in.

"You take the part, ducky. You be my Bonnie. I'm serious," he said. "It'd be bloody brilliant with a girl as young as you. It'd change the whole vibe."

The entire VIP room of this club was done up like an opium den—gauzy fabric hanging from the ceiling, thick velvet chaises, lots of giant silk pillows on the floor. There were even three-foot-tall hookahs to smoke our pot through.

"Don't you already have a lead actress?" I asked. "You start shooting in two weeks."

"Well, of course I do," he said. "I'll can her."

I burst out laughing, and so did Edward Dowling, who lay next to Callum, staring up at me. Edward was a total drug addict, far as I knew, so I figured this probably wasn't the best place for him to be. But he was also a brilliant actor, so nobody cared about the drug stuff except the insurance companies. He was on his third comeback, and he was going to be the Clyde in Callum's film.

"Who is she?" I asked.

"A British girl, ducky, nobody you know. And you'd act the pants off her." Callum tugged on the little fringe that hung from the ankle strap of my stiletto sandal. "Say you'll do it."

"You are so lucky my agent didn't come tonight," I told him. "She would lecture you till you wanted to kill yourself." As if Nika would be caught dead partying like this. Truth was, she didn't have a fun bone left in her body. She'd spent the whole week schmoozing and networking and going to meetings, while I sat on the beach or by the pool or went shopping, with my horde of fans and photographers following me everywhere. I never wanted the film festival to end.

But it would end, tomorrow night.

And then I'd be back in Los Angeles as if nothing had changed.

IM

CHLOE: I won! Trav, holy shit, I won!

GAMBLEGOAL: Shut up!

GAMBLEGOAL: Congrats, Clo. That's unreal.

CHLOE: I beat Anne Lynch! I'm Best Supporting Actress!

GAMBLEGOAL: I can't believe I'm not there.

CHLOE: Work comes first, TV rock god.

GAMBLEGOAL: Truth.

GAMBLEGOAL: But good news here, too. Texas court threw out
  Daddy's petition.

GAMBLEGOAL: They said we earned $ in CA so we filed for
  emancipation there, no problem.

CHLOE: HA! I win twice today!

CHLOE: 3 times, actually. I saw Kimber @ the awards ceremony. Loser.

CHLOE: She had to kiss my ass. Was awesome.

GAMBLEGOAL: Sasha says congrats.

CHLOE: Tell her to watch her back! Later—gonna go celebrate.

CHLOE: ☺☺☺☺☺☺☺

"Chloe, where are you? What the hell—where are you?" Nika's
voice practically screamed on my voicemail. "I'm at the airport.
Call me. Now."

I hit delete and stared at my cell. Nika was going to kill
me, so why call her back? She'd find out soon enough where I
was. Still, I didn't want her calling the cops to report me missing. I texted her:

TAKING A SIDE TRIP TO DUBAI WITH CALLUM.
CALL YOU TOMORROW.

Then I turned the phone off. Callum and Edward had
borrowed Harlan's jet, and we all knew the pilot wanted cells
off during the flight. It wasn't my fault if Nika couldn't reach
me until we landed in the United Arab Emirates.

It was no side trip. The flight would take all day and even

Harlan hadn't been too thrilled about it until I offered to chip in. Then he just laughed like I was adorable and said it would be a gift to me for winning a prize at Cannes.

I'd have to find out how much it cost to fly a private jet to the Middle East, maybe I'd be able to pay him back one day. Anyway, he was off shooting his next movie in Prague, so he didn't need his plane right away.

"What's this guy's name again?" I asked. "Your friend?"

"Damn if I know, it's at least ten words long," Callum replied. "I call him Ali."

"And he's a sheik? For real?"

"Absolutely, ducky, a crown prince. The great-grand-nephew of one of the biggies in Dubai, or some such thing." Callum shrugged. "He's a movie buff. He studied film at NYU. And he could buy you, me, and even Harley, ten times over. If he loves me enough, he'll pay for my whole film. But he doesn't, so I'm just hoping for a sizable donation."

"He's going to take us skiing. In the desert," Edward said. He had two days' growth of beard and his eyes were bleary, but I couldn't help noticing how full his lips were, and wanting to plunge my hands into his thick, dark hair. Edward was a fuck-up, no doubt, but he was hot as they come.

"In a mall," Callum added, shaking his head. "It's an entire bloody ski slope, inside a mall. Dubai is like a playground on acid. You won't be sorry you came."

"I don't do sorry," I told him. "Anyway, I'm an award-winning actress. If I want one last party before I go back to work, who's gonna tell me no?"

"You were very touching, I thought," Ali said to me that night, while Edward and Callum swam in the Olympic-size pool on the roof of the skyscraper he owned. "The award was well deserved."

"You said you didn't go to Cannes," I said, sipping his five-thousand-dollar-a-bottle wine. "How did you see *Frontier*?"

Ali shrugged. "I asked for a print to be sent to me. I have a full-size theater in my home, of course. Film is my first love."

My head was spinning from the jet lag and the wine, and I had no idea what time it was or even what day it was. All I knew was that this sheik had more money than all the Texas oil barons I'd ever heard of, and he couldn't be more than thirty years old. I laughed.

"What's funny?" he asked, leaning toward me.

"I'm trying to picture you in a college dorm," I said. "Callum said you went to NYU."

"I lived in my own home in New York," he said. "The dorm rooms were a bit too . . . cozy."

He was funny, and he didn't have a trace of an accent, and he was wearing jeans and a T-shirt—jeans that probably cost a thousand bucks and a T-shirt by Dolce & Gabbana—and he was nothing like what I'd ever thought an Arab sheik would be like.

"You're not what I expected," I said. "Are you really worth a billion dollars, or am I being punked?"

"Who can say what another person is worth?" he said. "It changes from day to day, doesn't it? You, for instance, are worth more today than you were yesterday."

I frowned. "You been checking my bank balance?"

"Yesterday you were an aspiring actress. Today you are an acclaimed actress. Your value has increased."

"You think I'm worth more as a person because I'm famous?"

"Don't you?" he asked.

Before I could answer, he suddenly leaned forward, resting his hand on my thigh. "Let me give you an example. I can have any woman I want, any time I want. Paying for sex is not a thing I must do."

"Okay," I said. "Thanks for sharing."

"My point is this: you are a desired woman now, known and wanted the world over. You have a higher value than an unknown person."

"Because more people want me," I said.

"Exactly. Didn't you know? That's what fame is, why we all want it. To be famous is to be wanted, to be valuable." He squeezed my thigh. "A year ago, Chloe Gamble, you were worthless. I would not have wanted you. But now . . ."

"Now?" I couldn't decide whether to be offended by this guy or what. I'd never felt intimidated by money or power before, but he was on a whole different level.

"Now it would be worth quite a lot to spend a night with Chloe Gamble. The woman everyone wants, at the moment of her greatest worth, when she is full of potential . . ."

"Are you saying it would be worth a lot of *money*?" I asked.

"I would give you . . . two million dollars," Ali said.

"For sex," I said.

He nodded, his hand still on my leg. I stared at him for a long, long moment. "It don't matter how rich you are, that's no way to talk to a lady," I said. "My mama would kick your ass." She'd also take him up on the offer in a heartbeat, but I kept that to myself.

Ali laughed, and he sat back and took his hand away. "I am merely making a point. It is not right, but it is the way of the world. Fame equals value. More fame? More value."

I glanced over at Callum and Edward messing around in the pool. How much were they worth?

"Are you going to finance Callum's movie?" I asked.

"That depends. Are you going to star in it?" he replied.

"I can't. I have a two-year contract with EdisonCorp to do my TV show," I said.

"Then why are you here?"

"Callum's a friend," I said. "I'm just tagging along before I go back to work."

"There is no one who believes that, Chloe," Ali said. "Including you. So I ask you again, are you going to star in his movie?"

I pictured Nika, and Sean, and Marc . . . and I knew what they would all say—NO. But I was famous now, I was worth more than any of them, and I was worth more than some little TV show for kids.

"Yeah," I said. "I am."

chapter nine

Nika Mays's Manuscript Notes: Apocalypse

Just so everyone understands the facts: Chloe Gamble taking a role in Callum's film was the absolute worst thing that anyone had ever done in Hollywood during the entire time I'd been in the Business. Britney shaving her head, Lindsay turning carjacker, Joaquin "retiring"—nothing could hold a candle to Chloe bailing on her *Cover Band* contract. The rest of that crap was just bad publicity.

What Chloe did was bad business.

EdisonCorp had already sunk money into planning

her Pay-Per-View concert—they'd paid the stage staff, the choreographers, the lighting and sound crew, the camera crew, the director, and all the support staff. They'd paid for the promotion, the arena, and the insurance on it. They'd paid for the wardrobe. They'd paid for the weeks of rehearsals that Chloe and her costars had already done. And they had deals in place for airing the concert on TV.

On top of the concert, EdisonCorp had put money into developing the *Cover Band* movie—they'd paid writers and hired a director, and they had people working on finding locations and preparing to shoot. They had also started preproduction on the second season of the *Cover Band* TV show. The soundstage was being prepped, the crew was gearing up with lighting, sound, makeup, and wardrobe tests, and an entire writing staff was working day and night to churn out scripts . . . fast. A hundred people worked on that show, and EdisonCorp was paying their salaries.

All of this money was being laid out based on the understanding that Chloe Gamble would return from Cannes and get right to work. Based on the understanding, that is, that Chloe Gamble was a professional who would honor her contract.

Looking back, I can see where maybe I should have noticed the signs that Chloe would do something so monumentally awful. But at the time, I was more shocked than I've ever been. It took me days—weeks, probably—to grasp what she had done.

Sean got it right away.

"I will destroy that girl so completely that there is nothing left!" he hollered at me over speaker phone the morning that I told him Chloe wasn't coming back from Europe. I'd spent two days begging, pleading, threatening, and screaming at her on the phone. She wouldn't budge. She was having fun, she was prepping for her completely inappropriate role in Callum Gardner's movie, and if I didn't like it, too bad.

It wasn't hard to see where her new attitude came from—Callum wouldn't even return my calls. He had always been a bad boy, which was why he hadn't been more successful even though the critics loved him. I had no doubt that he had convinced Chloe to do this, and she seemed to trust him more than she trusted me.

"Calm down, Sean," I said. My own heart was pounding, and Marc, in my guest chair, looked like he might puke. "It's just Chloe acting out the way she always does. I'll handle it."

"How? You going to try to renegotiate our contract with her again?" he snapped. "We're not putting up with another tantrum, Nika. Either she comes back to work or we'll see you in court."

It made me furious to hear him calling EdisonCorp "we." Every other time Chloe went up against this company, Sean had been on my side. He'd been there to help me navigate the legal ins and outs. But now he was on the other side, and he knew every detail, every word of Chloe's contract—because he'd written it himself.

"You can't sue her," I told him. "You're invested in *Frontier*, and Chloe just won an award for that movie. She's got buzz from Cannes, which means your movie has buzz. If you sue her, you'll torpedo the film and risk losing money."

"Plus you'll have to answer to Matthew Greengold," Marc put in. "He doesn't care about *Cover Band*, but he sure as hell cares about *Frontier*."

Sean was silent for a moment, and I knew he was thinking through the argument. The public doesn't care much about lawsuits, so how bad would the backlash against *Frontier* really be? On the other hand, Chloe was a master manipulator, and she could make herself out to look like the sweet kid going up against the megacorporation. Sean had seen that himself, when we used her to convince Dave Quinn to renegotiate.

"Fine," he said finally. "I'll give you two weeks. We'll postpone the concert and halt pre-production on the rest of it. You get her back by then and we're in business. Otherwise she owes us every cent we've spent on this property."

"We can put out a rumor that she's sick and that's why we're postponing the concert," Marc said. "We'll use her tweets to back it up."

"Callum's movie won't start shooting for another week, and they're in Monaco so the Hollywood media aren't paying much attention," I said. "We'll do our best to contain it and I'll get Chloe back if I have to drag her by the hair myself."

"I'm giving you the time to get Chloe under control, Nika," Sean said. "But I'm going after that movie right away, and we'll shut it down immediately if we can. Don't try to play us against Callum Gardner."

He hung up without saying good-bye, and I felt a stab of loneliness. Sean was supposed to be here helping me through this, a friend rather than an adversary.

"What can he do to Callum's movie?" Marc asked.

I sighed. "If he can find evidence that Callum encouraged Chloe to skip out on her *Cover Band* deal, that would show intentional interference with contract. It's against the law. He could threaten to sue Callum's movie for a gazillion dollars."

"Would Callum even care? He lives for that kind of stick-it-to-the-corporation shit," Marc said.

"He wouldn't care, but probably some of his financers would," I said. "People give money to independent filmmakers just to get their names in the credits as producer. They don't want to get into a legal battle with one of the biggest companies on earth."

"So Sean gets the money guys to pull out, and Callum can't pay for production, and the movie stops," Marc said.

"And Chloe comes home." I dropped my head into my hands. "God help us, but that might be the only way we'll get her back."

"What does Daniel Shapiro think of this?" Marc asked.

"He thinks it's my headache," I said. "By which he means that he wants to keep award-winning Chloe and lose contract-breaking Chloe, and he's going to let me do the dirty work to make that happen. If he keeps his hands clean, he's safe from the fallout."

"But you're not safe and neither am I," Marc said. "Chloe could ruin all of our careers with this."

"Hal told me so, that's what kills me," I said. "Hal told me if I let her get her way with *Frontier*, I would never be able to control her again."

And when it came to the Business, Hal Turman was always right.

H METER BLOG

BUZZING UP: KIMBER REEVE, getting rave reviews in the indie film *Forget Me Not*, written and directed by the married team of Moore & Brody. Everybody loves Kimber in this flick, so nobody's talking about her rumored dalliance with the male half of that married team. . . .

BUZZING UP: Golden boy TRAVIS GAMBLE, blazing across America's TV screens as the long lost brother/psychopath on CBS's popular show *Legacy*. He seemed so nice for his first three episodes, and then BAM! Travis brought the crazy. We didn't know he had it in him!

BUZZING DOWN: But speaking of Gambles, we hear that Trav's sister CHLOE GAMBLE isn't faring so well. The Cannes queen has postponed her big *Cover Band* concert and is rumored to have checked in to a clinic in Europe to be treated for exhaustion. Chloe's official fan page on Facebook claims that she's "devastated" about moving the concert back.

BUZZING UP: As if TY BOSWELL wasn't hot enough, his agent NIKA MAYS confirms that he's just signed on to headline next summer's tentpole movie *Neverland*, a 3-D apocalyptic action flick. We always knew he'd save the world.

CRAZY FUN

"Beautiful, ducky! I almost cried. See? There's a tear, a single tear, right here." Callum pointed to his cheek, grinning.

"That's why she's a genius," Edward said, stretching his lanky body across the filthy couch in the filthy room on this tiny soundstage. He didn't have a damn thing to do in this scene except lie there and listen to my monologue about how I longed to return to the idyllic house where I'd grown up—which was something I couldn't even imagine. But the entire time I was talking, Edward inched toward me until he ended up curled around me like some kind of human blanket.

The monologue was easy. I just pretended I was Kimber Reeve, who came from a nice home in Connecticut, and that somehow I ended up living in drug-addled squalor. It made me happy to picture Kimber like that. But the part with Edward freaked me out every time.

"Still, love, as moving and brilliant and goddesslike as that was, you're going to have to let him touch you eventually," Callum said.

"I know," I flung myself onto the couch and covered my eyes with my hands. "But it makes me feel like fire ants are crawling all over me."

Edward's eyes widened and Callum laughed until he coughed.

"You shouldn't flatter Eddie like that, it'll embarrass him," one of the cameramen called.

"Yeah, he can come put his fire-ant hands all over me," the sound guy agreed. He was a giant, burly man who had to be at least six foot five. He licked his lips and gave Edward a pretend sexy look that set Callum off into another fit of giggles.

"How'm I supposed to be serious when y'all are so stoned you can't keep a straight face?" I asked.

"No worries, ducky, we've got what we need for now," Callum said. "That's a wrap for the day, boys and girls."

There was a lot of joking around while the crew packed up, and I lay on the couch next to Edward, just watching. This set was nothing like the set of *Frontier*, which had been run like an office, or at least what I figured an office must be like. My daddy's air-conditioner repair shop didn't count, and besides, he ran that place more like a whorehouse.

But Callum was nothing like Matthew Greengold. The entire crew felt like a family—we all ate together, smoked together, drank together. Far as I could tell, the production assistants got as much respect as me and Edward did. It wasn't

Hollywood, but it was down and dirty and a million times more fun than *Cover Band* had ever been.

"Listen, Chloe, this is a raw role," Callum said, dropping down next to us on the couch. "It's not for the faint of heart. You have to check your intimacy issues at the door."

"I usually go over the hard scenes with my acting coach, but he's a million miles away," I said. I could call Alan, but I figured I'd hear the same disapproving sound in his voice that I heard in Nika's, and Trav's, and I'd had just about enough of it. Besides, even the best coach in the world couldn't teach me how to stop feeling my own skin crawl.

"You did a sex scene in *Frontier*, ducky, what's the problem?" Callum said.

"This ain't sex," I said. "It's just . . ."

"Love," Edward put in. "Honest, naked love between these two."

"How do you do it?" I asked him. "You're so intense all the time. It's like I can't shake you off."

Callum chuckled. "It's the Method. You've not even met the real Edward Dowling yet. He's really very boring and straightlaced."

"You're a Method actor?" I asked. Alan had mentioned something called Method acting back when I used to take classes instead of private coaching, back before I had any money. "What is that?"

"I live the character," Edward murmured. "All the time."

I chewed on my lip, staring at him in all his scruffy, gorgeous glory. He was a drug addict, everyone said so. The last thing he should be doing was playing a drug addict in a movie. But he was convincing, and he was also high all the time. It didn't matter, his acting was still brilliant. Because he wasn't acting—he was simply being his character, 24/7. Strung out and big-time in love with me.

"So I just live like my character?" I said. "I forget about being me and just be her?"

"That's the general idea," Callum said. "At least for a bit, until you get her into your psyche."

"You experience your character's reality, not your own," Edward put in.

"Try it, ducky. Many of the greats were Method actors." Callum got up and left, and I looked at Edward.

He pulled out a bottle of pills and shook one out onto his hand. "Ecstasy?"

"Well, my character likes it, right? So I guess so," I said. "What else we got to do?"

Edward grinned, inching over toward me on the couch. And this time I let him.

IM

CHLOE: Nika, WTF? Callum says we're shut down.
CHLOE: Did Sean do this?

NIKAMAYS: Of course he did.

NIKAMAYS: Clo, come home. EdisonCorp won't stop.

CHLOE: I love this movie. I'm @ whole new level of acting. Method.

NIKAMAYS: Method is no excuse for being an idiot, Clo. Come home.

CHLOE: Screw Sean.

NIKAMAYS: Where are you now?

NIKAMAYS: Clo?

NIKAMAYS: Clo?

"Thailand," Callum said. We were all squeezed into a bar in Monte Carlo, the entire cast and crew of the movie, and everyone was wasted—we'd started drinking the night before, about two minutes after Callum announced that our funding was gone. "We can shoot there."

"You crazy?" Edward said. "With what money?"

"I've got a mate with a house there, he'll let us stay, he owes me a favor." Callum winked at me. "And Ali will wire enough money to keep us going for a week—he loves a good fight with the Americans."

"Is that long enough?" I asked.

"Long enough to get my lawyers fighting back," Callum said. "Long enough to get through all the interiors in Act Three."

"Long enough to get a trunk full of opium," Edward put in.

"Don't be an ass, I'm not getting thrown in a fucking Thai prison," Callum said. "We can trick out the house as a set, take a skeleton crew with us. It'll be fun. You won't believe the beaches there, Chloe."

"Thank you," I said, my head spinning a little. "For keeping me around. I'm not even making money for you—I'm losing it."

"You're family," Edward said, taking my hand. "We stick together."

"Y'all are in this mess because of me—if you kept your first actress you'd still have your funding."

"True, ducky," Callum said, "but it wouldn't be nearly as exciting."

STAR CENTRAL BLOG

Blind Item: What up-and-comer is pulling the wool over fans' eyes with a tale of poor-me sickness and exhaustion while actually partying her ass off? This girlie has been on the A list for about a minute and she's already falling into a life of dissipation. Rumor has it she's left a cushy TV gig for a hardscrabble movie. She's playing roulette with her career—she wants the cred, but if she's not careful, she could lose this gamble.

My cell phone woke me up in the middle of the night, or at least I thought it was night. But the sun shone on the beach outside, and I saw Clem the sound guy wandering around naked in the surf.

The phone was somewhere near my head, so I turned to

look for it. There was a girl in bed next to me and Edward. She looked kind of familiar, though I didn't remember where we'd met her. I finally found the cell under one of the pillows. It was Anne Lynch.

"Hello?" I said, yawning.

"Little Chloe." Her voice sounded a million miles away. "I haven't seen you since we left Cannes, and your people keep telling me you're unavailable, as if I can't call you myself."

"Sorry, I'm shooting in Thailand," I told her.

"Well, Nika didn't say that. I had to wait an entire day for her to even call me back, very rude. It reflects badly on you, you know. My agent would never do that."

No, her agent—Joe something—would treat me better. I should call him, he'd basically told me to, back in London. He was an experienced guy, he wouldn't have let my film get shut down. Nika couldn't handle Sean, probably because she was too used to seeing him naked.

"When do you get back, little Chloe? It's only a month until the premiere of *Frontier*. You and I are booked on the *Today* show next week."

"Um, I'm not sure of my travel schedule yet," I said. Did she really think I couldn't see through her? She was calling to nag me, just like everyone else who called these days.

"Get your people on it, darling, the publicity tour is a must," Anne said. "I'll see you in New York? My daughter is dying to meet you."

"Me too," I lied. "See you there."

I hit end and tossed the phone on the floor. As if I would haul ass to New York just to sit on a couch and spout marketing copy at Matt Lauer. *Frontier* was a surefire hit no matter what. No way was I going back now.

I was having too much fun.

"Mama, just what the hell do you think you're doin'?" I asked. Me and Coop showed up at her Oakwood apartment to see her lugging an armful of dresses out the door. One of the photographers who followed us around had told Coop that my mama was up to something, but I hadn't expected this.

"Hey there, sugar," Mama said. "Y'all can help me load the car. Cooper, you take these things." She sent him off toward the parking lot with a pile of crap in his arms.

"Where's Alex?" I asked.

"He's got a shoot today, the man is a hard worker," my mama said, heading back into the apartment. The place was a wreck, with shoes and jewelry scattered all over, and poor Amanda trying her best to shove everything into suitcases.

"Hey, Mandy," I said.

"Travis, you have got to tell your mother that we're not ready to load the car yet." Amanda gestured around the room. "I have a day's worth of packing here."

"First somebody has to tell me where she's going," I said.

"I'm movin' in with Alex, darlin'," my mama said, pouring

herself some wine. "It don't make no sense for me to pay rent on this dump when he's got that big ol' house."

"Chloe told you she'd cut you off if you moved in with him," I said.

My mama waved her hand in the air. "She can just keep her opinion to herself. Ain't no money coming from her lately anyhow."

"What do you mean?" I asked.

"Snap stopped payment on her last check," Amanda told me. "Until Chloe shows up for work, she's in breach of contract. Again."

I sighed. "Sorry, Amanda. You're not being paid, either?"

"We're all on indefinite leave." Amanda pulled out a cigarette and lit up right there in the middle of the mess. "This is twice now. Even if your sister shows up, a lot of the crew won't come back. She's unreliable, and it messes with our livelihood."

There wasn't much to say to that, so I didn't try.

"Mama, if you don't want to stay at the Oakwood, you can come live with me and Coop, least until Chloe gets back," I said.

"It ain't about the Oakwood. I am a woman in love," my mama declared. "I been staying here 'cause Clo told me to, but I'm done listening to her."

"You're in love? With that cockroach?" I shook my head.

"Darlin', I got to look out for myself. You and Clo went and got yourselves declared adults. Well, you ain't my problem no more. I'm takin' care of me now," Mama said. "I'm makin' my own choices."

"You been takin' care of you since the day you were born," I told her. "Daddy's dragging you through the mud every chance he gets. You really want to move in with a porn producer in the middle of your divorce?"

"Alex says he won't let Lonnie hurt me no more," my mama replied. "He says we got to be Zen and ignore your loser of a daddy."

I glanced at Amanda. She rolled her eyes. "I told her that's not what Zen means."

"Trav, you've got Nika in half an hour," Coop said, appearing in the door. "We gotta roll."

The place was a mess, my mama was a mess, and everyone attached to Chloe's show was a mess. I couldn't do a damn thing about any of it. Chloe was the one who cleaned up messes, not me. And she hadn't even answered my last three calls.

"You know what? Good luck with the move, Mama. I'm done with this." I picked my way through what used to be my living room—and my bedroom—and I walked out of the Oakwood apartment for the last time.

When we got to Beverly Hills, Nika smiled and kissed me hello at her office door, but she didn't look happy. "Have you talked to Chloe?"

"Not for a week," I said. "You?"

"She calls and yells at me sometimes, but she won't listen." Nika perched on the edge of her desk. "It's really bad, Trav, and I can't get through to her. We've got six days left before Sean pulls the plug on the *Cover Band* concert. She's got *Frontier* promo duties starting up. And she's AWOL."

"*TMZ* says she's in Thailand," Coop put in, clicking around on the iPhone I'd bought him as a joke on Secretary's Day. "But Perez Hilton claims they moved production on *Roulette* to Amsterdam. Nobody's even pretending to believe that she's sick anymore."

"Marc's doing everything he can," Nika said. "We need your help, Trav."

"I don't know what you want me to do," I said. "I told her she was acting dumb and she said Sasha is poisoning me against her. Sasha won't even discuss Chloe anymore."

"Okay." Nika took a deep breath. "That's not why you're here, right? Let's talk about you. I've got the most amazing news of your life."

"Bring it on," I said. Anything to get my mind off my sister and her disastrous disappearing act. Chloe and I had been together since before we were born, but I didn't even know where in the world she was. It was like reality had turned to quicksand, where the one person I counted on had turned into the biggest flake in history.

"*Thicker Than Water* made you an offer. It's a three-year contract." Nika stopped and waited for me to react, like maybe I should scream and clap or something.

"*Thicker Than Water*, the soap opera?" Coop said.

"Longest running show on the air today," Nika replied. "They loved your guest stint on *Legacy*—who didn't?—and they want to write a similar character for you. It's incredible."

"A soap opera?" I asked. My brain must've turned to mush, because I couldn't understand what she was talking about. What was so amazing about this? Chloe would've known right away, but I didn't get it.

"Travis, it's a three-year-long gig. At least. You'll make six figures every year for doing a nine-to-five job," Nika said. "It's like the holy grail of an acting career."

"Chloe never even said a thing about soap operas," I said.

"Chloe doesn't care about stability. Obviously," Nika said bitterly. "She wanted to be a movie star. But you didn't."

"No," I said. "I was just riding the wave. I'm no big-time artist like Clo. I didn't even think the showrunners liked my acting on *Legacy*."

"They loved that you took a risk with that role," Nika said. "It's one of the directors from that show who recommended you for *Thicker Than Water*."

"Hang on." Coop was laughing. "You want Travis to be a soap star? For reals?"

"Yes." Nika frowned at him. "It's a steady job. Guaranteed money. Do you kids even know how rare that is?"

"Did you just call us kids?" I said, shocked.

"I did, didn't I?" Nika looked shocked too. "I really am turning into Hal Turman."

"Nah, you're way hotter," I said. "So you think I should take this role."

"Trav, have you ever heard of David McNabe? He's a soap star."

"Yeah, he's in the magazines Chloe reads," I said.

"Right. He's a client here at Virtuoso, and he makes us more money than half the primetime TV list combined," Nika said. "He's got a house in Beverly Hills and a ranch in Santa Barbara. He owns a chain of restaurants in ten cities. He's set for life."

"But he's in a soap opera," Coop said, still smirking.

"Oh, grow up," Nika snapped. "He's rich and famous and he doesn't have to spend every minute worrying about his career and whether or not he'll get that next role or else end up as a has-been doing a reality show."

I stared at her. Nika was stressed, more than I'd ever seen her. But she wasn't thinking about my twin right now, she was really focused on me. "You'd be an idiot not to take this job, Trav. It's the best offer you'll ever get. You can be secure and happy with a lot of money, or you can be constantly searching for the next thing, like Chloe. You want to be an actor? Those are your choices."

"We got trouble," Coop cut in. He was staring at his iPhone, and he wasn't smiling anymore. "It's your daddy, Trav, he just put some more pictures up on his blog."

"Tell me my mama's not actually naked in them this time," I said.

"It's not your mama, it's Chloe. She's at Glastonbury, and she's got track marks on her arm. Your daddy has it blown up so you can see them."

"Are you serious?" Nika said. "She's at a music festival? In front of everyone?"

Her phone was already ringing out at her assistant's desk.

"This is what your daddy's blog says," Coop went on. "'Just got these pics of my baby girl looking like a drugged-out hippie at some European concert when she ought to be working on her show. Chloe's spending time with men twice her age and where's her mama? Oh, right, moving in with her porn-star boyfriend.'"

"Alex isn't a porn *star*," I said.

"'I don't want to hurt my Chloe with these photos, I just want the world to see what I've been saying—that she needs an adult looking out for her interests.'" Coop lowered his iPhone and shook his head.

"Oh my God, he's right," Nika whispered. "Lonnie's right."

"Nika, Marc is on line one," her assistant buzzed in to say. "And Sean Piper is on two. And Daniel Shapiro is on his way in from The Ivy; he wants to meet as soon as he gets here."

Nika's face was ashen: that's the word they'd use in a book. Just sort of pale and sick-looking, like she might puke. Coop's eyes were wide and alarmed, and I knew I should be panicking like they were. But all I felt was numb.

"Put Sean through," Nika said.

I reached over and hit the speaker button on her phone. It was my twin sister, my family, my business. Nika didn't stop me.

"Nika. Chloe's partying in public when her fans think she's too sick to perform at her *Cover Band* concert." Sean's voice was cold, as if he'd never been our friend. "She's making a mockery of her contract. We're filing suit against her first thing tomorrow morning."

"You said I had two weeks," Nika replied weakly.

"This is just a courtesy call so you have time to protect yourself," Sean said. "That's the best I can do."

He hung up, and Nika sat there stunned.

"What happens now?" I asked.

"Now Chloe gets destroyed," Nika said.

chapter ten

Nika Mays's Manuscript Notes: Protection

The reason an actor has an agent is for protection. The agent's job is to protect the client—from the producers, from the lawsuits, from the press, from the truth. But when a client is behaving badly, the main thing they need protection from is themselves.

"At least we know where she is now," I told Marc, hurling my clothes in a bag. I couldn't think straight. For all I knew, I'd packed twenty pairs of panties and one shoe. "This time tomorrow there'll be a freeze on her accounts because of the lawsuit. She'll be trapped in England, and we can talk sense into her."

"Where is Lonnie getting these pictures?" Marc asked, staring at his laptop. "The ones of Early at that porn convention, these ones of Chloe. They're not paparazzi shots."

I hesitated. "You think he's got someone following them?"

"I think he's got a private investigator," Marc said. "That lawyer of his is used to dealing with nasty divorces, right? You can't do a divorce in Hollywood without a scummy PI taking pictures. She probably hired one to dig up dirt on all of them—Early, Chloe, Trav . . ."

"I want one," I said. "That famous one, the PI that corporations use to spy on each other, what's his name?"

"Jimmy Pannolizza," Marc said.

"Hire him, tell him to follow Lonnie. I have had enough of that man, he's really fucked things up this time," I snapped. "It's time to fight back."

"Finally," Marc muttered. "Done."

Lonnie had managed to find Chloe before I did, and I was especially angry about that. Why didn't I think of a PI? How could that ignorant rodeo loser be smarter than me? Sean and Travis and Coop, they'd always said I didn't take Lonnie seriously enough, and I guess they were right.

"What about Greengold's people? We've already rescheduled two interviews for *Frontier* and they're getting pissed. They know Chloe's not sick and she's not having time conflicts. If she doesn't start doing promotion soon, they'll jump on the breach-of-contract bandwagon," Marc said. "The movie premieres in three weeks."

"You've got to hold them off. Tell them she *is* sick," I said. "I'll know more when I see her."

Marc walked me to the door of my house. "Do you think it'll work?"

"If I get her back home, we can bring her in to apologize in person. She might not get *Cover Band* back, but at least we can escape the lawsuit," I said. "We've still got *Frontier*. She's got Oscar buzz for that movie: EdisonCorp can't ignore that."

The car service was waiting outside to take me to the airport.

"Good luck," Marc said. "You'll need it."

"You've got three hours before your flight," Coop told me. "I sent a limo to get your mama, then it's coming here for you. Nika's meeting you at the airport, and so is Jude."

I nodded. "Thanks. You sure you can't come?"

"It's not my place," Coop said. "Chloe never wanted to hear anything serious from me. I'm just comic relief."

I slapped him on the back and went over to look out the front window of our house in the hills. I'd moved in here with Chloe but we hadn't spent more than a week here at the same time ever since.

"One more thing, Trav." Coop's voice sounded so serious that I turned right back to look at him. He was staring at the rug. "I'm not gonna be here when y'all get back."

"What?" I said. "Why?"

"I'm goin' back to Texas," he said. "I figure I'll spend a semester at Spurlock Community, then I can transfer to A&M in January."

I felt like the wind had been knocked out of me, like when I took a hit in the gut during a soccer game. "College?" I said, baffled.

"Yeah." Finally Coop looked up at me. "This ain't real life, Trav. All this . . ." He gestured around the house. "I'm havin' a great time, and if you want to go be a soap star and be rich and stay in this world forever, good for you. I'll come visit and get myself laid 'cause you're famous, you can count on that."

"Soap stars need assistants too," I said.

"And I'm a damn good one. But I don't want to be that for the rest of my life," Coop said. "It's too much for me, Trav. Look at Chloe. She's not even the same person anymore. The way y'all live, it's insane."

A horn honked outside. My car was here, my mama was probably already mixing herself a drink in the back.

Coop came over and hugged me. "You tell Chloe to behave," he said.

"I will," I said. "See you, Coop."

INTERVENTION

"Where next?" I asked Callum in the car back from the Glastonbury Festival. We'd camped out there for three days, but I could hardly remember what had happened. It all blurred together into a nice mix of music and sex and X, and a lot of mud.

"London, ducky," he said. "I've got a friend who'll let me use his editing bay for a bit. I'll see how much we've really got, should we ever emerge from the black shadow of our corporate enemy."

I let that roll around in my mind for a while before I decided I had no idea what he was talking about.

"But where are we going to shoot the rest?" I asked. "All the casino stuff has to really be in a casino, doesn't it?"

Callum frowned. "I'm out of ideas, I'm afraid. *Roulette* is going to have to wait."

Edward sat up suddenly, twisting around from the front passenger seat, where he'd been slumped while Clem drove. "Crap, Callum, you saying I have to go back to fucking LA?"

he said, sounding way more annoyed and way less strung out than I'd ever heard him sound.

"Sorry, kiddies, the money is gone. The financiers are running scared. The lawyers are circling," Callum said. "We knew we were operating on borrowed time. And borrowed money, for that matter, but I never mind about that."

His voice was as cheerful as ever, and he didn't seem to be bothered by what he was saying, but I couldn't shake my confusion. "So where are we going now?"

"Home, I suppose," Callum said. "And if you can work out your legal issues quickly, ducky, we might be able to finish our little film sometime this decade."

"Nice." Edward shook his head. "You could've given us a little warning."

"Now come on, don't be like that. I paid for us all to have a lovely time at the music festival, on my own dime. A little vacation before we go our separate ways for a bit." Callum slung his arm around my shoulders and kissed me on the head. "Don't worry, we'll find each other again someday soon."

When I woke up at The Four Seasons where I'd stayed when I was shooting *Frontier*, my hair was still caked with mud from the festival. And my brother was sprawled on the couch.

"Trav? What are you doing here?" I asked.

"I got here last night," he said. "But I guess you don't remember that."

"No," I said. "I let you in?"

"You and your pal Edward, and you were both shitfaced on champagne," Travis said. "Or worse."

I frowned and looked around the room. "Where is he?"

"He left," Travis said.

"But what are you doing here?" I asked again. "Did you tell me you were coming?"

"No, Chloe, and it wouldn't have made any difference if I did 'cause you don't listen to messages and you don't return calls." Travis got up and went over to make coffee, banging things around angrily. "You know what you looked like last night? You know how I felt? I felt like I was pouring Mama into bed after one of her benders."

"That's enough," I snapped. "You barge into my room and start yelling at me? You're out of line. You can't sleep on my couch *and* lecture me, Trav, you got to pick one."

"I slept on your couch to make sure you didn't OD on whatever the hell you were taking," he said. "I make my own money, Clo, I don't need yours. So don't go pulling that crap on me."

He shoved a cup of coffee into my hands and went to pick up the room phone.

"Who are you calling?" I asked.

"Everyone else." Trav mumbled something into the phone, then hung up and turned to me. "Go take a shower. You smell."

I went into the big marble bathroom, feeling numb. Used

to be I'd tell my mama to go get cleaned up. Nobody ever had to tell me.

When I got out, Trav had company. Nika was there waiting for me, and Jude. And my mama.

I burst out laughing. "Well, look who it is—everyone who's been living off me for the past year. Y'all here to drag me back home and make me be a good girl?"

"We're here to help you, sugar," Mama said. "You been messing things up real good."

"For you, you mean?" I asked.

"For yourself, Chloe." Nika didn't even get up from the couch. "Do you have any idea of the shitstorm you've created? EdisonCorp is suing you for all the money they've spent on *Cover Band*. You won't be able to repay it in a hundred lifetimes."

"So fix it," I said. "That's what I pay you for, ain't it?"

"You can't pay me if you have no income," Nika said. "Chloe, you have to stop this behavior now. We can still say you were sick, you can go to a hospital and dry out—"

"I'm not going anywhere." I cut her off. "I'm done with that stupid show."

"It made you a star, Chloe. It's the reason you got the part in *Frontier*," Jude put in. "You promised to go back."

"I don't care," I said. "I went back, and it was boring. I want to stretch my acting muscles, like on *Roulette*."

"Is that what you call it?" My mama smirked. "From what I hear, all you been doin' is partying."

"Don't you dare say a thing to me," I said. "All you've ever done is party. What are you even doing here?"

"Look, Chloe, nobody is trying to upset you. But people are mad, and it's because of you. I asked Amanda to come here with me and she wouldn't," Jude said. "She's lost her job twice now just because you wanted to do something else."

"And Marc couldn't come because he's too busy trying to manage your image," Nika added. "If this behavior goes on much longer, it will impact *Frontier*." She shook her head. "You were brilliant in that movie, Chloe. Why would you ruin it?"

"I've heard this all before. It's the only thing you know how to say these days," I said. "What do you want?"

"I want my sister back," Travis said.

"I want you to come home and salvage your career," Nika said.

"Well, I want a little gratitude," I said, grabbing my bag. I needed to get out of there and find Edward or Callum or anyone from *Roulette*. And besides, I had a pill bottle in my purse. "Y'all are a bunch of parasites, and you have some nerve coming here. You'd be nothing without me."

I didn't look back as I headed out the door. They could kiss my Texas ass. I didn't need a single one of them.

chapter eleven

CELEBRITY FREEFALL—
WHERE THE STARS FALL TO EARTH

It's official! We've been hearing rumors about CHLOE GAMBLE for months now—that the hot blond starlet was partying too far out of her weight class. But Clo-Clo kept it all in Europe, and we all know that what happens in Europe . . . oh, let's face it, it just doesn't count. On American soil, Chloe's public image remained spotless. Her Snap show, *Cover Band*, geared up for her return with a concert, a movie, and new episodes. Her Facebook and Twitter talked nonstop about how excited she was to get back to the role that made her famous. Her big-screen debut, *Frontier* (because nobody remembers her blink-and-you'll-miss-it role in the horror flick *Ritual*), was a triumph at Cannes. Chloe herself won an award and was rumored to be an honest-to-God good actress.

BUT . . .

Turns out she hates *Cover Band* and they hate her! Her Twitter was fake! And she wasn't just partying in Europe—she was on a full-blown multinational bender!

That's right, she's spiraling the drain. And we all know what that means: WELCOME TO CELEBRITY FREEFALL, CHLOE GAMBLE!

Here's the list of disasters so far. We'll keep it updated as the freefall continues:

▶▶ When the press in London asks for a comment on *Cover Band*, Chloe tells reporters that she's "never going back to that show," and claims she's way too huge for TV now.

▶▶ In New York, Chloe has lunch with biggie agent JOE HANDELMAN, prompting talk that she's shopping for new representation.

▶▶ Chloe appears to be stoned while on the *Today* show promoting *Frontier* with an appalled ANNE LYNCH.

▶▶ Chloe and SASHA POWELL throw down at Calico Jack's in Manhattan. Sources say Chloe's brother and Sasha's boyfriend, TRAVIS GAMBLE, is the cause.

▶▶ Chloe waits until EdisonCorp, owner of the Snap network, wins an injunction against her for breach of contract . . . and THEN she returns to Los Angeles. Excellent timing!

▶▶ Virtuoso's NIKA MAYS drops Chloe as a client, which everyone knows is a way to distance the agency from Chloe's legal woes. But Mays manages to mention that Chloe's own family recently held an intervention for her—and it didn't work. Way to torpedo her chances at landing a new agent!

▸ With only weeks to go before the Hollywood premiere of *Frontier*, Chloe's publicist cancels almost all of her promotional appearances.

▸ Chloe's credit card is denied when she tries to buy mouthwash at a Target. Brilliantly, the resulting tantrum is caught on tape by the paparazzi.

▸ Chloe's father, LONNIE GAMBLE, takes to his blog to rant about how much he wants to save Chloe from herself, and completes the post with several photos of his "little girl" snorting coke in a bathroom with a paparazzo. Nice parenting job.

▸ Chloe shows up at ex-boyfriend MAX TYRELL's show, argues with an audience member, and then forgets her car in the club's parking lot. No one knows how Chloe gets home, but the car is there until her brother TRAVIS GAMBLE picks it up two days later.

▸ Rumor has it that Chloe can't even get meetings on new films. MATTHEW GREENGOLD continues to praise her work in the upcoming *Frontier*, but insiders say he's furious because her behavior has soured his relationship with EdisonCorp, one of the film's major funders.

▸ Chloe and old flame JONAS BECK attend the MTV Movie Awards together, and are tossed out halfway through for picking a fight with KIMBER REEVE. Onlookers say Kimber started the fight, but Chloe was "scary and strung out"—which wins every time.

▸ LONNIE GAMBLE, citing Chloe's increasingly erratic behavior, files for legal conservatorship over Chloe, seeking complete control over her decisions, personal, professional, and financial. Given Chloe's bizarre behavior, odds are he'll get it.

E-MAIL FROM TRAVIS GAMBLE

Coop, you home okay? Sorry I've been out of touch. I guess you know why. Anyway, it's all bad here. Chloe's gone again. My daddy filed for conservatorship, and if he wins, it'd be like Chloe was a minor. I don't know what she'd do if he got put in charge of her, man. I'm kinda scared. He's sadistic.

So she took off, she's been gone for two days. Nika totally bailed on us, she cut some deal with the guy who runs EdisonCorp, I think. She was afraid her big agency would fire her for bringing Chloe on as a client when now she's turned into such a disaster. But that don't make sense to me, because the whole reason they hired Nika in the first place was 'cause they wanted Chloe as a client. It's like they just don't remember that, even though it was less than a year ago.

I can't find my sister and she didn't take her phone with her. Jesus, Coop, it's like living with my mama at her worst. Half the time Chloe's not even conscious, and the other half she's not home. Jonas hangs out here a lot, and I think he's doing heroin. And then him and Clo go out with all these people I don't even know. I'm not sure Chloe even knows them, really. She just hangs with anyone who says what she wants to hear.

Sasha took off back to New York. She says this kind of scene makes her nervous. Like, nervous for her reputation. Which, okay, but she's supposed to be my girlfriend and she's leaving me to deal with it all alone. So I think we're through.

My mama is hiding at her porn dude's house and she is PISSED at my daddy about the conservatorship thing. Pissed she didn't think of it first, probably. Usually, I'd think no judge in the world would consider either one of them a fit parent, but Chloe is so out of control that it could happen.

Anyway, Marc told me he's got a PI tailing my daddy, and he'll ask the PI to switch to Chloe for a while. To try to find her, I mean. So that's good. But dude, there's a PI following my daddy. WTF? And get this—Marc says it's because my daddy had one tailing Chloe and my mama, and maybe even me. All those pictures Daddy puts on his blog are from this sleazebag hiding in the bushes or whatever PIs do. He's just lurking and trying to catch us all doing bad things. Freak.

Marc said it was Nika's idea to hire our PI, and she still pays him because she's still my agent. But I told her to turn down that soap opera offer. After I got back from London, I couldn't shake it—my sister is like a stranger. She's not even Chloe anymore, Coop. And it's because of all the attention. The fame. She wanted it, but it ruined her life. Why would I want to stay in a business like that? I'm no actor. You're right, it's all just bullshit. I don't know about college. I never even finished high school. But I know I'm not staying here.

Nika hasn't called me even once after that. You'd think she would still want to check in, right? Make sure we're not dead? But no. Jude can't deal with Chloe anymore, and neither can Amanda. But they're trying to help find her, at least, calling everyone to see if they know where she is.

You still have your contacts from when you were here? Can you call a few people? I need help.

H METER BLOG

BUZZING DOWN: LUCE BRODY has filed for a quickie divorce from STAN MOORE, citing infidelity. Sources tell us that KIMBER REEVE is named as Moore's partner in adulterous crime.

BUZZING UP: KIMBER REEVE, who may be a homewrecker, but she's also set to star in boyfriend STAN MOORE's next film, a(nother) remake of *Sabrina*.

BUZZING DOWN: CHLOE GAMBLE, out of sight for days, finally turned up at a police station in Las Vegas after crashing her BMW into the wall of a parking garage. Sources say the car was a rental and no one was hurt, but you can bet ANNE LYNCH won't want to sit next to Chloe at the *Frontier* premiere on Wednesday.

SEA CHANGE

"How'd you get me out of that?" I asked Travis as he drove the Escalade through the desert toward Los Angeles. "That cop kept screeching at me about how I was a menace." I laughed. "I'm a menace to parking lots, watch out!"

"It ain't funny, Clo," he said.

Buzz kill. My brother was no fun anymore. He never wanted to go out, never wanted to spend time with my friends, never wanted to do a single thing except lecture me and look disappointed. I could have a better time hanging out with my mama.

"I called Sean. He told me what to say to the police," Travis said. He kept his eyes on the road, which meant he was scared to look at me.

"You asked for help from the guy who's ruining my life?" I asked. "Sean is trying to take all my money!"

"He's the only one I know who can handle this stuff," Trav burst out. "I was freakin' terrified that you were dead somewhere, Chloe. You didn't take your phone, you didn't say where you were goin', you just ditched me. So, yeah, I called Sean. He's not ruining your life, *you* are."

"I can't believe you're on his side," I said.

"Shut up, okay?" Trav snapped. "I'm on *your* side. I just needed a hand."

I shut up. I would shut up all the way back home and he'd see how much he liked it. It had always been me and Trav together, but he had changed. I closed my eyes and tried to ignore the sick feeling working its way up from my stomach. I must have left my bag back at the police station in Vegas, 'cause it sure wasn't here in the car. Or maybe it was in the hotel room? I tried to remember, but I honestly didn't know what hotel I'd been staying at. I couldn't remember much of my trip—only reason I knew it was Vegas was that the cops told me so.

"There's something else," Travis said after a while. "I asked Sean for help with colleges. I have to take the SAT still, but I got all my soccer experience, and now I have the TV and movie stuff to set me apart."

"What?" I said.

"Sean knows a guy at Notre Dame, and they're a great soccer school. He pulled some strings for me," Trav went on.

"What the hell are you talking about?" I said. "You're going to college?"

"In two months. It's in Indiana."

"But what about work?" I cried. "Ain't no acting jobs in Indiana."

"I'm done with that garbage," Travis snapped. "Look, I made a lot of money and that's real nice and I'm grateful. But now I'm gonna use it to pay for school. It's what you always wanted me to do, not that I expect you to remember that."

"What about the house? What about me?" I asked.

"Know what? I can't even look at you these days," Travis said. "We been living separate lives for months anyway."

When we got home, Trav put the car in park and waited for me to get out. "You're not coming in?" I asked.

"No. I need some space. I'm gonna go tell Mama that you're back, and you got to get ready for the premiere." Trav looked over at me. "It's tonight, Chloe."

"I know that," I said, but it was a lie. Truth was, I had no idea what day it was and no idea what time it was, but there was no need to tell Travis that, he was pissy enough already.

"Here." Trav pulled a crumpled up piece of paper out of his pocket and thrust it at me. "I found this in the stuff Mama sent over from the Oakwood. You might want to read it."

I opened it up and looked. It was my handwriting, and it was my list. My Don't Do list.

"Remember the girl who wrote that?" Travis asked. "She

would laugh her ass off at you. How many more of those things are you gonna do before you come to your senses?"

"Screw you," I said. I crumpled the paper back into a ball and tossed it on the floor before climbing out of the car. Travis peeled out when I was only about two feet away.

Inside the house, I went straight to my room. My cell phone was on top of the dresser, and my stash of pot and pills was in the top drawer. Thank God, because the long drive and my disapproving brother had shot my nerves all to hell. I lit up and checked my messages. Almost all of them were from Marc. I didn't bother listening, I just called him back.

"Chloe, thank God. I don't even want to hear about it, we're officially ignoring your little fender bender until after tonight. You're not bringing a date, are you?"

"To the premiere?" I asked. It was hard to wrap my mind around the fact that my movie would be on the big screen at the Arclight tonight, with an audience made up of A listers like Anne and Harlan.

Harlan! I can go out with him and his friends after, I realized. I hadn't heard from him since I left Europe. It would be nice to see a familiar face.

"Can Travis go with you?" Marc sounded worried. "It's a big deal, Chloe, all eyes will be on you."

"I know," I said happily.

"Not in a good way," he said in his bitchiest voice. "Every

photographer in the world is hoping they'll catch you falling down without your panties on."

"Y'know, you were more fun when Nika was around," I told him.

"Then fire me. Please," Marc said. "What are you wearing tonight?"

"I haven't decided." I wandered over to my closet and stared at the clothes on the hangers. Nothing looked right, nothing was perfect. And tonight I had to be perfect. I had to look gorgeous, and act charming, and prove to everyone that Nika was wrong, and so was Sean, and Dave Quinn, and all the gossip blogs that kept saying I was doing things I wasn't doing. Or at least things I didn't remember doing.

"I'll go get Amanda to dress me," I said. "I don't have anything amazing at home."

"Fantastic," Marc said sarcastically. "Good luck with that."

CELEBRITY FREEFALL—WHERE THE STARS FALL TO EARTH

File Under: CHLOE GAMBLE

Breaking: Where's Chloe? The stars are out for the Hollywood premiere of Matthew Greengold's epic *Frontier* . . . but where's Chloe Gamble? The trainwreck is supposed to be fantastic in the film, shot before her transformation into the drug-addled nightmare she is today. Chloe's publicist insists that we'll see the old, brilliant Chloe on the red carpet tonight, even though she was busy crashing her car in Vegas this morning.

Harlan Reed is in the house. Anne Lynch, too. Matthew Greengold has even arrived. But no Chloe.

OMG. Is she skipping out on her own movie premiere?!

"Shut up already," I mumbled, reaching for my cell. The damn thing had been ringing forever, but I felt so peaceful. I didn't want to answer it.

It rang again, and this time I managed to find it, on the floor near the brake. I sat up quickly and that was a mistake, because my head was spinning. Forget the phone. I leaned back against the drivers' seat and closed my eyes until the dizziness passed.

I was in the Mercedes, the car we'd leased for Coop to use when he was living with us. Travis hadn't returned it, even though it was pretty clear Coop wasn't coming back. It was just as well, because how else was I supposed to get over to Amanda's when Trav took off in the Escalade?

Amanda didn't want to dress me for the premiere.

Suddenly I was really awake. I had gone to Amanda's, and she slammed the door in my face. The memory was fuzzy, but it was definitely true because I still felt angry. She'd actually slammed the door on me, after everything I had done for her.

So then I went shopping, though that memory wasn't as clear. I knew I'd gotten some Valium from Jonas's dealer on

Sunset, because I was stressed out by Amanda and I wanted to be relaxed for the *Frontier* premiere. And I sort of remembered being in a jewelry store.

"Crap," I muttered, grabbing the door handle. I must have fallen asleep in the car. God only knew what time it was, but I needed to clean myself up before I went to the premiere. I would wear jeans and a T-shirt if I had to, I could make any look work.

The car wasn't exactly in my driveway, but it was close enough. Only the rear bumper stuck out into the street. The Escalade wasn't here, so either Trav never came home, or he'd gone back out. The sun was sinking over Los Angeles, bathing the city in pink light, and I could see the whole gorgeous view from my driveway. What I mostly noticed, though, was the fact that it was sunset. It was late, and I was supposed to be on a red carpet.

I hurried toward the house, then stopped. There was another car here, not the Escalade. It was a little convertible, parked right up close to the house. And the front door was open. Did I leave it open when I left? Maybe Marc had come to drive me to the premiere?

"Hello?" I called, going inside. "Marc? I just need five minutes." I grabbed a bottle of water from the fridge and headed for my room, trying to ignore the panic rising in me. I could not miss this premiere, I could not. The blogs said such terrible things about me lately, and none of the agents I'd called would call me back. I had to show them all I was on top of my game, or else I'd end up with some bottom-feeder agent and no money.

The French doors to the pool were open. "Marc?" I called, veering over there. He was the only one who still worked for me, and I couldn't remember for sure, but I had the feeling I'd been a bitch to him earlier.

He was in the pool. Well, halfway between the pool and the hot tub, hanging over the low stone divider that separated them. Just hanging there, with his face in the water.

But it wasn't Marc. It was my daddy.

And he was dead.

chapter twelve

Nika Mays's Manuscript Notes:
Witch Hunt

When the cops showed up at my door that night, the first thing I thought was that Chloe Gamble had finally ended up dead in a pool of her own vomit, ODed on painkillers and heroin and God knows what else. Just like we'd all been expecting for months now.

It was the thing all the paparazzi were waiting for. The thing that the millions of people who devoured the Chloe gossip all secretly wanted—the final, shocking scene in the movie of Chloe's life. And I always knew they would come to me first. I'd cut off all contact with her, I was categorically not her agent anymore.

But the world knew that I represented Chloe Gamble. When the worst happened, they would look to me for answers. They would want someone to blame.

"Lonnie?" I said to Detective Lopez. "*Lonnie* is dead?"

"He was found drowned, and the circumstances are suspicious," the cop replied. "I'm sure you understand that we have to investigate every lead we have."

"Okay," I said, trying to process the information. So Lonnie was dead, and it looked like murder.

"Are you familiar with Chloe Gamble, the victim's daughter?" he asked.

"Of course I am," I said.

"And would you be willing to answer some questions about her . . . and her relationship with her father?" the detective asked.

He didn't sound upset, or accusing, or even very interested, but all of a sudden I realized why he was here.

"Chloe is a suspect?" I said, realizing the truth. "You think she's the one who killed him."

It's funny, but the first thought that popped

into my head was that I should call Sean. He was our lawyer, he'd know what to do. But he wasn't our lawyer anymore, he wasn't even a member of Team Chloe. And neither was I.

"I'll answer any questions you have," I told Lopez. "But I don't have any inside information on Chloe Gamble. I don't know anything about her anymore."

"But you can tell me whether or not she had a difficult relationship with Lonnie," he said.

It wasn't really a question. All you had to do was read a magazine to know that Chloe hated Lonnie. "Yes," I said with a sigh. "I can tell you about that."

The story was too good to resist, and nobody tried. Even the real newspapers and websites had Chloe splashed all over their front pages, with headlines like "Lonnie's Little Girl" and "Daddy Drownedest." It took them two days to arrest Chloe, and then her mugshot hit the Internet and appeared on every single so-called news site in the world within an hour. She looked like crap, of course, dirty and freaked out and wasted.

Nobody seemed to care that she wasn't arrested for killing Lonnie. She was arrested because she had a pharmacy's worth of drugs in her house, and most of them weren't prescribed to her—and some of them weren't even legal. She also had a bunch of outrageously expensive jewelry that Harry Winston claimed they'd lent her and she hadn't returned. Chloe claimed the bling was given to her. Who knows the truth? She had no grasp on reality by that point—even if she really believed those things were hers, that didn't mean she was right.

Marc showed up with a bottle of vodka at nine the next morning, and we spent two hours convincing ourselves that this wasn't our fault. He didn't even try to spin the mess—he just quit as the Gamble publicist. What was the point anymore? How could he make Chloe look good when the revered Matthew Greengold was publicly calling her a disaster?

There was nothing for us to do except to lay low.

I didn't need Hal Turman to tell me that when Anne Lynch goes on Letterman and says that Chloe didn't have even one responsible adult in her life, well, it's best if the adults in Chloe's life just keep quiet.

It's hard to believe that I didn't even visit her in jail. She called me, too. She called and cried on my voicemail. And I didn't call her back.

It was bad, and I'm not proud of myself for the way I handled it.

But that wasn't the worst part about the Lonnie Gamble murder.

The worst part was that I couldn't help myself—I was glad that bastard was dead.

VALUES

When I walked out into the lobby of the jailhouse, the first face I saw was Alex. He had my mama with him, and my twin brother, but he was the one who smiled at me.

"They treat you okay? You look okay," he said, holding his arms out a little bit, like maybe I might hug him.

"Why is the cockroach here?" I asked my mama, ignoring him.

"You be nice, Clo, you ain't in no position to judge no more," Mama told me. "Why, Alex even wanted to pay your bail."

"Probably just so you could keep your gravy train running," I said.

"Clo, you ain't been making much gravy lately," she said. "But it don't reflect well on me to have my child in jail."

"Nice, Mama," Travis muttered. "I paid it, Clo. I'm not about to let you be in debt to the porn king. But it was a lot of money."

He was looking at me funny. "Thanks," I said.

"And if I'm goin' to college, I can't afford to lose it," Trav went on. "So don't go jumping bail, Chloe. Promise."

"I'll pay you back, don't worry," I snapped. Used to be the two of us always had each other's backs, and we didn't need to lecture each other about it. "Let's just get out of here. Will they let us go out some side entrance?"

"It wouldn't matter, the paps have the whole place surrounded," Travis said. "The house, too."

"So where'm I supposed to go?" I said. My hands were shaking, and I needed a drink or a hit. I'd been in the holding cell overnight, but it felt like a year. All I wanted was to wake up from the nightmare.

"To Mama's house," Travis said.

"You mean Alex's house," I replied. "No thanks."

"Chloe, we can't go home. It's a crime scene." Travis sounded tired.

I pushed the memory of my daddy's body out of my mind. It didn't seem real, anyhow—it was all jumbled together with the premiere I missed, and Amanda yelling at me, and Travis getting me from Vegas. How had I managed to be in two different police stations in a week?

"Ready?" one of the cops asked.

I nodded. Travis opened the door and immediately the cameras started clicking. I couldn't count how many paparazzi were there, it was a sea of people all yelling things to me, and my heart began to pound. Back in the day, the photographers were friendly to me, but this was a whole different energy.

In the car, Travis reached for my hand, but I pulled away.

The cops had given me my cell phone back along with my clothes. I pulled it out and dialed Callum.

"I need a place to stay," I told him as soon as he answered. "Everyone has gone insane here."

"I heard about your father, Chloe, my condolences," he said.

"I hated that sonofabitch, and I'm glad he's gone," I said, ignoring the look Trav gave me.

"Oh. Well, cheers then," Callum replied. "Listen, ducky, I'd love to help you out, but I'm off to Bruges in the morning."

"Are you shooting?" I asked.

"Not quite." Someone was talking to him in the background, and he wasn't paying attention to me. It didn't matter. He wasn't going to help. I hung up and stared out the window. We were stuck in traffic on the 101 freeway, and so what? At the end of the road was a porn producer's house and a new life of living with my mama, which was no kind of life at all.

"Did you do it, Clo?" Travis's voice was so quiet I almost couldn't hear it. "Did you kill him?"

Travis could've stabbed me in the gut and it would've felt better.

"I ain't even goin' to answer a question like that," I said. I looked down at my phone. This one, I would text. It was none of Trav's business, anyway.

IM

CHLOE: $2M

CHLOE: Offer still stand?

FILMLOVER: Where are you?

CHLOE: LA

FILMLOVER: Van Nuys airport. My jet will be there tomorrow.

I smiled and leaned my head back against the seat. I could handle one night with my mama and her disgusting boyfriend. At least she had wine.

"I ain't staying long," Travis said. "You can come to Indiana with me, but you got to wait till the legal stuff is worked out first. Last thing you need is to jump bail on top of everything else."

"I did not get out of Texas to live in Indiana," I said.

"It's a nice place. You can stay clean there, without all the Hollywood stuff to tempt you. These people don't live right."

I snorted. "Says the guy who's been livin' the life for a year now."

"And I realized it ain't for me," Travis said.

"Well, thanks but no thanks," I said. "I got other plans." The cops didn't want me to leave the state, and they sure as hell didn't want me to leave the country. But I figured that don't matter, not when a crown prince sends a private jet for you.

* * *

"Miss Gamble, the plane is waiting," Ali's butler said. Or maybe he was just an assistant, or a manservant . . . I had no idea what to call the people who worked for Ali, there were too many of them. But this guy was the main one—he'd met me at the door when the Rolls dropped me off at Ali's palace, he'd shown me the closet full of lingerie in my room, he'd taken my dinner order and brought my drinks and lit my hash pipe and woken me up in the morning.

"Where's Ali?" I asked. I hadn't expected to be getting on a plane again quite so soon. Maybe we were going someplace else, someplace even more exotic than Dubai.

"I'm afraid he had some business to take care of this morning. He asked me to see you safely to your flight," the butler said smoothly.

So Ali was blowing me off. He didn't even have the decency to say good-bye after what we'd done last night. Well, I could handle it, especially since the butler was pretending it was all normal and nice.

"You been taking acting lessons?" I asked him. "You never let me see a thing behind that polite smile of yours."

For the briefest instant, his grin grew wider, and then he was back to being professional.

He walked me to the door of the palace and opened the car door. I climbed in and relaxed against the leather seat. It wasn't so bad. Ali hadn't been weird or anything. Nobody would ever know. And I'd have two million dollars to live on until I found a new agent and landed another movie role.

The butler leaned in the window and handed me an envelope. "I'm sorry," he said softly.

As the Rolls pulled out, heading for the Dubai airport, I opened the envelope and found a check and a note. "We spoke of a person's worth, how it changes from day to day," it read. "Your value is no longer what it was. Ali."

I looked at the check. A hundred thousand dollars.

The tears spilled from my eyes and fell onto the check, smudging the ink. But I couldn't stop crying.

CELEBRITY FREEFALL—WHERE THE STARS FALL TO EARTH

File Under: CHLOE GAMBLE

It's getting crazy now! We all know that CHLOE GAMBLE is in the middle of the biggest Hollywood scandal of the year, the mysterious death of her father, LONNIE GAMBLE. In her swimming pool. Found by Chloe alone. After filing for conservatorship of Chloe.

The LAPD hasn't named Chloe as a suspect. But they also haven't named anyone else.

The investigation led to drug and theft charges lobbed against our little Clo-Clo, and she spent a night in LA County jail before being released on bail. So what did Chloe do then?

That's right—she skipped town! Left the country, in fact. She's a bail jumper! Run, Chloe, run!

UPDATE:

▸ Breaking news from Van Nuys airport! A private jet has been held on the tarmac for an hour now, and our sources put CHLOE GAMBLE on the plane. Since it's a private flight, the manifest hasn't been released, but it is definitely an international arrival, and the LAPD are on the scene.

▸ It is Chloe! The cops are bringing her off the plane in cuffs. Photos coming soon.

▸ Chloe is back in jail tonight. She jumped bail and now will not be released until she appears before the judge tomorrow.

▸ Here we go—Chloe is in the courthouse now. Brother Travis is nowhere to be seen. But EARLENE GAMBLE is in the front row and she's brought her adult producer boyfriend, ALEX BOBROV.

▸ REHAB!!! That's right, 17-year-old Chloe Gamble has been ordered by the court to check into drug rehab or face prison time.

▸ For the first time in months, Chloe talked to the press. When asked about rehab, she simply said, "I have nowhere else to go."

It's come to this, people. While celebrity meltdowns are our *raison d'etre*, we don't have hearts of stone. Poor Chloe Gamble isn't even 18 yet, but her life is in the toilet. So let's all join hands and say a prayer that this is the end of the Chloe Gamble freefall. May we never make another entry about her on this blog.

Get healthy, kid!

chapter thirteen

IM

COOPERMAN: You okay, man?

GAMBLEGOAL: On my way to family day at rehab. Fucked up.

COOPERMAN: Did you find a place near Notre Dame?

GAMBLEGOAL: I think I want to live in the dorm.

GAMBLEGOAL: Spent two weeks @ soccer camp with the team. It
    felt good.

GAMBLEGOAL: But weird to plan my life without Chloe.

COOPERMAN: You staying in LA for a bit?

GAMBLEGOAL: Two days. Crashing on Jude's couch. I'll say hey for you.

COOPERMAN: Hang in, Trav. Tell Clo I love her.

GAMBLEGOAL: Yeah. Thanks, Coop.

"You heard they got the guy who killed Daddy?" I asked my sister. "They found him in a ravine off Mulholland Drive."

"Yeah?" Chloe barely sounded awake, and she didn't even look at me. She just stared off across the lawn of the rehab center in Malibu.

"His car crashed, they think maybe he was . . ." All of a sudden it hit me that I shouldn't talk about driving drunk. Chloe drove drunk a lot. Was I allowed to bring it up with her in rehab? "Uh, they think he lost control and drove his car off the cliff."

"Daddy owe him money or what?" Chloe asked.

"They don't know. He was dead when they found his car, but he had Daddy's belt buckle, you know the one."

"His rodeo belt?" Chloe finally met my eye. "This guy took Daddy's precious rodeo belt?" And she started to laugh.

"Yeah. He had a record for breaking and entering. They figured there's no other reason he'd have the belt buckle," I said. "It's pretty random."

Chloe ran her hand through her long hair. "Who was he?"

"George Brown," I said, watching her face to see if she recognized the name. She didn't. "Just some guy, I guess. Followed Daddy and killed him."

"I still don't know why Daddy was at our house. I can't shake the image of him." Chloe leaned forward on the stone bench, gazing out over the green grass. The place was gorgeous, more like a golf club than a hospital. "Isn't it weird? More than all the bad things I did, it's Daddy that keeps sticking in my mind."

"Chloe . . ." I began.

She reached over and took my hand. "I did a lot of horrible stuff, Trav, I stuck needles in my arms and I sold my own body. But I did not kill Daddy. I hope you believe me now."

"I never should've asked you if you did," I said. "I wouldn't have blamed you, you know. He deserved it."

My sister just shrugged.

"You okay, Clo?" I asked. "Really?"

"I'm sober," she said.

"I went to soccer camp," I said. "At Notre Dame. It felt real normal."

"That's good. I always thought you should be normal," Chloe said. "But I ain't livin' in Indiana, Trav."

I'd known that all along. I just didn't want to think about it. "What are you gonna do, then?"

"I don't know. I never wanted to do anything but this." Chloe stood up from the bench and wrapped her arms around herself. "But I fucked everything up real good."

What was I supposed to say to her? She was right. And she was always the one with the plan, not me. She'd been right when she said I didn't have a thick enough skin for Hollywood. She'd been right when she said I should play soccer and go to school. Chloe always made plans for me along with herself. I wanted to do that for her, now, but I didn't know how.

"There's my baby!" My mama's voice cut through the quiet of the lawn. "Chloe, they treatin' you good, sugar?"

She came bursting out of the glass doors from the lobby, her hair done up and her makeup perfect, and she threw her arms around my sister like she actually cared. That piece of garbage Alex was with her, and he was wearing a suit.

"Mama, what's he doin' here? It's family day," I said.

"Alex is family. We might get hitched, now that your daddy's gone," Mama said. "I am a free woman."

"I can't go to college and tell everyone my stepdaddy is a porn king," I said.

"I'm thinking of expanding," Alex said. "If Chloe's interested."

"Excuse me?" my sister said.

"I have money, and I'll spend it on you," Alex told her. "You need a comeback. I'll fund it."

"You are not seriously suggesting that Chloe does porn?" I took a step closer to the guy, but he backed right off.

"No. I'm talking about legit stuff. We'll start a production company, keep it separate from my adult work. We'll find a movie script to relaunch Chloe." Alex grinned. "I am a producer, you know."

"Just stop it," Chloe said. "I am trying to get better in here. I don't need to be propositioned by my mama's boyfriend."

"I'm trying to help you," Alex said. "It tears your mother up to think of you so sad, and I love your mother. So let me help."

I expected some kind of typical sharp comeback from Chloe, but instead she just sighed. "I've sunk low enough already. The minute anyone finds out I'm in business with you, it turns into another story of Chloe Gamble doing something sleazy. I can't take any more of that. It's bad enough that everyone will always think I killed my own daddy."

"They won't," I told her. "They know who did it now."

"You think that'll matter?" Chloe said, shaking her head. "Thanks anyway, Alex."

Alex actually looked disappointed, like he honestly cared. "Well, the offer stands," he said.

"I can't believe it," Chloe said, peering off toward the front of the rehab center. "There's a camera crew on the driveway. The paparazzi are supposed to be banned from here."

"I'll go get security," I said.

"No, sugar, they're with me!" Mama cried. "It's my camera crew. The center won't let them in the building, but they're allowed to shoot me from a distance if I'm outside."

"What the hell, Mama?" Chloe said.

"They're doin' a reality show about me!" my mama said. "I am a well-known woman, and I am adjusting to life as a widow. And I got a kid in trouble."

"If they're doing a show, it's about Chloe," I snapped. "They're trying to get to her, and you're letting them!"

"Oh, hush up, Trav, I got to take care of myself somehow," my mama said. "Y'all are no help anymore."

"We were never supposed to be, Mama," I said. "You're supposed to support us, not the other way around."

"Just get out." Chloe turned back toward the doors. "I been

exploited by everyone else, Mama. I will not be exploited by you."

"The show would welcome you on any time," Alex said. "You, too, Travis."

"You really want to help me?" Chloe said to him. "Take my mama off my hands for good. You take care of her, I don't care where your money comes from. She don't need to go doing things like this if you just support her. You love her, right? Go get married and let her sit around and drink all day. I'm done."

"Chloe," I started.

"I'm tired, Trav." She kissed me on the cheek. "You go on back to school and have a nice life."

And then she was gone.

But if I was being honest with myself, I knew that Chloe had been gone for a long time now. And maybe she wasn't ever coming back.

Nika Mays's Manuscript Notes: The Answer

"George Brown," Marc said, lounging on my office couch with the *LA Times* open on his laptop. "An ex-con with Lonnie's belt buckle. What's that all about?"

"Don't know, don't care," I said, channeling Chloe. "I'm turning a new page. I signed my statement for the police this morning, I asked the cute detective out for coffee, and that is the end of my obsession with the Gamble family."

"Mine, too. From now on, only clients with functional families," Marc said. "You're dating a cop?"

"I've never gone out with a cop before," I said, shrugging.

"You know what's weird? This article says that Brown was a big guy with a mangled ear," Marc went on.

"You can't even stop Gamble-ing for two seconds," I said.

"No, it's just that I saw a big guy with a mangled ear," Marc said. "I was in a Red Mango with Travis and this yogurt worker had no ear. You think it's the same one? Maybe he overheard us talking—Early and the porn king were there too, and you know she never shuts up about money. He could've just been in Trav and Chloe's house to rob them, and Lonnie showed up."

"Kimber Reeve is here, Nika," my assistant buzzed in to say.

"Sorry, time to work," I told Marc. "You want to go have coffee with Detective Lopez? You can tell him all your Sherlock Holmes theories."

"Don't tempt me. I've never gone out with a cop, either," Marc teased. He shut his laptop and stood up. "Remember, if you land this one, you need to get me in there as her publicist. She needs one."

Later on, though, I found myself reading the *LA Times* article about Lonnie's killer. And the *TMZ* posts. And the wild conspiracy theories at *The Enquirer*. I was no better than Marc—I might want to be done with the Gamble family, but they still sucked me in. They sucked everyone in. The media was desperately spinning stories, trying somehow to attach the earless guy in the car wreck to Chloe Gamble and her massive fall from grace. They didn't want to make sense of Lonnie's death, they just wanted to make it more interesting. More about Chloe.

And it *was* interesting that Chloe's name had been cleared. Not that I ever really thought she'd killed her father . . . although she probably wanted to, and was messed up enough to. But she was the only real suspect, and as long as the doubt was out there, she'd never be able to start over.

Now she could.

I never told Detective Lopez about the private investigator I'd hired to tail Lonnie. He had never asked. The truth was, I'd stopped even reading the PI's reports around the time that

Chloe completely melted down. I didn't need dirt on Lonnie to keep him from destroying her—she was destroying herself.

But the reports were fascinating, once I dug them out. I guess it was creepy to spend my whole night reading about the comings and goings of a dead guy. Lonnie Gamble was as bad as Chloe always said he was—a different girl every night, some of them not even legal. And sometimes Lonnie went to Early's apartment and tried to seduce her, or threaten her, or drive her to drink—which wasn't hard.

And one time, he found Alex Bobrov there instead of Early. And Alex threatened to kill him if he kept bothering Earlene. Lonnie laughed it off, according to the PI. Lonnie laughed everything off; he thought he was untouchable. He was like Chloe that way.

It didn't take the PI long to find the connection, not once I asked him to. George Brown with the mangled ear (from a prison fight) worked at a Red Mango when he was paroled. Alex Bobrov had a good eye for desperate people willing to do desperate things for money—he was a pornographer, after all. And Alex liked Red Mango tea. He was a regular, he saw that he could manipulate George, and, somewhere along the way, he hired George to kill Lonnie.

Who knows how George's car ended up driving off a cliff, conveniently preventing him from telling anyone about Alex?

Here's the thing: Alex loved Earlene Gamble, and she loved him. They were a couple of horrible people, but they actually seemed happy together. And Lonnie had been a bad guy, willing to destroy his entire family just to make a few bucks. Instead of helping Chloe when she was spinning out of control, he tried to exploit her.

Even if Chloe spent the rest of her life as a has-been actress, she would be better off than she had been with her father alive. Travis could go off and have a normal life. Early could finally get the attention she so desperately wanted. They could all stop running away.

Lots of people will think I'm just making it up so this book will sell. I don't have any proof, and I don't need any. I know what I know, and that's enough. I simply didn't see a reason to sic the cops on Alex, or to make life worse for the Gambles. I had already done plenty to contribute to their mess.

Looking back, all I can see are the ways I

let Chloe down. I never meant to. I loved her, I considered her a friend, and I wanted her to take over Hollywood. But I treated her like a teammate instead of a client. I thought she knew what she was doing. And she didn't.

Chloe was always in such a rush to grow up and be in charge of her life—and the rest of us were in such a rush to let her grow up and start earning us money. I think we all forgot that she was a kid. She was a smart kid, and one who was mature beyond her years, but she was still only seventeen. And she was swimming in waters that were way over her head.

Chloe watched her friends make dangerous choices and take big risks, and it looked fun and daring and exciting, and I bet it was. But Callum Gardner was a grown man. He'd been around the block. He knew where to draw the line between reckless fun and flat-out self-sabotage. And so did Harlan Reed and his posse of frat-boy friends and sycophants. As for Edward Dowling, not so much. But the world is willing to forgive a bad boy more than a bad girl, and that was one more thing that Chloe was too young to realize.

Lonnie was right. If Chloe had had adults around her, watching her back and drawing that line for her, she would've ended up as a supernova instead of a Z-list joke. But she didn't have any real grown-ups on her side. Not Early. Not Lonnie. And not me.

The best I can say is that I've grown up now. I'm not sure I'll ever get over the guilt about what happened to Chloe. Then again, if I hadn't been so close to her, I wouldn't feel so responsible. Hal Turman always said not to make the client your friend. And Hal Turman was always right.

That's why when I signed Kimber Reeve as a client, I knew it would work out fine. She was my client, not my friend, and I didn't love her. And together we were going to take over Hollywood.

This Is Me Now

"Good luck, Chloe."

The rehab nurse closed the door behind me and there I stood, alone in a driveway in California, sober enough to know how truly screwed I was.

The taxi would be here any minute, and hell if I knew where I would tell it to take me. The Oakwood? Jude's place? She was the only one who'd visited me in rehab besides my so-called family.

She won't let me stay there, I thought, and I knew it was

true. I'd been nothing but trouble for all my friends. Nobody wanted the disaster of Chloe Gamble and her throng of vulture-like photographers in their house. I couldn't go to Indiana with Travis. He couldn't be a normal college student with a sister like me. Besides, it would be jumping bail to leave the state.

I couldn't go stay with my mama and the porn king. I wouldn't. I'd seen myself on Mama's reality show, telling her to get out of my life. The camera crew used a telephoto lens, and my mama must've had a microphone on her somewhere. Of course, they edited the footage so that Mama looked sweet and supportive and I looked like a bitch.

Take a deep breath, I told myself, closing my eyes. *Just breathe.*

Back in the day, I used to stand there alone before I walked out on a pageant stage. At that moment, it was all on me, and nobody could help me if I messed up. This was the same. It was all on me.

The sound of an engine filled the air. My cab was here. I opened my eyes.

It was Travis's Escalade.

"Welcome back to the world," my twin said, coming around to hug me.

"Aren't you supposed to be at Notre Dame?" I asked, blinking back the tears in my eyes.

"Turns out Pepperdine is right here in Malibu, so the girls

will be going to classes in bikinis, probably," he replied. "I'll have to play club soccer, but I will absolutely be the best one in the league." He opened the passenger door and waved me in.

"Travis. You don't have to do this," I said, when we'd been driving for a few minutes.

"I ain't doing a thing," he said. "My money is enough to pay tuition and rent on a one-bedroom apartment in the Valley. You get the couch."

"Okay," I said.

"I'm not taking modeling jobs or acting jobs or party-hosting jobs or anything. I'm done with that," he went on. "I'm going to school."

"Good."

"And you're paying half the rent, so find yourself a waitressing gig. Or some day job, anyway."

"Okay," I said. Was it really possible? Could I have a normal life now, like Trav? "Maybe I'll take some classes, too, find a way to get myself into college with you."

Travis snorted. "Don't be an idiot. You got all clean in rehab, but you can't change who you are. You're a star, remember?"

"Not anymore," I said.

"So you'll start over. Do it all again. You've still got it, Clo."

I stared out at the hills alongside the road, the Pacific ocean gleaming in the distance. All I had ever wanted was right here in Hollywood. "You think I can?" I asked my brother.

"You write any new songs in rehab?" he said.

"Yeah. Of course I did," I said, a smile coming to my lips for the first time since I didn't remember when. "I always write songs."

Trav glanced over at me, then nodded toward my guitar case in the backseat. "We got a pretty long drive."

I laughed, and got out my guitar. I strummed for a minute, thinking. Then I sang.

"This is me now.
I'm not sure how
This me can be
In love with you

I'm all new now
And it's true how
I'm not the girl
You thought you knew

I'm grown up now
And I know how
To walk away
When things are through

So good-bye now
Soon you'll see how

This is me now

Not lovin' you."

After I stopped singing, Travis was quiet.

"You hate it, huh?" I said after a while.

"We'll put it on YouTube," Trav said. "It's perfect."

I shook my head. "I don't have a team of friends to help anymore," I said. "I don't have a way back in."

"So you'll get an agent. Get some buzz for your music first, and then you can call Nika. She owes you."

"No," I said, thinking it through. It felt good to fire up my scheming muscles again. "Not Nika. This time I would go straight to the source."

Travis shot me a questioning look.

"As soon as we get home to our apartment in the Valley," I said, "I'm going to call Hal Turman."

Jude's photography studio was empty and dark except for the lights she'd designed to make me look good. I'd done my own makeup this time, but that was okay. I knew how after so many hours in makeup chairs for *Cover Band* and *Frontier*.

"Let me just do one last sound check," TJ said. He'd been the sound engineer for all the songs I recorded with Max, and miraculously he didn't hate me. I figured I had no one left who I hadn't burned bridges with, but TJ showed up with no questions. And his wife, Sharon, came along and did my hair.

"Ready to go?" Jude asked me.

"Born ready," I said. I went over to the stool we'd set up in front of the cameras, and Travis brought me my guitar.

"You're going to kill it," he told me. "Forget about the rest of this Hollywood garbage and sing your song. That's always been where your strength was, anyway."

"Trav." I caught his hand. "If you hadn't come back, I don't know what would've happened to me."

"You took care of me for a good long time. I figured it's my turn," my brother said. He squeezed my hand. "You and me against the world."

I nodded. "Same as it's always been."

And then the lights came on, and the camera started up. And I began to sing.

About the Authors

ED DECTER is a producer, director, and writer. Along with his writing partner, John J. Strauss, Ed wrote *There's Something About Mary*, *The Lizzie McGuire Movie*, *The Santa Clause 2*, and *The Santa Clause 3*, as well as many other screenplays. During his years in show business Ed has auditioned, hired, and fired thousands of actors and actresses just like Chloe Gamble. Ed lives in Los Angeles with his family.

LAURA J. BURNS is a television and book writer who once dreamed of being an actress, so she's thrilled to live vicariously through Chloe Gamble. She lives in California with her husband and children.

Like what you just read?
Check out

Getting
REVENGE
on Lauren Wood

by Eileen Cook

Last night I dreamed I dissected Lauren Wood in Earth Sciences class. She was wearing her blue and white cheerleader outfit, the pleated skirt fanned out and the sweater cut right down the middle. She lay there, unmoving, staring straight up at the ceiling tiles. She was annoyed. I could tell from the way her jaw thrust forward and her lips pressed together in a thin line. I opened up her chest, peeling her ribs back like a half-opened Christmas present, and the entire class leaned in to get a good look.

"As I suspected," I declared, "no heart." I pointed with my scalpel to the chest cavity, where nothing but a black lump of coal squatted in the lipstick-red center. The class leaned back with a sigh, equally appalled and fascinated. The mysterious inner workings of Lauren Wood exposed for all to see.

"Earth to Helen."

My Earth Sciences teacher, Mr. Porto, was staring at me, waiting for an answer. Someone behind me snickered. I hadn't heard the question. I had been reliving my dream from last night and must have spaced out. I looked at my desk in case the answer was there, but the only thing on my page was a doodle of an anatomically correct heart. I didn't think Mr. Porto would be impressed with my artwork at this particular moment. I prayed for time to speed up and make the bell ring, but the clock kept on ticking one second at a time.

"People, I know vacation begins in a few days, but at the moment you still need to worry more about your final exam than about your summer plans. Can anyone else list for me the six kingdoms of the scientific classification system?" Mr. Porto asked.

He looked around the room for a victim. I slouched down in my seat and attempted to resume my train of thought and natural state of invisibility.

Before the incident there hadn't been a single moment of my life without Lauren in it. We were born in the same hospital, her the day before me. They placed us side by side in the nursery, our first sleepover. Helen Worthington right next to Lauren Wood. Even alphabetically, Lauren came before me. Lauren was in every one of my birthday photos—from age one, when she has her fist buried in my cake, to fourteen when we are both posing supermodel style for the camera,

Lauren's outstretched arm covering part of my face. Looking back, I can see how she always had to be front and center.

Speaking of needing to be front and center, Carrie Edwards must have been running for star biology student. She waved her arm like she was flagging down traffic until Mr. Porto called on her.

"Eubacteria, arche bacteria, protists, fungi, plants, and animals," Carrie spouted off. She paused as if she expected applause. I drew a cartoon of a cheerleader on my paper. I gave her a giant mouth. My eyes slid back to the clock and watched it tick over the final seconds. The bell rang out, and everyone stood up together and jostled toward the door.

"Be sure to look over chapter twenty-two before the exam! I don't want to hear anyone saying they didn't know they were supposed to know the material. Consider this your last warning," Mr. Porto yelled to everyone's back. The volume in the hallway seemed even louder than usual. Everyone was excited to see the year come to an end. Next year we would be seniors, on top of the world. I slipped through the hallway by myself. A few people nodded in my direction, but nobody said anything to me.

It had been the end of the school year when it happened three years ago, only a few days after my fourteenth birthday. Sometimes I look at the photo from the party to see if I can find any clues. Lauren and I are both smiling. My smile is easy to explain—I didn't know what was coming—

but Lauren would have known. She had already put pieces of her plan into action, but there isn't a sign of regret on her face. No hesitation at all, just her wide smile. I suppose she expected me to be grateful that she let me have my birthday before she brought the world crashing down around me. It was the least she could do. After all, what are friends for?

Up in the attic there are four secrets hidden.
Blond, beautiful, innocent little secrets,
struggling to stay alive. . . .

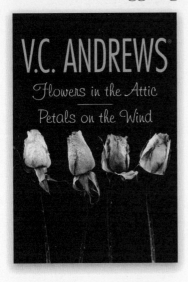

And find out how it all began in:

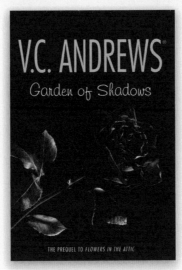

From Simon Pulse
Published by Simon & Schuster

Feisty. Flirty. Fun. Fantastic.

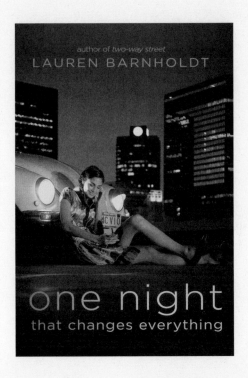

LAUREN BARNHOLDT

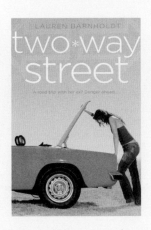

BROKEN HEARTS. JEALOUSY. REVENGE.

What's a little competition among friends?

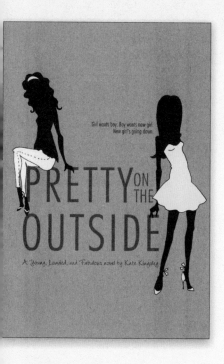

And look for:

FROM SIMON PULSE
PUBLISHED BY SIMON & SCHUSTER

Which will be *your* first?

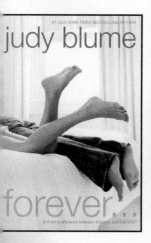

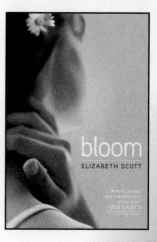

Need a distraction?

Lauren Strasnick

Serena Robar

Amy Belasen & Jacob Osborn

Charity Tahmaseb & Darcy Vance

Teri Brown

Eileen Cook

Nico Medina & Billy Merrell

From Simon Pulse

Published by Simon & Schuster